THE DUKE'S SHARPSHOOTER

The Duke's Guard Series
Book Fourteen

C.H. Admirand

ARE YOU SIGNED UP FOR DRAGONBLADE'S BLOG?

You'll get the latest news and information on exclusive giveaways, exclusive excerpts, coming releases, sales, free books, cover reveals and more.

Check out our complete list of authors, too!

No spam, no junk. That's a promise!

Sign Up Here

www.dragonbladepublishing.com

Dearest Reader;

Thank you for your support of a small press. At Dragonblade Publishing, we strive to bring you the highest quality Historical Romance from some of the best authors in the business. Without your support, there is no 'us', so we sincerely hope you adore these stories and find some new favorite authors along the way.

Happy Reading!

CEO, Dragonblade Publishing

Rescued by the Lyon
Captivated by the Lyon
A Lyon's Word of Honor (Novella)
The Lyon's Saving Grace
A Lyon's Promise

Historical Cookbook
Dragonblade's Historical Recipe Cookbook:
Recipes from some of your favorite Historical Romance Authors

Dedication

DJ, you stole my heart all those years ago and took it with you. I miss you, babe.

For my loyal readers who remind me that the men in the duke's guard have been ignoring my plots since the first book! Proof that you've fallen in love with my hardheaded Irishmen as much as I have. Thank you for making my heart smile.

Acknowledgments

A special thank you to my wonderful editor Arran McNicol. I appreciate your time and talents picking those nits!

Dear Reader:

I am so grateful for your comments and encouragement. During my June takeover of the Dragonblade Reader's Group, I asked if readers were ready to say goodbye to the men in the duke's guard. I was surprised the response was a resounding no! Apparently, I won't be the only one having a hard time letting go.

A few months ago I was writing, and the image of the ballroom at Wyndmere Hall popped into my head. Every man in the duke's guard was in attendance and standing—not dancing—with a wary look in their eyes. They were shifting uncomfortably as the duchess narrowed her eyes at each man in turn. And I knew they were going to have to do something totally out of their comfort zone. No weapons needed—well, other than their devastating smiles. The duchess ordered them to attend the ball, smile, and dance with the wives and sisters-in-law...or else! LOL!

Here's the good news: Kathryn loved the idea and accepted my proposal for my November 2027 novella: The Duke's Yuletide Ball. *The O'Malleys, Garahans, and Flahertys will be in rare form, as they always are whenever the brothers and cousins get together. There will be just a bit of mayhem, settled with a bare-knuckle bout or two. You can read the working blurb on my website.*

Oh, and don't worry—there will always be one of the Garahans, Flahertys, or O'Malleys interrupting when and where he is not supposed to be, answering the call from Captain Coventry when the men he has hired to work undercover need assistance in my next series: Wyndmere's Warriors.

Until then, find a comfy seat, pour a cup of tea (or coffee), and relax while I tell you a story...

C.H.

CHAPTER ONE

R ORY FLAHERTY DID not mind the rain. He'd known when he saddled his gelding earlier that at some point, between the village and Wyndmere Hall, it would start to fall. Hadn't he and his horse caught the scent of it—and discussed it—when the predawn breeze shifted?

"Well, laddie, we're in for a good soaking." The answering whinny had him chuckling. "Aye, there'll be an extra cup of oats for ye at the end of our patrol. Don't be distracting me now."

Not for the first time, Flaherty cursed having to wear a frockcoat, waistcoat, and the bloody cravat. But His Grace had been immovable on the subject. The men in his private guard were to wear their full uniforms at all times—as the duke had reminded them on more than one occasion, appearances mattered. At least he and his brothers and cousins had had a say in the color. They chose one that wouldn't easily show bloodstains and would blend in with the shadows. The duke's guard spent a good part of their time in the shadows. Unrelieved black from head to toe, with one small exception: the embroidered word *Eire* in bright green over their hearts and the gold Celtic harp beneath. Both symbols of the land of their birth.

The O'Malleys, Garahans, and Flahertys, families, bound through marriage, had spent generations digging their roots deep into the fertile soil of their island home. Loved ones had bled and died protecting their land in an endless cycle of hardship and toil laced with sorrow and joy. Rory and his brothers had been as determined as their cousins to save the family farms that had withstood the loss that bled down from one generation to the next. Following in the footsteps of so many young Irishmen, they'd left to find work abroad...the only option left open to them. They'd learned to live without the sweet smell of the rain-washed dawn and peat fires burning, the sight of standing stones and faery forts as dawn broke over horizon, sunlight glistening off the dew-laden fields dotted with sheep. The sound of his ma's voice calling his da, him, and his brothers in for the hearty meal that would fuel them while they worked the land.

His throat tightened with emotion a bit too close to the surface, so he tucked thoughts of home safely away as he scanned his surroundings. Nothing out of the ordinary on either side of the road. The breeze stilled as he reached the halfway point to town. Birds heralded the first few drops of rain. He breathed in the scent, comforted. It reminded him of home. He had expected to receive a letter from his ma last week and was surprised to receive one instead from his new sister-in-law, Mary Kate. He'd already been apprised of the situation his eldest brother had been embroiled in involving Viscount Chattsworth with the flurry of messengers arriving from Sussex—and London. Thankfully, cooler heads prevailed and the duke's guard had held strong.

"Did ye ever think Seamus would marry?"

His horse snickered—or if a horse *could* snicker, that was what Rory imagined it would sound like.

"'Tis my opinion as well."

Rain soaked him through to his waistcoat by the time he rounded the bend and saw the roof of the inn. While not a small village, there was a good-sized inn, and a few shops between the innyard and the church on the other side of the village green. It was early yet, and only a few souls were out and about in the rain, mainly the stable hands that worked for the inn's hostler.

He raised a hand to Scruggs. The middle-aged hostler was

well liked, and had a gentle hand with the horses...and children.

Children...

Flaherty's thoughts turned once again to Mary Kate's letter. It had been full of news—some good, some disturbing. He and his brothers had agreed years ago not to marry before their thirty-fifth year. Seamus marrying a few years before then wasn't as much of a shock as the startling news that the duke's distant cousin, Viscount Chattsworth—the family member Seamus and two of the O'Malleys protected—would challenge Seamus's decision to check on his recently injured wife before giving his report to the viscount.

Riding past the inn, he wondered what man in his right mind would not want to see with his own eyes that his wife was well. For feck's sake, the detour could not have taken more than a quarter of an hour! His temper flared in righteous indignation on his brother's behalf before the rain soaking into his hair cooled his head. All of the Flahertys had tempers, and Seamus's was the hottest of the four of them.

"'Tis lucky we were that Captain Coventry took our measure when he hired us, was pleased with and planning to use our tempers to his advantage." The captain's decision to separate the Flaherty brothers from one another—and the same with the Garahans—had been a good one. The O'Malleys weren't as quick to rile, nor did they hold a grudge for long. To their credit, they could be paired with any one of their brothers or cousins.

He snorted. Good thing, as there were eight O'Malleys—four from Cork and four from Wexford.

The men in the duke's private guard were beholden to Coventry as well as the duke. Working long hours with little time away from their duties hadn't bothered them. Time away was time to think of home and dream of when they'd someday return. Dreams were for children. Flahertys were known to be fertile as well as hot tempered.

He slowly smiled, as pride filled him. If he knew Seamus, his brother had already planted the seeds of the next generation of

Flahertys. Rory looked forward to becoming an uncle.

Passing by the shops, he noted all was quiet, as expected. The shopkeepers in the village opened their establishments midmorning to provide a service to travelers staying at the inn. The habit proved to be economically sound, as most were doing a brisk business by eleven o'clock in the morning. At this hour, not a lamp had been lit, nor curtain drawn back to greet the day.

"Not everyone enjoys the rain like we do, laddie." His horse snuffed in response.

Flaherty did not expect to see anyone out and about this early, and was immediately on guard when a shadow shifted by the base of one of the tall oaks by the corner of the graveyard. His gelding reacted to the reflexive tightening of Flaherty's quadriceps. He was ready to defend, or chase down a vagrant.

"Who goes there?" The shadow shifted, and Flaherty got a better look at the figure as it turned to flee. "Stop! By order of the duke!"

The figure obeyed. Flaherty dismounted and strode toward whom he deduced to be a lad, given his height. "Turn around and show me yer hands."

To his shock, the wide green eyes, smallish nose, and full lips were decidedly female. Her face was a bit too thin, as if she had not had enough to eat recently.

"Are ye after riling me, lass? Show me yer hands." She lifted one small hand. Frustrated, and for a moment concerned, he asked, "Have ye only the one, then?"

"I have two. The other one's busy."

He snorted, and tried to cover his laughter. "Well now, if it's a blade or pistol ye're hiding beneath yer cloak, ye'd best turn it over to me now. Then I'll escort ye to the constable. The duke won't be happy if ye're here to cause trouble."

When she didn't move, he sighed. "Me name's Flaherty. I'm one of the Duke of Wyndmere's private guard. What's yer name, lass, and who have ye come to visit?"

She relaxed her stance. "I do not know anyone in the village.

I'm looking for work."

Flaherty's frustration doubled. "Did ye arrive by mail coach?"

"We did."

The coach would have come and gone by now. He glanced around her, and behind himself, though he would have heard if anyone were behind him. "Ye're trying me patience, lass. State yer name, and show me yer other hand and be quick about it!"

"Temperance."

"Well now, 'tis a fine quality to have, but I'm asking yer name."

She lifted her chin and narrowed her rain-drenched eyes at him. "*Mrs.* Temperance Johnson."

"Ah, so when ye said we, ye meant yer husband. Why didn't he leave ye at the inn, where ye'd be warm and dry?"

The fire in the lass went out. "He's dead."

When she shivered and wavered on her feet, Flaherty reached out a hand to steady her. "Ah, lass. I'm sorry for yer loss. Is that why ye're sitting in the rain alone, at the edge of the graveyard?"

Her eyes met his, and something shifted inside of him, as if to make room for the feelings he normally controlled. Compassion, and the need to protect, surged through him.

A muffled cry, like the sound of a small animal, had him staring at her cloak. Had it moved? And then it hit him—*eedjit*, she was protecting a babe!

"Come with me over to the inn. I'm well known in the village, and have the duke's approval to aid anyone I deem in need of it in His Grace's name." She tried to shift out of his hold. "Here now, Temperance, I'm after helping ye. Ye need to get dry, mayhap to feed yer babe. How old is he?"

"*She* just turned four. Her name's Madeline."

Worry lanced through Flaherty. Why was the lass hesitant to accept his offer? Normally people cried out to him for help.

He was about to ask when a tiny hand pushed the cloak aside. "Mum, I'm hungry."

Utterly charmed by the curly-headed tot in Temperance's

arms, Flaherty smiled. "Well, now, wee *cailín*, I'll escort ye and yer ma to the inn for tea and cake."

"That's not my name."

"You have to excuse Madeline," Temperance said. "We've traveled a long way, and I am too weary to walk back to the inn."

Flaherty sensed that there was something more the lass was leaving out. "Begging yer pardon, Miss Madeline. Ye see, *cailín* is Irish Gaelic meaning 'young girl.'"

The tiny lass wrinkled her nose. "My name's Maddy."

Charmed, Flaherty smiled. "'Tis a lovely name—sounds similar to the duke's housekeeper. Her name's Merry. You'll like her, and Constance, too."

"Who's Constance?"

"The duke's cook. She has a fine hand with sweets. Lavender scones are a favorite of Her Grace and her twins, Richard and Abigail. But they're half yer age."

Maddy's little face scrunched up. "Half?"

"Aye, Miss Maddy. If ye had one kitten for each one of yer years, ye'd have four kittens." She nodded, and he continued, "Half that would be just two kittens—one for each hand."

The little darling batted her eyelashes at him. "I always wanted a kitten. Mum said no."

"Well now, one of the cats that lives in the stables just had a litter of kittens. Three orange-and-white-striped ones, and one tiny black one. 'Tis the runt of the litter." Before the inquisitive tot asked, he explained, "The smallest of the bunch."

"Could I see them?"

From Temperance's frown, Flaherty expected her to say no. "Mayhap. First we need to count how many coins we have left. If I don't find a position soon, we'll have to push on to the next village."

"Here now, let me take ye to the inn for that tea and cake. As me ma's fond of reminding meself and me brothers, 'tisn't wise to make any decisions on an empty belly. I've a mile more to go on patrol before I head back into town. I'll stop at the inn on me way back and take ye with me to Wyndmere Hall. No one will bother ye if they know ye're under me protection, but there are those in the village who are wary of vagrants."

The threat of being apprehended for being homeless or jobless sparked her temper. "I'm not a vagabond!" As if she regretted raising her voice to him, she added more quietly, "I would not want to put you out, Mr. Flaherty."

"I'd rather know the two of ye were safe and sound, warm and dry at the inn, than being mistakenly identified and hauled before the constable."

"But wasn't that what *you* threatened a few moments ago?"

She had him there. "Aye, but that was before I knew ye weren't armed and hiding a dangerous weapon."

The lass sighed. "Thank you for your concern, but Madeline—"

"Maddy," her spitfire of a daughter reminded her.

"Maddy is dry, but I'm soaked, and do not believe we would be welcomed at the inn."

"Ah, there's where ye'd be wrong then, lass," Flaherty replied. "The hostler, Scruggs, is a friend and has a soft spot for little ones and horses. The innkeeper is a fair man who is known for his hospitality."

Maddy patted her mother's face and reminded her, "I'm hungry, Mum."

"It'll be me treat for two lovely, damp lasses on a soft spring morning."

"It's cold and raining," Maddy complained.

"Rain makes it a lovely morning. The flowers will be drinking it up, and when the sun comes out, they'll be opening their blossoms to show them off. If ye wait right here, I'll whistle for me horse. The lad is partial to little ones and would be honored to give ye a ride to the inn."

"It's not that far a walk," Temperance protested.

"I thought ye were too tired to walk. Isn't that why I found ye sitting here in the rain?"

She shrugged.

He would wager—and win—that her reason for leaving the inn had more to do with the fact that she and her little girl were traveling without an escort than a lack of coin. It would raise questions she might not be up to answering, especially if her husband had died recently. More often than not there were folks who judged a woman alone harshly, and a woman with a young child or babe harsher.

He'd be asking her the details later. For now, he intended to see them settled at a table near the fire in the inn's taproom. "Leave it to me—I'll see that ye have tea and cake, or whatever yer mum feels is best."

"Cake!"

When Maddy's mother did not answer right away, he said, "Cake it is, Miss Maddy." He whistled for his horse, chuckling when the ladies gushed over how smart and handsome the gelding was. "Shall I set ye on me horse first, while Maddy stands beside me, or Maddy first?"

"Maddy first," Temperance said.

He nodded and told his horse to be still, while he lifted the little one onto the animal's back. "Now then, Miss Maddy, grab hold of the saddle, while I help yer ma up."

"I can manage," Temperance insisted.

"I don't doubt it, but me horse is used to me movements, not the excess fabric of yer cloak and gown fluttering against him. If it's me ye're skittish about, ye have no worries. Me ma would have me hide if I forgot me manners or mistreated a lady." He put his hands around her too-thin waist and decided he'd order a full breakfast for the both of them. "Up ye go."

After he'd settled them on his horse, he praised the animal, "There's a lad. We'll detour back to the inn, settle the lasses inside, finish up our rounds, stop back, and take them to meet the duke."

"Oh, but I never said we'd go with you to Wyndmere Hall," Temperance protested.

"Don't ye want Miss Maddy to meet Merry and Constance?"

"Another time. I need to secure a position first."

The desperation underlying her tone told Flaherty all he needed to know. They were likely down to their last few coins. They weren't vagrants as long as they had a few in their pockets, but he had a feeling they had been treated warily—mayhap even badly.

"I'll introduce ye to Scruggs first, as he'll want to spoil me horse with an apple, as he does every time I pass through the village on patrol. After we get ye settled by the fire with a meal and hot tea, we'll ask the innkeeper if he needs kitchen help."

"Thank you, Mr. Flaherty."

"Ye'd be welcome, lass, and it's just Flaherty." He walked his horse to the inn, grateful the rain had let up. He was worried about the lass and her little girl.

"What have you got there, Flaherty?" Scruggs called out as he led his horse into the innyard.

"Mrs. Johnson and her daughter, Maddy."

"It's a pleasure to meet you, missus—and you too, Maddy."

Flaherty pitched his voice low, so only the hostler would hear. "They're under me protection, Scruggs, and that of His Grace. Will ye keep an eye on them for me while I make the loop around and return for them? I wouldn't want anyone accusing them of being vagabonds."

Scruggs squared his shoulders and gave a nod. "I understand. You can count on me."

Relief filled Flaherty. He'd known he could rely on the honest hostler. "They're chilled to the bone. I'd appreciate it if the innkeeper or his sister would sit them by the fire and serve them tea and breakfast. 'Tis on me." Flaherty reached into his waistcoat pocket, withdrew a few coins, and handed them to Scruggs. "I have a mile or so to go to finish me patrol, then I'll swing back to pick them up and take them on to Wyndmere Hall."

Scruggs nodded toward the side of the inn. "Harkness is settling an issue with a delivery of ale. I'll let Miss Susana know."

Flaherty nodded and turned to smile at the little girl. "Hold on tight to the saddle while I help yer ma down."

The wee one nodded.

This time when he wrapped his hands around Temperance's waist, she stiffened and he shifted in his hold. *Bollocks*, he could feel her ribs! This widow needed his help, whether she knew it or not, wanted it or not. "Easy now, lass," he soothed. "Let me help yer little *cailín* down." Maddy held out her arms and giggled. "Aye, ye're a charmer for sure, lass, just like yer ma."

He passed the little girl into her mother's arms. "Now then, I'm sure ye heard me asking Scruggs to take care of ye while I'm gone. I won't be more than three-quarters of an hour. Time enough for ye to warm up next to the fire and fill yer bellies."

"Oh, but I don't—"

"I've already taken care of it," Flaherty interrupted. Holding her worried gaze, he continued, "Scruggs here will see to it that Harkness and his sister know that ye're under me protection and that of His Grace. They'll take good care of yerself and little Miss Maddy."

Watching Scruggs escort them to the inn, he patted his horse's neck. "Now then, laddie, ye'll have a bit of a wait for the cup of oats I promised." Fine animal that he was, the gelding lifted his head and whinnied. "Good lad." Flaherty mounted and rode off.

CHAPTER TWO

T EMPERANCE THANKED MR. Scruggs, unnerved by the way the innkeeper's sister looked at her. For Maddy's sake she did not let her unease show as she smiled and thanked the woman. The fire was hot, and her cloak was mostly dry. While they waited, others had arrived and been served. This was not the first time this had happened to them. She had discovered that traveling with her daughter—without a male escort— immediately raised suspicion. In the few years she'd been widowed, she had been unable to secure steady work. Whenever anything went wrong, she was the first to be blamed, though she had a strong work ethic. Since leaving her last position, she had even been accused of stealing Maddy, who was the image of her late husband with her curly blonde hair, but with Temperance's green eyes.

"Mum, my belly aches." The tiny hand on her arm had her temper simmering. Scruggs had relayed Flaherty's message to Miss Harkness, so why had she been ignoring them in favor of other travelers who had arrived after they had?

"Breakfast will be here soon, Maddy."

Her daughter abandoned her chair. She climbed onto Temperance's lap and leaned her head against her breast.

"You're such a good girl to wait so long. Thank you."

Maddy's breathing slowly evened out until she began to

snore. The little girl was just as exhausted as Temperance was.

She wondered if she should have left the merchant's employ sooner. She'd been hired to assist the man's cook. He paid her well, and agreed to let her keep Maddy with her while she worked. After a few months, she'd begun to think that maybe this was where she and Maddy belonged. She relaxed her guard—and that was when he'd cornered her in the pantry and locked the door. The cook had warned Temperance that it was not *if* he would add Temperance to his list of conquests, but *when*. She suggested Temperance carry a knife in her apron pocket, and thank goodness she had! The coward had covered his face with his hands and backed away, begging her not to stab him. She'd packed up Maddy and left a short time later, but not before Cook handed her a small bag of coins. Temperance had nearly wept. She couldn't remember the last time she cried. There had simply not been time.

She had spent most of the coin on their journey south in the hopes of finding another position. Rocking and quietly humming, she reaffirmed her vow that her daughter would not go hungry ever again. Temperance had worked her fingers to the bone trying to provide for Maddy and was at a loss as to what else she could do to earn money, short of selling herself.

Shame filled her for even thinking it. Her husband would never have wanted her to stoop so low. *Lord, what else can I do?*

Humiliation stained her cheeks as she realized heads slowly turned as the other patrons stared at her and whispered. It had taken less than an hour this time before the rumors and speculation began. Temperance refused to allow one more self-righteous person to cast aspersions on her daughter or herself. They were dry, and Maddy had fallen asleep. It was time to leave.

She rose to her feet. Head high, she skirted the tables and, without a backward glance, walked out the door.

"I see your little tot fell asleep," Mr. Scruggs called to her as she walked toward him. "A full belly more often than not has me feeling sleepy myself."

She decided not to tell him what had happened inside. "Would you please tell Mr. Flaherty that it was too crowded to stay inside?"

"No sense getting wet again after you've already dried off. Why don't you wait inside the barn?"

"Maddy would be terrified if she woke up surrounded by so many horses, but thank you for your kindness, and please do thank Mr. Flaherty for us."

The older man's frown was fierce, but facial expressions were the very least of what worried Temperance. A person's smile while passing on false rumors and innuendo was far more threatening. She had no one to stand beside her while she fought against those who sought to slander her good name. Those that had did not know her or her husband.

She felt the weight of her sleeping daughter between her shoulder blades and in her lower back. The aches were welcome, as they served to remind her that no matter what anyone else thought, her husband had loved her—and would have loved their daughter. She shifted Maddy in her arms and dug deep for a smile for the only other person in the village to show her an ounce of kindness. "Thank you, Mr. Scruggs."

"I gave my word to watch over you and Maddy, Mrs. Johnson."

"But you have a job to do, and three carriages arriving on the heels of one another required your attention. I'm grateful that you took the time to see us settled in the taproom and spoke to the innkeeper's sister on our behalf. You have no control over when and how many carriages arrive at the inn. I shall always remember your kindness. Goodbye, Mr. Scruggs."

Someone hailed the hostler. Short of tying them up, Temperance knew he had no choice but to let them go.

Her footsteps were steady, but slow. She'd learned to conserve as much energy as she could in order to walk the long distances required in searching for employment. Half a mile seemed much longer when her daughter was fast asleep. Awake,

Maddy would have her arms around Temperance's neck, clinging to her like a bur, and would not feel as heavy.

Tears pricked the back of her eyes, but she refused to let them fall. "Tears solve nothing. They make my eyes swell and my nose red."

Annoyed with herself, she slipped on a patch of deep mud along the edge of the road. It was time to find shelter and rest. She could not afford for Maddy to become ill by exposure to the wet and the damp, chilly air. A copse of fir trees off to the right would have to do.

Aware that her steps were faltering, her body straining from the weight of the precious burden she carried, Temperance prayed for her guardian angel to protect them while they rested.

Beneath the cover of the trees, she found a dry spot among the fragrant pine needles. She set her daughter down, then lay beside her, tucking Maddy against her heart where no cold air or dampness would touch her. Fingers stiff from being wet and cold, gown sticking to her legs, Temperance fought the urge to shiver.

Her eyes drifted closed as she prayed, "Lord, please help me find a way to feed my little one. She needs to eat and somewhere warm to sleep."

"WHAT DO YE mean they've gone?"

Scruggs shrugged. "We had a number of coaches arrive at the same time right after I tucked Mrs. Johnson and her daughter in the taproom next to the fire. I passed along your message to the innkeeper's sister as three carriages pulled in. I offered to let her stay in the barn out of the wet, but she insisted it would startle her daughter to wake surrounded by horses."

Flaherty had a bad feeling in his gut. "Did she say where she was headed?"

"She mentioned it being too crowded inside, and I can well

imagine it with the number of people in the packed coaches. Besides, if she and her daughter had finished eating, they would be obliged to give up their seats."

Flaherty scrubbed a hand over his face. "How long ago did she leave?"

"Half an hour, maybe more." Flaherty turned to leave, and Scruggs called out, "She said to thank you for your kindness and headed out of town with Maddy sleeping in her arms."

Flaherty knew a sleeping—or unconscious—body felt as if it weighed more. The lass had looked dead on her feet when he'd had to leave her to finish his rounds in the village. It had taken a bit longer than anticipated. He'd stopped to help one of the tenant farmers' sons, who'd gotten stuck halfway up a tree, unable to climb down.

Gaining his saddle, he prayed, "Lord, I could use Yer help finding them."

Three-quarters of a mile up the road, the heavens opened up. He wiped the rainwater out of his eyes and noticed a copse of fir trees off the side of the road—and deep, small footprints, indicating someone was carrying a heavy load. It had to be Temperance.

Dismounting, he walked his gelding over to the trees and called her name softly, not wanting to startle the lass. When she didn't answer, he told his horse to wait for him, brushed the branches aside, and stepped into the small shelter the thick branches provided.

The pair he sought were huddled in a pile of pine needles. Temperance was shivering in her sleep, while her little one slept peacefully snuggled against her. He crossed the distance and knelt beside them. "Wake up, lass, 'tis Flaherty. I've come to take ye home."

Neither one stirred. He repeated the words, louder this time. A sliver of fear snaked up his spine. Placing the back of his hand to the lass's forehead, he felt the heat radiating off her. Worry filled him. Maddy was much smaller, and he used two fingers to check her for fever. She was warm, but not as hot as her ma.

A sense of urgency filled him. How long had she been fevered? Why hadn't the stubborn lass at least waited in the barn for him? A scared child could be soothed, but at least they'd have been dry and warm.

Though the inn was closer, and he was familiar with Scruggs and Harkness, he knew the duke and duchess would never turn away anyone in need—especially a widow and her small child. Decision made, he slipped his arms beneath the lass and started to lift her.

Maddy opened her eyes. "You found us."

"That I did, little Miss Maddy."

"Mum's tired, and we're hungry."

"We'll take care of that when we get to Wyndmere Hall. Let me help ye to stand up. I'll need to put ye on me horse first, then yer ma. How brave are ye, wee *cailín*?"

"I'm the bravest. Mum said so."

"There's a lass. Now then, I've got a spare shirt and coat in tucked in a leather bag behind me saddle. I'm going to get them and wrap ye and yer ma in them to keep ye warm while we ride. All right?"

Her green eyes sparkled like gems. "All right."

"Stay close to yer ma." He grabbed the bag. "We've a big job ahead of us, laddie," he told his gelding. "The lass is fevered, and we need to take her to the duke." The intelligence in the horse's eyes settled him. "Good, lad. Ye know how important it is for haste. Though the weight of us combined will be a chore for ye." In answer, his horse snorted.

If Flaherty had not been so worried, he would have laughed. Instead he rushed back to lasses. "Let me wrap this around ye, Maddy." She watched him wrap his shirt around her. "Now then, let's see if we can rouse yer ma and tuck ye into her arms. Then we can wrap me dry coat around the two of ye."

Wide green eyes stared up at him. "How will we get on your horse?"

He tapped the end of her nose. "I'll lift ye up. Now then, let's try to wake yer ma."

"When I'm really hungry—like now—I wake her up like this." Maddy cupped her mother's face in her tiny hands and kissed her cheek. "Wake up, Mum, I'm hungry!"

"I know, sweetheart. I'm sorry." The lass's eyes opened and so did her mouth.

Flaherty touched the tip of his finger to her chin. "Close yer mouth, lass." She blinked a few times as if she could not believe what she was seeing, then obeyed. He assured her that she wasn't dreaming. "I followed after ye. Why didn't ye wait?"

"The lady didn't like us," Maddy whispered.

Flaherty strove to keep the anger out of his voice. "Which lady?"

"The inn lady. She fed other people. Not us."

Anger tore through his guts at the notion that Miss Harkness would take his coin and not take care of the two lasses. He knew Scruggs would have delivered his message to her. "She'll be sorry she didn't take care of ye."

"It's not her fault," Temperance told him. "The inn was busy."

"'Tis no excuse. From what Scruggs told me, ye were there first and should have been served first."

"But—"

"Ye can argue yer point later. Right now I need to take that wet cloak off ye and wrap yerself and Maddy in me frockcoat."

"We're fine right here."

"Ye're not thinking clearly—'tis the fever, lass. Would ye rather let yer daughter stay out in this damp and rainy weather?"

Her green eyes filled with worry before gut-wrenching sadness replaced that emotion. "You're right. My head is muddled."

He helped her out of the cloak and wrapped them in his frockcoat. Flaherty was thankful that the duke insisted on the finest wool. The tight fibers kept the cold—and most of the elements—out. Unless it was a downpour, which had been happening off and on since he rode out of the stables at the duke's estate.

When Temperance stood shakily and started walking, he scooped her off her feet and into his arms. Maddy giggled. It took no time at all for him to reach his horse's side and set the lasses on the animal. "Thank ye, laddie. There'll be the cup of oats I owe ye, an apple, and two carrots when we get to the stables."

His gelding snuffed out a bold breath. Maddy's eyes widened in surprise. The little lass was a joy to watch.

"Now then, snuggle up tight to yer ma, while I mount behind ye." Seated, he pulled the lass and her pixie-faced daughter into his arms. "Close yer eyes now, and dream of the butter cake and scones Constance will have ready and waiting for ye."

"And tea?" Temperance whispered.

"Aye, lass, and tea."

CHAPTER THREE

F LAHERTY GAVE A short, sharp whistle as they rode toward the stables behind Wyndmere Hall. Patrick O'Malley and Aiden Garahan rushed toward him—O'Malley from behind the stables, Garahan from the rear entrance of the house.

"What's happened?" O'Malley demanded.

"Who's that?" Garahan asked.

A tiny gasp sounded from the bundle in Flaherty's arms. "Later." He bent his head and whispered, "Ye've nothing to fear, Maddy-lass. Me cousin O'Malley will take ye inside."

"To Constance's tea and cake?"

"Aye. She'll feed ye till yer belly's full." He met the intensity of O'Malley's gaze. "Take the wee *cailín* to the kitchen. I've promised her tea, butter cake, and scones."

O'Malley opened his arms and took the little lass from Flaherty. "Me daughter Deidre would love yer curls, and the duke's twins will want to play with ye."

The curly-haired moppet stared up at the blond-haired, green-eyed guard. "Your eyes are like mine and Mum's." When O'Malley smiled at her, she told him, "I'm hungry."

Flaherty could not contain his worry. The poor little mite had waited patiently at the inn after he'd promised they'd be fed…and they hadn't been. He vowed to get to the bottom of the issue. The coin wasn't much of a concern—justice was imperative for the poor widow and her daughter.

"Garahan, hold me horse." After Flaherty dismounted with the lass in his arms, he nodded to Garahan. "I've promised the lad a cup of oats, an apple, and two carrots. He didn't get his oats at the inn. There's a situation there that we need to handle, immediately."

Garahan started to walk the horse to the stables but then stopped. "Why don't ye tell me now?" Temperance moaned in Flaherty's arms, and Garahan's eyes locked with his. "Me wife will be along to help shortly. Emily won't mind sitting with the poor woman while Merry and Constance decide if the physician is needed."

Flaherty's throat felt like the round shot from an eighteen-pounder gun was lodged in it. Garahan seemed to be waiting for his agreement. He inclined his head and finally managed to swallow the imaginary munition, then strode toward the rear door to the house, shifting the lass in his arms to reach for the doorknob. It opened as the duke's butler Humphries ushered him inside.

"Constance is helping little Miss Maddy wash her hands before she feeds her."

"Thank ye, and please thank Constance for me."

"No thanks necessary, Flaherty. His Grace would expect us to lend aid whenever and wherever needed."

As Flaherty's gut burned with indignation on the lass's behalf, he stepped into the room with the cot and healing supplies. "I left them in the care of Scruggs with instructions to see them inside and to ask the innkeeper's sister to let them sit by the fire and to feed them."

Humphries scoffed. "Mr. Harkness is the affable one of the pair."

"I thought it a family trait," Flaherty said.

The butler shook his head. Before Flaherty could question him further, he noticed the duke's housekeeper bustling about the room, smoothing fresh linens on the cot, setting out drying

cloths and a new round of soap. "Bring her over here, Flaherty."
Merry stepped back while he gently placed the lass on the cot.
"Poor woman—what happened?"

"I noticed someone by the base of one of the oaks next to the
graveyard. When I called out, she stood and tried to run."

"I take it you stopped her," Humphries said.

"Aye. I judged her to be a lad, given her size, but when she
turned and looked at me…I saw her face."

A footman arrived with hot water. "Add it to the pitcher and
the bowl," Merry instructed him. When he finished the task, she
thanked him.

"Scruggs is a good man," Flaherty continued. "I left the widow and her daughter in his care and gave him coins for their
meal. He agreed to escort them inside and promised to hand Miss
Harkness the coin I gave him to feed the lasses, while I finished
me rounds. I asked the lass to wait and she agreed, but when I
returned, they had gone." His temper boiled. "Why did the
innkeeper's sister take me coin and not feed the lasses?"

Merry shared a telling look with Humphries. "We'll find out,"
she said, returning to the cot and the woman that had Flaherty's
guts tied in knots. She placed a hand to Temperance's forehead.
"You'll have to leave, Flaherty. We need to get her out of these
damp clothes immediately."

Flaherty brushed a lock off Temperance's forehead and promised, "I'll be back, lass."

"Humphries, tell Francis I need her—Emily, too," Merry
continued. "If Garahan demands to know what task I have given
her, please let him know she will not lift anything heavier than a
linen cloth."

Humpries followed Flaherty out of the room. "Garahan dotes
on his wife," Flaherty commented as they walked toward the
kitchen. "I'm thinking it's been some time since someone doted
on the lass."

"Miss Maddy ate every bit of food I gave her," Constance told
Flaherty as he strode into the kitchen. He smiled seeing the wee

lass sitting on top of two cushions the cook must have placed on the little one's chair. She smiled before taking a huge bite of butter cake.

"Easy, now," he warned. "Ye'll not want to be worrying yer ma by choking."

Duly chastised, Maddy slowed her chewing until she finished the bite she'd taken and pushed the plate of cake away from her. "Mum hasn't eaten in a day or so, and it's my fault."

Her tear-filled eyes tore at his gut. He walked over, knelt by her chair, and mopped her tears with his handkerchief. Handing it to her, should she need it again, he tried to think of what to say to get her to stop crying. "Yer ma needs ye to be strong for her—can ye do that?"

Blonde curls bounced with the movement of her head.

"That's grand. I'm thinking she'd be wanting ye to clean yer plate. Am I right?"

"How did you know?"

"Ma always insisted me brothers and I not leave a crumb. We needed to eat to keep our strength up to help our da with the chores."

"Chores?"

"Aye." He used the tip of his finger to move the plate within her reach. When she picked up the fork, he nodded. "There's a lass. A chore is a task...a job. On me parents' farm, there are plenty of jobs. Tasks that never end." He handed her the napkin next to her plate. "Ye missed yer mouth with that last big bite. Need help wiping yer face?"

She shook her head, wiped her mouth, and set the cloth on the table. Her eyes shone with what she was feeling with her belly full and her ma being taken care of—relief.

"I'll bet Constance has the beef broth ready for yer ma to drink. It'll warm her from the inside out. Later, when her belly's ready, we can give her broth-soaked bread."

"How do you know what she needs?"

"Ah, lass. 'Tis the saddest of tales, but I'll tell ye that 'tis a crime for a person to go hungry when there are those with more than enough food to prevent such a thing."

Maddy's brow furrowed, as if she were thinking about what he'd said. Her green eyes widened as she asked, "Were *you* ever hungry?"

"A time or two, but that was once me brothers and I left home to find work here in England. We had to so our folks wouldn't lose their farm."

She frowned as she chewed the last bite. "But who does your chores?"

"We have cousins who have been helping around the farm. Now then, did ye drink yer tea?"

"Every drop," Constance assured him. "Would you like more, Miss Maddy?"

Maddy smiled. "Thank you, Miss Constance."

"Yer ma would be proud of ye for remembering yer manners."

The cook agreed with him and told the little girl so.

"Can I see Mum now?"

"Not yet—Merry, Francis, and Emily are helping yer ma out of her wet clothes before helping her dress in something warm and dry."

She sniffled as her eyes filled again. "I don't want Mum to be alone. She cries at night when she thinks I'm sleeping."

Flaherty's heart ached at what the pair had been through. "Thank ye for taking care of this wee sprite for me, Constance. We're going to knock on the door and see if her ma's ready for a visit."

The cook gave a nod. "Let me know when I can send the broth and tea to her."

"Thank ye, Constance." He looked down at the child and asked, "Ready to get down?"

"Yes, and I can climb by myself." He'd been prepared to pick Maddy up, but waited, understanding the little one's need to prove she could handle the task. She wiggled off the chair and looked up at him before he offered his hand. He had to bend over so she could reach it, but Flaherty did not mind. He was proud of her resilience, and the way she skipped toward the room where her mother was being cared for.

"I'm glad Mum can finally eat. She always has me eat first. I tried to eat less so I could share, but she insisted that I needed it more so I could grow up to be a mum someday."

The sadness entwined with hope in Maddy's voice entranced him. She might be tiny, but she was mighty and far too worldly for her age. A four-year-old should not be able to understand that her mother was starving herself so that her daughter could eat. He'd seen it and heard tales of it back in Ireland. Maddy should be running across the meadow chasing butterflies, or picking wildflowers while she walked through gardens holding her mother's hand. If she were *his* daughter—

Flaherty's heart knew then what his head had not yet accepted—the tiny, green-eyed pixie had him firmly wrapped around her finger. "Me ma always saw that the four of us ate our fill first, too."

"I love my mum. Do you love yours?"

"Aye, lass, to pieces."

She was giggling when they reached the room where Temperance was temporarily being cared for. Flaherty knocked, and the door swung open. Merry beamed at them. "Just who we were coming to look for. Your mum is asking for you, Miss Maddy."

Flaherty let go of Maddy's hand, and the little girl rushed toward the cot. "Mum, you're awake!"

"Have you eaten?" Temperance asked.

Maddy nodded. "I sat on two pillows and had stew and bread with butter and cake and tea."

Temperance's eyes glowed, but Flaherty had a feeling that most of it was from the fever. "Where did you fit it?"

Her daughter patted her belly. "Right here."

Flaherty smiled at the pair. "Well now, as I'm no longer needed, I'd best return to me duties. 'Tis me shift guarding the perimeter." His eyes met Temperance's. "Eat what ye are able to, lass. Little Miss Maddy will be in good hands while ye rest."

"Thank you, Mr. Flaherty."

"Just Flaherty, lass. If ye need me, Humphries knows where to find me." He turned and walked to the door, only to stop when something plowed into the backs of his knees.

Maddy wrapped her arms around his legs. "Thank you for saving us, Just Flaherty."

Warmth filled him as he stared down into the face of the pint-sized angel. *I'm thinking 'twas yerselves that saved me, lass.* He had not been around children since leaving home, where there were always younger cousins to mind in between his chores. He'd forgotten how they would say exactly what was on their minds and were not afraid to show emotion. Flaherty and his cousins were loath to reveal what they were thinking or feeling. His Grace depended on them to be emotionless when dealing with those who sought to discredit or defame the duke and his family. Most everyone they came in contact with were left to wonder what they were thinking.

Maddy tugged at his heart until he felt as if the walls he'd built around it cracked. Going down on one knee, Flaherty hugged the wee lass to his heart. "'Twas me pleasure, lass." Easing her out of his arms, he urged her back to her mother's side and turned to leave.

He'd always thought that he could hold off falling in love for another few years. Walking away from that room, he knew he'd given his heart—nay, it had been snatched from his chest—to the tiny, curly-haired *cailín.*

Flaherty knew then that he was in big trouble. He had to convince her ma that he was worthy of protecting them both. He had feelings for the lass and knew he was not far from giving the rest of his heart to her. First he had to prove he was up to the task of providing a home for the pair. He'd show Maddy and her ma that he was skilled at handling all manner of weapons—especially a rifle and pistol. His moniker of "the duke's sharpshooter" had been earned.

The challenge would be convincing the lass that he was worthy of her daughter's love—and hers!

CHAPTER FOUR

TEMPERANCE DID NOT want Maddy to know how weak she felt, or how high her fever was. Her daughter would worry. At times she appeared to be far older than her four years, never questioning when Temperance packed their meager belongings into the battered portmanteau—the only thing of value remaining after her husband perished in a mining accident in Cumberland a few months before Maddy was born. Her sweet girl never complained. It was as if she somehow sensed that to question things would only add to the burden weighing heavily on Temperance's shoulders.

Constance set the cup of water within reach on the small table by the cot. "Try to rest, Mrs. Johnson."

"But Maddy—"

"Has been helping me bake," the cook interrupted. "Haven't you, Miss Maddy?"

"She lets me borrow a special apron. I help her stir the batter, Mum."

Temperance fought to keep her voice steady, her concern hidden. "I don't want her to get underfoot—"

"Your daughter has been a ray of sunshine in the kitchen and the nursery. You've raised her to respect her elders, and to be patient, caring, and solicitous of others. I cannot imagine that your daughter would be anything but helpful." Constance frowned. "Has someone on the staff complained? Tell me now, and I shall ask His Grace to have a word with them."

Temperance's fear for her daughter receded. The housekeeper and cook were constantly urging her to let Maddy go off with them to help. More than once, Their Graces' nanny Gwendolyn had asked for her daughter to visit in the nursery and play with the twins.

Temperance's past experience working in different household positions had taught her to be wary of smiling faces—oftentimes they hid a darker intent. The memory of her little girl's ashen face and bruised wrist had had her protective side roaring to the surface, recalling how she had to coax what happened from Maddy. Finally her little one confided that one of the upstairs maids had been eager to let her help put away the linens. Maddy tearfully told of how she'd tripped on the edge of the carpet and dropped the pile she carried, and when she tried to pick them up, the maid grabbed hold of her wrist and yanked her to her feet, and threatened to take a switch to her.

Small hands patted the sides of Temperance's face. She realized her mind had returned to that horrible day and the confrontation—Maddy had come running back to the kitchen where Temperance was chopping vegetables for the cook. One look, and she knew her daughter had been mistreated. Temperance suspected it had to do with the freshly laundered bed linens.

"Mum, are you all right?"

Her head ached abominably, but she strove to ignore it to assure her daughter that she was fine. "Yes, quite all right, Maddy dear." She turned to the cook. "No one has complained to me. But please send Maddy back if she 'helps' too much. She can keep me company while I rest."

"One can never have too much help from willing workers," Constance replied. "Now then, Maddy, I could use an expert stirrer to help mix up a batch of scones."

The unabashed joy on her little girl's face soothed Temperance's soul. Maddy had been smiling ever since Mr. Flaherty—

No, he'd corrected them, and Maddy had been calling him Just Flaherty since he'd rescued them. Was it yesterday, or the day before? It was difficult to remember when one's brains were heated near to boiling.

"Rest now, Mrs. Johnson. Maddy and I have a mountain of scones to bake."

Curious, Temperance asked, "A mountain?"

Her daughter bobbed her head up and down. "We have to bake for teatime, and extra for the charmers."

Temperance frowned. Had guests that she was unaware of arrived? Not that she expected anyone to share that information with her—she was of no consequence. She would be the last person to be informed as to whether the duke and duchess were receiving guests. She was only here because of the kindness of the handsome guard with light-blue eyes that seemed to see into her soul.

Protective of her daughter's safety, thinking of some of the unscrupulous people she had worked for, she asked, "Charmers?"

"Those handsome-as-sin Irishmen who work for His Grace," Constance replied. Holding out her hand to Maddy, she added, "We'd best get busy, Miss Maddy."

The little girl's laughter echoed off the walls and filled the room with a lightness that had been missing.

"Well now," a familiar deep voice rumbled from the doorway. "There's a welcome sight of a morning."

"Just Flaherty!" Maddy rushed over to the guard, who bent down to catch her as she hurtled across the room. "We were talking about you."

He was smiling—was he amused at the way her daughter had taken to calling him Just Flaherty? Temperance would have to explain to Maddy that Flaherty did not want to be addressed as *Mr.* Flaherty, but wasn't sure if her little one would understand. "Were ye now?" His gaze sought Temperance's. "No doubt expounding on tales of how I rescued two lovely lasses halfway between the inn and Wyndmere Hall."

Maddy giggled. "No."

"No?" He brushed a hand over Maddy's curls—so like Temperance's late husband's. Unbidden tears filled her eyes and threatened to fall. Flaherty's expression changed in an instant. He hugged Maddy, motioned for her to return to Constance, and strode toward the cot.

As if the cook sensed what the guard wanted to ask, the woman held out her hand a second time. "Come, Miss Maddy, we've baking to do." With a nod to Flaherty, she warned, "I'm leaving the door open. You may have five minutes, Flaherty—no more. Mrs. Johnson needs her rest."

When they were alone, his expression darkened—was it concern, or something altogether different? Pretending not to notice how intently he stared at her, Temperance shifted her gaze to the doorway. "I hope Constance is not exaggerating, and that Maddy is a help, not a hindrance."

"Yer daughter could never be a hindrance. Constance doesn't exaggerate—'tis Francis who is given to exaggerating, and she uses it to great effect when making up stories to tell Richard and Abigail—little Deidre too—when it's her turn in the nursery."

Temperance could well imagine. Maddy repeated everything the young maid said.

It had been a very long time since she'd felt the pull of attraction to a man. She paused to wonder. Why him? Why now? She did not believe it was because she was more or less a captive audience when he visited her—which seemed to happen whenever the guard changed shifts.

Uneasy with the way she reacted to a man she hardly knew, and concerned that her daughter had formed a friendship with him, she repeated her concern. "In my experience, children are frowned upon when one is widowed and looking for work. I will not repeat the phrase I heard repeatedly from those who turned me away without the courtesy of an interview." The words were etched in her brain: *Children are insufferable, loud, annoying, and a hindrance to those of us forced to deal with them!*

➵➵➵❮❮❮

FLAHERTY HAD A few minutes to spare and sensed there was more to the lass's comment. Something that carved deep worry lines on her forehead. "Do ye mind if I sit? I have a moment or two before I'm to report to the rooftop for me shift."

"I do not mind, but please do not be late on my account. You've done so much for us."

Flaherty sat. "I'm thinking there are those in yer recent past who have not done enough for ye." He wasn't one to mince words, and had had his fill of trying to discern the meaning of what most of those in the *ton* had said. Thankfully, His Grace was a man who believed in speaking his mind and getting to the point.

Now, telling a tale over a tankard of ale, or sharing a flask of whiskey, was another matter altogether. That would be the time for adding a wee bit of exaggeration to enhance a tale to get a reaction from his brothers or cousins.

When she didn't respond, he prompted her, "Ye've no worry that I'll be repeating what ye tell me in confidence, if that's what's holding ye back." Her eyes lifted, and the mix of pain and worry lanced through to his soul. He reached for her hand and patted the back of it. "Growing up, Ma was always telling us not to hold troubles too close to our hearts, but to share them to lighten our burdens."

"Share them?"

Her hesitation worried Flaherty. Had someone spoken harshly to the lass? He'd need to question Merry, Constance, and Francis closely, as they'd been caring for the lass during the worst of the fever that had held her in its grip these last few days.

Decision made, he was determined to get Temperance to open up and share her worries with him. He wanted to be the man she shared them with. His shoulders were broad enough to handle the load he carried working for the duke, as well as any burden this slip of a lass had. "Do ye have a close friend, sister, or brother ye share yer woes with?"

She shook her head.

"Have ye any kin?"

Again, she shook her head, but this time she looked away from him.

"None at all?"

No answer this time. Moved by the fact that the lass and her little girl were all alone in the world, Flaherty scooted the chair right up next to the cot and brushed a strand of ink-black hair out of her eyes. When she did not flinch or move away from him, he lightly traced the tip of his finger from her prominent cheekbone to the hollow beneath it...evidence that the lass had not been getting enough to eat.

"That would explain why ye look as if ye're starving yerself, Temperance."

Her gasp and irritated gaze were just what he'd hoped for. Her full attention was riveted on him. Flaherty intended to have at least one of his questions answered.

"When was the last time ye ate yer fill?" Temperance hesitated just long enough to ignite his temper. "'Tis plain to anyone with an ounce of sense and clear vision that yer darling daughter has been eating well. She's got roses in her cheeks, a joyful expression on her face, and runs Merry, Constance, and Francis ragged trying to keep up with her."

When she remained silent, he leaned closer than was proper—but he needed her to understand how dire her situation was. "Me grandda worked his fingers to the bone to feed his family when their potato crop failed two years in a row. Da and his brothers helped, but Grandda went too long without eating to ensure that me da and uncles ate their fill. He never fully regained his strength. You'd know how important the growing years are to a child, because sure as I'm sitting here staring at yer hollow cheeks, I recognize the signs."

She closed her eyes and turned her face to the wall.

Flaherty shot to his feet. "Ye've a right to care for yer daughter the way ye see fit, but to refuse food when it's offered to ye is a sin!"

He spun around, intending to leave, and froze. "Yer Grace. I didn't know ye were standing there."

The duchess frowned. "I hope you haven't spent the last few minutes haranguing Mrs. Johnson. She needs her rest, Rory, not to be chastised by the man who rescued her and her daughter."

"I beg yer pardon, Yer Grace."

"I believe you should be begging Mrs. Johnson's." She leveled him with a look he was more than familiar with, having felt the weight of it whenever he'd disappointed his ma.

He inclined his head and turned around. The look of surprise on Temperance's face had him wondering: Had the lass been mistreated by her employers? "Her Grace is right." He glanced over his shoulder to add, "And usually is." When the duchess's frown faded, he turned back to the woman on the cot. "Forgive me for taking me worry ye out on ye." Raking a hand through his hair, he groaned. "'Tis been eating at me gut since I found ye beneath that oak by the graveyard. But ye need to understand—"

"Where in the bloody hell are ye, Flaherty?" O'Malley's voice echoed through the hallway. "I'd best not find ye've been sweet-talking the lass when ye're supposed to be relieving Garahan from his shift on the rooftop!" His cousin's sharply indrawn breath and immediate apology, when he saw the duchess, almost had Flaherty smiling. But one look at the duchess's face and he swallowed the grin.

"Apology accepted, Patrick," the duchess replied. "However, you should know that Rory was in fact raising his voice to Mrs. Johnson."

The intensity and temper in the duchess's eyes had the head of the duke's guard turning his ire on Flaherty. "Report to yer post immediately. Ye're not to stop and speak to Mrs. Johnson again without permission."

Flaherty's back went up. "You cannot tell me—"

"Explain yourselves," a deep voice boomed from behind

them. "At once!"

"Were you looking for me, Jared?"

The duke entered the room and paused to study his wife's face. "You know you are to keep your emotions on an even keel." Sliding his hand around her waist, he pulled her close and pressed a kiss to her forehead.

Flaherty had had a feeling that Her Grace was with child, and the duke's words confirmed it. A glance at O'Malley was telling. He already knew of the duchess's condition. No wonder he was issuing orders he normally would not have.

"Your Grace?"

The high-pitched voice had Flaherty wondering what Constance had been thinking to send Maddy into what could turn into a loud *discussion*. Every one of the duke's guard knew that the duchess had been slow to recover after discovering she was carrying again…only to lose the babe a few weeks later. He held his breath and prayed that the duke would temper his anger-laced worry when speaking to the little girl.

Relief speared through Flaherty at how quickly the duke's frown vanished. "Miss Maddy, did Constance send you with an important message for me?"

She nodded and clapped her hands together. "Tea's ready!" She stepped closer to the duke and motioned for him to bend down. When he complied, she whispered something in his ear that had the duke smiling.

"Indeed! Well then, my darling duchess, it seems I am to join you shortly. Miss Maddy will escort you to the sitting room. I shall be along in a few minutes." The duke watched the little girl take the duchess's hand and lead her away from the room.

"O'Malley, inform the men that they are to moderate their voices to an even tone and volume. Any and all outbursts will have to wait until they are away from the house. Differences will be settled in the outbuilding, and no one—I repeat, *no one*—will arrive for their shifts with blood on their faces or knuckles. Understood?"

Flaherty knew then that the duke was terrified his wife would miscarry again. Before his cousin replied, he assured His Grace, "Ye have me word that we'll moderate our voices to what Her Grace likes to refer to as our *inside* voices."

"And the men will not let their tempers show in front of Her Grace." O'Malley paused and nodded to Temperance. "Or yerself, Mrs. Johnson. Forgive me for losing me temper in front of ye, when ye are still recoverin'."

Flaherty watched her shocked surprise smooth into an expression of wonder. "There is nothing to forgive, Mr. O'Malley. I should not even be here, and will hopefully be able to leave tomorrow."

"What's this?" the duke asked. "You have barely recovered. It would be unconscionable for my wife or me to let you leave before we are assured that you will not have a relapse. I shall summon the physician to see you again. I have no doubt that he will reiterate his diagnosis that you require at least a sennight to recover."

"Please do not go to the trouble. I'm certain that I'm well enough to know—"

Flaherty interrupted, "Do not argue with His Grace."

"Oh, but I wasn't arguing. Your Grace, please forgive me, but I do not want you to feel that I am overstaying my welcome."

The Duke of Wyndmere sighed. "My darling duchess reminds me when she is disagreeing with me that she is not *arguing*, simply has a point to make that requires my full attention."

O'Malley snorted, trying to cover his laughter, but the duke heard. "I would not be so quick to laugh, O'Malley. I know for a fact that your wife has adopted my wife's way of thinking." Turning to Flaherty, the duke added, "Strong women like to have their way, but still need coddling."

"Aye, Yer Grace."

The duke bade Temperance goodbye and left the room, O'Malley following in his wake.

Flaherty saw his opportunity to fully explain why he had

raised his voice to the lass, but then his cousin reappeared in the doorway. His frown fierce, O'Malley bit out, "Rooftop. Now!"

With a brief glance at the woman staring up at him, Flaherty spun around and strode from the room. He would have that talk with the lass later. She would understand—and capitulate!

CHAPTER FIVE

MADDY WATCHED THE duchess with unabashed awe. The light from the window shone on the duchess, magically adding streaks of blue to her black hair. Mum had the same color hair, but she'd never seen blue in it. Unable to help herself, Maddy reached out to touch the duchess's hair, but quickly drew her hand back. "You have blue in your hair."

The duchess nodded. "The sun must be coming in the window behind me."

Wonder filled Maddy. "How did you know?"

"I've never seen it happen, because it's always scooped up on my head, but other people have noticed and told me."

Maddy remembered Mum telling her about faeries with dark hair and green eyes. But did they have brown eyes, too? Was the duchess a faerie in disguise? "Did the faeries put it there?"

When the duchess smiled at her, Maddy felt warm inside. The duchess had a pretty face and a soft voice, like Mum. Maddy liked her. She smiled, watching the duchess set her teacup on its saucer and place it on the table between them.

"I often wondered if they had," the duchess replied. "It is a question I have asked myself more than once over the years."

Maddy frowned. "Did yourself answer?"

"I haven't," the duchess replied. "Although I have been waiting for another chance to sneak down to the rose garden and wait for dawn to break. And do you know why?"

Hearing the excitement in the duchess's voice, Maddy bounced in her seat. "Why?"

"The *tween* times—when the clock strikes on the half-hours—are when the fae can be seen," the duchess confided. "At dawn, they come to our gardens to wash their faces in the dew that settles on the flowers overnight."

Maddy gasped and covered her mouth with her hands. The beautiful duchess who had been so nice to her and her mum must be part faerie!

"Do you know what they do then?"

Maddy shook her head, blowing at a curl that flopped into her eyes. "What?"

"They lift their faces to catch the first hint of the morning breeze, spread their arms, unfurl their wings, and dance upon the air."

Maddy slowly flipped onto her tummy, scooted to the edge of the chair, and slid off the chair. She rushed over to stand beside the duchess. "Mum says there's magic in the air..." Her voice trailed off, and she frowned. Maybe the duchess didn't have a mum anymore. Maddy's mum didn't. She knew Mum disliked it when people asked her questions. But if Maddy didn't ask, how could she find out what she wanted to know? "Mum says we gotta believe to see it."

"Your mum is a very wise woman, Maddy."

Maddy nodded. "Can I watch for faeries with you?"

PERSEPHONE WAS CHARMED by the little girl's sunny nature and inquisitiveness. "I do not see any reason why you cannot go, but we shall have to ask permission from your mum." Watching Maddy's face, she was not surprised when the child's expression changed yet again. She had noticed the same swift shift from happiness to tears in her own children.

"She'll say yes."

"If she does, I hope you can be quiet as a mouse."

"I can!" Maddy covered her mouth with her hands, then slowly removed them, whispering, "I can."

"Wonderful. We shall need to be, when we sneak past the guards." Persephone sighed deeply, knowing how it vexed the men—especially Patrick—but what choice did she have? They'd sworn an oath to her husband that they would protect her and the children, and the rest of Jared's family. It was easier for the guard to protect them if they remained indoors.

Maddy seemed to be waiting for her to say more. The duchess decided to explain about her fierce protectors. "The guards have our best interests at heart, and their job protecting us has not been easy. I admire their diligence and efficiency in patrolling our home, the extensive grounds, and the surrounding land between our home and the village. But I do not like being told what to do."

The little girl tilted her head to one side, and Persephone could swear she could hear the cogs moving through the gears until Maddy's thought clicked into place. "Ask them."

Unable to resist, the duchess brushed a hand over the mop of golden curls. "For permission?"

Maddy nodded.

Persephone wished all of life's questions could be handled so smoothly by simply asking and receiving the answers. Not everyone appreciated being questioned, nor did they feel obliged to answer. "An excellent notion, but I should warn you, Miss Maddy, the men in my husband's guard will try to escort us right back inside if they catch us creeping outside at such an early hour."

"But we aren't bad people."

The duchess realized the little girl needed her to explain further. "The men in the guard are strong and brave and will insist that it is for our own good if we wait until the sun comes up to visit the gardens."

Maddy's little face showed every unspoken thought. The dear little girl reminded Persephone of her own daughter. Abigail loved picture books of faeries, elves, wood sprites, and water horses. Anything magical. Her twin Richard preferred books with knights on horseback holding shields and wielding swords.

Finally, Maddy asked, "Will the faeries hide if they see the men?"

Thinking of the tall, broad-shouldered, fiercely protective Irishmen standing shoulder to shoulder in a solid wall of protection, Persephone sighed. "They might."

"Maybe we could ask Just Flaherty to guard us. He can carry Mum outside. Then she can wait and watch for the faeries with us!"

The duchess was not surprised that the little one had already detected Flaherty's interest in her mother. If he were anything like his O'Malley and Garahan cousins, he would be wed before the month was out.

"Leave it to me," she said. "I'll see to it that Rory—Just Flaherty—accompanies us and carries your mother out to the rose garden."

"Thank you!"

The duchess smiled. "Now then, someone has to help Constance bake a batch of faerie cakes. Then we'll need some of her special dandelion wine. The fae are partial to it."

"Do you have tiny teacups?"

Utterly delighted with the child, Persephone paused to think about it. "I'm afraid I do not, but I once read that acorn tops turned upside down will serve as teacups, and tiny leaves can substitute for cake plates." Pleased with their plans so far, Persephone was reminded of the time Ladies Phoebe, Aurelia, and Calliope had planned a dawn adventure to wait for the fae. But they had been forced to cancel their plans when Wyndmere Hall was under attack.

"After we finish our tea, we're expected in the nursery. When we're there, we'll ask Francis and Gwendolyn to help us search for what we need in the herb garden. There's a huge oak tree near the stables. Oh, and of course we cannot exclude my twins, Richard and Abigail, nor Gwendolyn's daughter Deidre—they'll help decide which leaves to use."

"But Deidre cannot walk yet."

"True," the duchess agreed. "But faeries have been known to show themselves to little children and babes because of their pure and kind hearts."

The tiny hand that slipped into hers sent a surge of happiness through Persephone. The trust in Maddy's expression felt like a hug. She knew it would take some doing to slip down to the garden and wait for dawn. The longer they waited, the better the chances that someone would overhear their plans and tell Patrick or one of the other guards. They'd best enact their plan tomorrow.

"Can you keep a secret, Maddy?"

The adorable girl's curls bobbed as she dipped her head. "Yes!"

"His Grace should be arriving any moment, and it would be best if we did not mention our early morning excursion."

Maddy's brow wrinkled. "'scursion?"

"Our dawn trip down to the garden," the duchess explained. She paused and glanced up as footsteps approached. "That will be the duke." She mimed turning a key in a lock against her lips, causing Maddy to giggle.

"What a joyous sound. Mind if I join you ladies for tea?"

Maddy ran over to the duke and held out her hand, confident Jared would grasp it. When he did, she exclaimed, "We saved you sweets!"

The duke's attention to the tiny waif warmed Persephone's heart. Her husband truly loved all children—not just their twins. While Maddy chattered, and Jared listened, Persephone prayed that the babe sleeping beneath her heart was healthy and strong and would continue to grow to term.

Her husband helped Maddy to sit on the chair she had abandoned, then settled on one of the vacant seats. Persephone drank in the sight of the powerful Duke of Wyndmere conversing with the green-eyed pixie as if she were already part of their family. In that moment, the duchess wondered if they, and Flaherty, would be so lucky.

Maddy paused to sip from her cup, and Persephone felt Jared's eyes on her. Lifting her gaze, she saw the hint of concern that had taken up residence since that first morning she'd cast up her accounts upon rising a fortnight ago. "How are you feeling, my darling?" he asked.

Though his voice was couched in concern, she saw the hint of desperation in his gaze. He was worried for her, and their unborn babe. "Rested, thanks to Miss Maddy for keeping me company while we enjoyed our tea."

His deep blue eyes darkened, and she knew he was preoccupied with other matters...matters he had yet to divulge that were either dangerous or had the potential to become so. It was a blessing and a curse to be surrounded by protective men.

"Will you be lying down before the midday meal?"

Persephone did not bother to hide the exasperation she felt. "Were you not listening just now, Wyndmere?"

Her husband nearly choked on his last sip of tea. She always addressed him by his title when she was upset with him. She lifted her cup to her lips and met the intensity of his gaze over the rim.

Maddy tiled her head to one side to stare at her, and then the duke. "It's my turn to read to the twins."

"Read to them?" Jared asked.

"Maddy likes to use different voices as she tells the stories," Persephone explained.

"Indeed."

"Don't be so stuffy, Jared. Miss Maddy is a wonderful companion to Richard and Abigail—and little Deidre, too. There are plenty of picture books for her to read from."

Her husband set his cup on the saucer and placed it on the

table. "How does one *read* from a book filled with pictures?"

Persephone smiled at Maddy before answering, "With one's heart, and the gift of one's imagination."

"An overactive imagination should not be encouraged," he warned.

"Stifling an imagination should be a punishable crime," she retorted.

"What's stifling?" Maddy asked.

The duke raised his eyes to the ceiling and mumbled beneath his breath. He could count all he wished to. But it would not stop Persephone from seeing that neither their children, nor the any of the guards' children—and this precious child, for that matter— would feel stifled or be admonished for daydreaming!

He finished mentally counting and stared at her. She returned the look with one of barely veiled irritation. Lord love the man, Jared sighed and answered Maddy, "To stifle is to suppress something or someone."

"Suppress?"

The duke frowned, searching for another word to use. "Tamp down."

"What's tamp?"

Persephone's emotions were wont to shift dramatically when she was expecting. Right now, she wanted nothing more than to check on her children and spend the next hour or so cuddling them, while Maddy interpreted the picture books with smiles and funny voices. She rose to her feet and answered, "This." She followed the word with an exaggerated stamp of her foot.

Maddy's eyes widened. "Stamp rhymes with tamp!"

The duke chuckled. "Yes, it does, clever girl." Rising to his feet, he bowed to Maddy, before turning to lift Persephone's hand to his lips. The swift kiss arrowed straight to her heart. The wicked look he sent from beneath his lashes promised he would tire her out...later. "I shall be in my study, should you need me."

"Jared?"

He paused in the doorway. "Yes, love?"

"I shall always need you."

His potent smile assured her that he understood her mood shifts and expected them. "Until later."

The duchess drew in a deep breath and slowly exhaled. Rising to her feet, she walked over to the corner and called to Maddy, "Would you please help me ring the bellpull?" The little girl rushed over to her side. "Now then, place your hands here, and I'll place mine above and below yours. On three we shall give it a tug. One…"

"Two, three!" Maddy called out as she tugged the cord with all her strength.

The duchess barely had to pull before she felt it engage. "Well done. Thank you."

Maddy's smile was infectious. "You're welcome."

Persephone held out her hand. The little girl held on tight as the two walked to the nursery. There were babes to cuddle, castles to build out of blocks, and stories to tell.

CHAPTER SIX

T EMPERANCE COULD NOT help but worry. Maddy had been out of her sight for a good portion of the last few days. Whenever the little girl returned to the small room at the opposite end of the hall from the kitchen, she was bubbling over with tales of scones and teacakes, dark-haired, blue-eyed twins, books, and castles built with blocks.

Her daughter was inquisitive, constantly asking questions, from the time she awoke until she closed her eyes at night. Thinking of how quickly she had fallen asleep the night before, Temperance could not help but give credit to the persons responsible for the change. Maddy was more like her cheerful, joyous self. Gone was the reserved little girl who seemed to be shouldering responsibilities far beyond her years. Temperance was beyond grateful to Flaherty for coming to their aid, and to the duke and duchess for their kind offer of a place to stay while she gathered her strength.

She shivered knowing that if it were not for Flaherty, they'd still be sheltering in the middle of that copse of trees. Instead they were treated as if their existence mattered, safe and secure beneath the duke's roof. Their emotional, and physical, wellbeing thrived. Maddy had eaten her fill, and then some, since arriving. She was happier than she had been in a very long time. Still guilt threatened to pull Temperance under. She knew that her inability to secure a position for more than a few months at a time had led to their nomadic existence.

Temperance was adept at cooking and cleaning and had found more than one position. Keeping a job was the issue when it became apparent that those who hired her mistakenly thought, because of her marital status, she would submit to them when cornered. She had been married to a man who loved her and their unborn child, and had vowed never to allow any man to use her for his own pleasure, especially one who believed it his right as her employer. Temperance had fought back. It had been so unexpected that she had successfully evaded more than one employer's foul intentions, allowing her to scoop up her daughter and their bag and flee. The village had been her last hope. She'd hoped to find a position at the inn. There was a better chance that she could keep Maddy with her if she worked there.

Her thoughts returned to the sight of her four-year-old rushing into the room yesterday, brimming with excitement, announcing she had been hired as the sweets taster. The perfect job for Maddy, who loved anything sweet.

"You'd be so proud of our little girl, Paul."

Thoughts of her late husband started the unending circle of questions that had gone unanswered. Why had Paul and his brother stayed behind, bracing the weakened supports of the mine, when no one should have been working in those conditions in the first place? Why hadn't one of the other miners offered to stay and help while the others escaped to safety? Every time she closed her eyes, she could picture the two men standing on either side of the tunnel, feet spread, an arm braced on the support above their heads, and the other against the vertical supports.

Tears welled in her eyes, but she refused to let them fall. The very last thing she wanted was for the footman stationed in the hallway to hear her crying. She stifled the sob that rose in her throat.

Remembering that horrible day, and the ones that followed, she kept asking herself the same question: why had the owner let the miners continue to work in unsafe conditions? The answer that whispered in the back of her mind never changed: money. Coal was in demand and a valuable commodity. The owner had offered his trite, soulless condolences while tales of the Johnson brothers' strength and bravery had spread through the mining town. Survivors spoke of the Johnsons' courage while waiting for the brothers to rush out of the mine. Instead, those gathered outside the mine felt the ground rumble beneath their feet. The rumbling stopped, punctuated with a cloud of dust that belched from entrance to the mine. The survivors had bowed their heads, praying for the souls of the brothers who'd risked their lives only to perish as the tunnel collapsed.

It had taken a week to clear a path to retrieve their remains. Temperance knew that, if not for the valuable carload of coal buried with her husband and brother-in-law, the owners would have abandoned that shaft and concentrated their efforts on one of the others.

Merry bustled into the room and paused, staring at Temperance, who was not quick enough to hide the fact that she had been weeping. The kindly housekeeper walked over, reached into her pocket, and offered her handkerchief to Temperance. She sniffed and thanked the woman, who waited for Temperance to regain her composure.

"We have an extensive herb garden. I have no doubt that we have a herb to alleviate whatever ails you."

Temperance wiped her eyes. "I appreciate everything you have done for Maddy and me, but you have other duties. Please do not worry about me, Merry. I'm quite certain I shall be ready to leave in the morning."

Merry stared at her, pursed her lips, and nodded. Without another word, the housekeeper left the room.

Had Temperance unknowingly insulted the woman, after Merry had been kindness itself? Surely no one expected her to continue to take advantage of the largesse of the duke and duchess without repaying them. She was not used to accepting help in the first place, let alone from such a high-ranking member of the *ton*. Temperance had to apologize—at once!

She shoved the blanket off her lap and shot to her feet, ignoring her spinning head and fading vision. Pushing herself to follow after the housekeeper, she felt her strength lagging. *Not now!* Feeling the overwhelming need to be of service, and not be waited on, she forged ahead. Halfway to the kitchen, her legs wobbled. She tripped and threw her hands out in front of her to break her fall.

Strong arms wrapped around her from behind and she was saved from smacking her head on the floor. "I've got ye, lass." The familiar lilt of Flaherty's voice soothed her jangled nerves as he scooped her into his arms, settling her against his broad chest. "Before I set ye down, ye'll tell me what in blazes ye were thinking. Where were ye going?"

Defeated, she couldn't speak. She'd had a few years to find a way to provide for her daughter and failed miserably time and again. If not for this man finding them by the graveyard, demanding to know who she was and what she was doing, she had no doubt that they would have spent the last few nights on a bed of pine needles.

Growing up in the small mining town, she had never given a thought to foraging for food—there were local shops where her family purchased what they needed. Her father had been a miner, as had Paul's. Used to the way of life, she'd never given a thought to leaving their village. But after losing everything, she'd had no other choice. Faced with moving on again after leaving another untenable situation, Temperance had found herself in yet another town, no mine in sight. With little-to-no money, she'd had to resort to providing something to eat from the land around them, but had no idea where to begin. Which plants were poisonous, and which were safe to eat?

Flaherty's powerful chest expanded beneath her cheek, followed by an audible, exasperated sigh. She had not seen him these two days past. Given the circumstances, she had not wanted him to see that she was still not steady on her feet or strong enough to care for her daughter.

He mumbled something unintelligible beneath his breath, and she sensed he was extremely vexed with her. Afraid to ask, she remained silent. The heat pouring off Flaherty should have soothed her, but instead it added to the ache in her heart. It reminded her of the day her husband had swept her off her feet and into his arms, delighted with the news that she was expecting. His loss lanced through her as if it were yesterday.

Unable to hold them back, her tears fell, and she could do nothing to stop them.

"Ah, lass, don't be weeping."

The rumbling command had her turning her face into the crook of his neck. Memories she'd held off for too long bombarded her.

"Tell me what's wrong," Flaherty urged. "Then I'll fix it."

Words got caught in her throat as she finally accepted the loss of her husband, and began to grieve.

"FETCH MERRY AND Constance!" Flaherty barked. The footman did not need to be told twice. Flaherty could soon hear raised voices and was relieved. The women were accustomed to handling a bout of tears. But it was not only the housekeeper and the cook who rushed toward him, but Her Grace and Miss Maddy, too.

"What happened?" the duchess asked.

"Did Temperance collapse?" Constance asked.

Merry murmured, "This is all my fault."

"The lass was weaving on her feet when I stepped into the hallway," Flaherty told them. "I caught her as she tripped. How could that be yer fault, Merry?"

The normally even-tempered woman wrung her hands. "She

told me she and Maddy would be leaving in the morning. I turned and left without answering her, because I knew Her Grace would not want her to leave and had to tell her."

"You are absolutely right, Merry," Persephone agreed. "I do not want them to leave. It has only been a few days and the physician said it would take at least a sennight for Temperance to recover from the fever."

"A fortnight would be better," Constance added.

"Mum hardly ever cries during the day," Maddy whispered.

The tears welling in the little girl's eyes gutted Flaherty. "Here now, I can barely handle one woman's tears—not the both of ye. Someone has to stop. Now!"

Instead of the immediate reaction Flaherty expected, Merry gasped, Constance's eyes widened in shock, and the duchess snorted, trying to cover her laughter.

"What part of this do ye find amusing, Yer Grace?"

Persephone met his stern expression with one of irreverence. "Do all men expect someone to stop crying simply because you tell them to?"

Flaherty would rather be on the receiving end of Garahan's jaw-jarring right cross than admit that tears unmanned him. He was helpless trying to stop them. Most often he had no idea why a woman started to cry in the first place. On the defensive, he muttered, "'Tis me duty to fix this. Why can I not tell her not to cry?"

Merry's eyes danced with merriment, while Constance stared at him.

The woman weeping in his arms did not sound as if she intended to stop anytime soon. Flaherty had to admit that he had lost control of the situation. That was unacceptable. "Someone has to stop crying!" He raised his eyes to the ceiling and mumbled a curse he hoped the duchess would not hear. They had orders not to upset Her Grace, but he was in the middle of a maelstrom of tears that was slipping out of his control.

Maddy wiped her eyes with the backs of her hands. "I

stopped, Just Flaherty. See?"

"There's a lass," he crooned. "Now, if yer ma would only stop, we could all sit down with a nice cup of tea and chat." He stared at the women surrounding him, daring any one of them to contradict him.

Her Grace was the first to agree. "That last part of your suggestion makes more sense than the first." She turned to the cook. "Constance, the tea should have steeped by now. Have one of the footmen fetch it along with a plate of your lavender scones. They are delicious, and the scent is so soothing."

"At once, Your Grace."

"Merry, please join us. My darling duke will have no reason to complain that I have overexerted myself if you're with me."

"Of course, Your Grace." The housekeeper entered the room first, shifting chairs and retrieving the blanket that had fallen to the floor.

"Are ye wanting to sit, lass, or lie down?" Flaherty asked Temperance.

Maddy giggled, breaking through the tension in the room. "Mum can't sip tea lying down."

"Well now, Miss Maddy, 'tis an excellent observation. We'd best set yer ma in the chair." He leaned down and gently placed Temperance on the seat. Pulling his handkerchief from his waistcoat pocket, he wiped the tears from her face, stifling a groan when more welled up. "I'm thinking ye'll be needing a half-dozen linens if ye cannot shut off yer tears, lass."

The duchess placed her hand on his arm. "Thank you for arriving in time to prevent an injury, Rory. We'd better let you return to your duties before you are missed."

He inclined his head. "Aye, Yer Grace." Relief filled him when he glanced at Temperance, and she'd managed to stop crying. "If ye have need of me, I'll be patrolling the perimeter." Bending down, he brushed his hand over Maddy's curls. "Ye're a brave little lass. Keep an eye on yer ma for me."

Her expression shifted from worry to resolve. "I will."

"Faith, I know it. Thank ye." He strode to the door and steeled himself to not look over his shoulder and see if Temperance watched him.

Flaherty left the building, intent on retrieving his gelding. Striding toward the stables, he wondered if Temperance's husband had been able to easily halt her tears. His gut churned and his temper simmered as he reached for the door, and it struck him—he was jealous of a dead man! "Ye're a fecking eedjit."

The snort of laughter had him spinning around and tossing a punch. Garahan tilted to the side. "Yer aim is off." Frowning, he added, "Ye'd best get yer head on straight before ye ride out to guard the perimeter."

Flaherty curled his hands into fists before relaxing them. "Me head's fine." He grabbed hold of the handle and yanked the door open.

"Keep telling yerself that, boy-o."

Garahan's laughter grated, but Flaherty ignored it. The urge to pound on his cousin was strong, but his sense of duty was stronger. His horse was saddled and ready for him. He led the gelding out of the building, gained the animal's back, and headed toward the road that wound around the duke's estate.

A mile down the road, he couldn't remember if he'd thanked the stable master. The man took excellent care of the horseflesh the duke owned. Flaherty and the rest of the guard appreciated the man. The fact that he could not recall meant that his head was muddled. *I won't be admitting that fact to Garahan—or anyone else!*

Rounding the bend in the road, he glanced over his shoulder as the trees obscured his view of the duke's ancestral home. Once Wyndmere Hall was out of his sight, it was easier to set aside his worry for the distracting woman and the wee *cailín* aside. He'd left them in the care of the duchess—a force to be reckoned with when she wanted her way—and the duke's staunch housekeeper and cook. The older women and Humphries the butler had proven their mettle when Wyndmere Hall was under attack from the unhinged Viscount Hollingford.

Scanning both sides of the road was second nature to him. Alert to changes in the landscape, and the itch between his shoulder blades when he sensed danger, Flaherty covered the familiar ground, while memories from the attack two years ago added to his sense of unease.

At the time, the newly pregnant duchess had been the catalyst convincing Merry and Constance to put herself, the duke's sister, and two of her friends to work. They had gathered and sorted the linen to be used as bandages and retrieved herbs that would be needed, while water heated and threads were boiled. Willing hands helped chop vegetables and meat for the stew, soups, and meat pies Constance deemed necessary to feed the men defending the duke and his family. Loaves of bread and batches of scones were consumed while more were baking. Every single man and woman on the duke's staff had pitched in wherever needed, while tenant farmers fought alongside the duke, his brother the earl, and the sixteen men in the duke's guard.

Flaherty slowed at reaching the first of the handful of spots sharpshooters had used in the past. Satisfied that nothing was amiss, he urged his mount to pick up the pace. Riding through an open section with fields on both sides of the road, he admitted to himself that he missed that span of time he and his relatives were all stationed together. They had fought and bled side by side to uphold their vow to the duke. Not long afterward, the duke's brother had married, and the first of the duke's guard had been assigned to protect Earl Lippincott and his bride Lady Aurelia.

Movement to the left caught Flaherty's eye and had him slowing his mount to a walk. He slipped the rifle off his shoulder, took aim, and waited. The hedgerow moved close to the ground as a fox darted from beneath it. He exhaled, eased his finger off the trigger, and slung the rifle over his shoulder.

The rest of his patrol was quiet—eerily so. He'd be reporting that fact to Patrick, who'd relay the information to His Grace. They would no doubt discuss whether to request that additional men be sent north to increase their numbers. Captain Coventry, the duke's London man-of-affairs, and Bow Street Runner Gavin King would combine their resources and discuss who best to send to the Lake District.

Guiding the horse to the south, Flaherty let his thoughts return to the green-eyed, dark-haired woman who'd unknowingly tugged at his gut and whispered to his heart. The overwhelming need to protect her and her daughter surprised him. Having watched his cousins wrestle with needs that sometimes conflicted with their duties, he accepted that his head and his heart had never been captivated by a woman before—separately, yes, but never settling on the same woman.

Three and a half hours into his patrol, the lass was still on his mind, firmly wrapped around his heart—alongside her daughter. With half an hour left until the shift change, he knew without a doubt that the two lasses held the key to his happiness and the future they would make together.

"Rory lad, ye've finally done it," he mused as Wyndmere Hall was once more in sight. "Ye've given yer heart to the wee lass and her ma. God help me if they hand it back!"

CHAPTER SEVEN

T EMPERANCE COULD NOT help but stare at Flaherty as he left to man his post. She'd thought her husband was the only man with shoulders that broad or a chest that deep. Memories teased the edges of her memory, begging to be let back in, but she held them off until she was alone again. She needed to be a help, not a hindrance.

Constance returned, followed by one of the footmen bearing a large tray. "Please, set it over there." After the man bowed to the duchess, he retreated to the hallway. Temperance hoped he was not close enough to listen to their conversation. From the way the ladies relaxed, she decided if they were not bothered by a footman overhearing whatever they said, then she wouldn't be either.

"Mum, your nose is red."

Temperance sighed. "I'm certain that my eyes are too."

Maddy patted her mother's face and sighed. "They swelled up." She pressed her lips to Temperance's cheek and patted her face a second time. "Tea will help."

Constance smiled. "Tea is just the thing...the stronger, the better."

"Not too strong," Merry warned. "Invalid's diet. Remember?"

Temperance felt as if she'd been hugged. These women had showered herself and Maddy with attention and caring. She had to find a way to repay them.

"You are such a wonderful help to your mum," the duchess remarked. "Merry tells me you folded the linen cloths all by yourself."

Maddy beamed at her. "The hand ones…not the big ones."

"The size isn't important—the task undertaken and performed to the best of your ability is what counts, Miss Maddy."

Her little girl's happiness with the compliment was infectious, though Temperance worried her daughter's exuberance and lack of deference to the duchess's title would upset Persephone. Protective as a mama bear, she decided the direct approach would be best.

"Your Grace, may I ask you a question?"

Persephone frowned. "Of course. Ask me anything."

"I have become more protective of Maddy after having to leave my last few employers. I hope you do not think I'm trying to overstep. That isn't my intention, but Maddy is such a happy child that she sometimes forgets the proper way to address the people we meet." When the duchess merely inclined her head, Temperance continued. "Neither Maddy nor I have ever met a duke or duchess before. Please do not think we do not respect you or your title, Your Grace. We hold you in the highest regard, and are beyond grateful for your indulgence, allowing us to remain here for the last few days."

Persephone sighed. "If you are about to tell me again that you intend to leave in the morning, let me remind you that the physician has yet to return to reexamine you. Until he assures me that you are fully recovered, you are not leaving."

Temperance was surprised by the duchess's firm tone. She had not heard her use it before. "But surely we are in the way—"

"You are not. Jared and I are so pleased that you appear to be regaining your strength. Tomorrow morning, Merry will help you move upstairs. You and Maddy will have the yellow guest room. It has a lovely view of the rose gardens."

"Mrs. Duchess—" Maddy began, only to furrow her brow in

concentration and look at Temperance.

"It's *Your Grace*, remember, Maddy dear?"

The little one nodded, reminding Temperance of her husband's mop of blond curls. "Your Grace?"

"Yes, Miss Maddy?" Persephone replied.

"Did you forget about"—Maddy looked at the open door and turned back, lowering her voice to just above a whisper—"the faeries, the dew, and the flowers?"

Persephone's soft laughter filled the room, chasing away Temperance's worry. The duchess was nothing like the merchant's wife. She would never raise a hand to Maddy.

"I was waiting until everyone finished their first cup of tea. But now is the perfect time to discuss our plans. Would you please close the door, Maddy?"

Temperance watched her daughter bounce up, rush to the door, and, using two hands, close it. "Like that?"

"Just like that." Still smiling, the duchess refilled their cups while Constance served the lavender scones, adding an extra dollop of clotted cream to Maddy's. "Thank you, Constance, these are delicious." She finished off her first scone and turned to the ladies. "Now then, Miss Maddy and I plan to go to the gardens early in the morning."

Maddy clapped her hands together. "It's a dawn 'scursion."

The duchess nodded at the little girl. "An excursion because we're hoping to see faeries."

Maddy bounced on her chair and nearly fell off, but caught herself in time. "Faeries! Know why, Mum?"

"I believe I do," Temperance replied. "Your grandmother and I used to wait and watch for the faeries when I was your age."

"I don't remember her." Temperance held out her hand, and Maddy took it and climbed up onto her lap. Laying her head against her mother's breast, she sighed. "She and Grandfather are in Heaven with Papa."

Her throat tightened, but Temperance ignored it to answer, "Yes. So is Uncle Matt."

"He and Papa were brave."

"Aye, my love. The bravest."

"They saved miners," Maddy told the duchess. "'Cause the ceiling broke when the floor rumbled."

Understanding filled the duchess's dark eyes.

Before her daughter said anything further about the tragedy, Temperance said, "Maddy, dear, we can talk about Papa later, when we're alone."

Maddy shrugged, but thankfully fell silent.

Needing to distract her daughter before she started talking about her father again, Temperance said, "I saw a faerie with flaming red hair and green eyes. Her wings were as delicate as a spider's web."

The duchess smiled. "The one I saw had ink-black hair like yours, Temperance. Her bright-green eyes tipped up at the corners. Her smile was decidedly mischievous."

"'Cause they like to laugh and spin and fly up high!" Much to the delight of the other women, Maddy demonstrated by laughing, spinning, and throwing her arms out to her sides as she flew around the room.

"Maddy, you know you aren't supposed to run inside," Temperance scolded her.

"Just this once," the duchess said. "To show us how faeries fly. It has been some years since I was Miss Maddy's age."

Temperance crooked her finger, and Maddy slumped her shoulders and dragged her feet until she reached her mother's side. "Do I have to 'pologize?"

"You do."

Maddy sighed deeply. "To everyone?"

"You do, but you should address the duchess first."

"I'm ever so sorry, Your Grace."

"That was a lovely apology, thank you, Maddy," Persephone said.

"Sorry, Miss Constance, Miss Merry."

The older women inclined their heads, accepting the little

girl's apology.

"Well done," Temperance said.

"Can I have another scone, Mum?"

"You need to ask Her Grace," Temperance reminded her.

"Mrs.—Your Grace, can I?"

The duchess's warm smile was all the assurance Temperance needed that Maddy would be forgiven for running circles around them while she flew. "Of course you may. Do you have room in your tummy for one more with clotted cream?"

Maddy's eyes widened. "Yes!" When Temperance sighed loudly, Maddy remembered her manners. "Please and thank you."

While her daughter nibbled on the scone, Temperance asked, "Will we be able to watch for faeries without an escort?"

The duchess's eyes brimmed with merriment. "We shall certainly try—that is the fun part."

"Fun?" Temperance asked.

"Oh yes, outwitting Patrick O'Malley and his cousins will be a rare feat, but I believe we are up to it."

"Your Grace?" Maddy asked.

"Yes, what is it?"

"You forgot Just Flaherty."

"Maddy, dear," Temperance began, "his name isn't Just—that was his way of telling you he wants to be called Flaherty."

"He said it twice, Just Flaherty. 'Member?"

When the duchess stifled her laughter, Temperance gave up. She would try to explain later. "What about Flaherty?"

Maddy frowned at her mother, but before she could say anything, the duchess chimed in, "We discussed asking Flaherty to carry you outside, if you were too weak. Maddy didn't want you to miss out on our excursion."

"'Cause I love you, Mum." Maddy scooted closer and pressed a feather-soft kiss to Temperance's cheek.

"I love you too, Maddy."

"Now that that's settled," the duchess said, "I suggest you

rest, Temperance, just for an hour or so."

"Oh, but I'm not tired."

"When I tell Mum that, she makes a face."

The duchess's lips twitched, and Temperance appreciated that Her Grace did not want Maddy to think she was laughing at her. "Does she?"

"Uh huh. Like this!" Maddy scrunched her face until her eyes were tiny slits and her chin was jutting out.

"I see. Do you think it would work if I made that face at her?"

"Yes! Do it!"

Temperance could not believe how wonderful the duchess was with Maddy—but then, she was a mum herself, though her twins were younger. When the duchess made the exact same face as Maddy, Temperance bit her bottom lip and hung her head. "I'll rest, Your Grace."

"See?" Maddy exclaimed. "It worked!"

When Constance and Merry started stacking teacups, saucers, plates, and utensils on the tray, Temperance said, "I do have a question for you, Your Grace."

"What would you like to know?" Persephone asked. Temperance glanced at her daughter and back. The duchess must have sensed that she did not want her daughter to hear the question. "Miss Maddy, would you please help Constance put away the tea things?"

"Yes, Your Grace!" The little one skipped out of the room.

"Now then, ask me," Persephone told Temperance.

"I have a few pence left that I will gladly give to you for taking us in, but it's not enough. I need to fully repay you. I cannot in good conscience continue to stay without repaying you somehow."

Persephone sighed deeply. "What do you have in mind?"

"I can help in the kitchen, or with any of the housemaid's tasks. I would be honored to help Gwendolyn in the nursery, too."

The duchess was silent for a few moments before she nodded.

"I think we can arrange something. Mayhap an hour or so in the nursery tomorrow afternoon. After you rest from our morning—as your daughter put it—'scursion.'"

"Thank you, Your Grace!"

"However, if I feel it is too taxing, you will rest for another full day before you attempt to help again. Is that clear?"

"Very. Thank you, Your Grace."

"We could still ask Just Flaherty to carry you tomorrow morning."

Temperance felt the flush creep up her throat to her face. "I am quite certain he has other duties."

The duchess held her gaze and slowly smiled. "We can make an exception tomorrow morning."

"I wouldn't want to bother him."

Persephone's light laughter hinted at something she knew that Temperance did not. "Oh, it won't bother him in the *slightest*."

Temperance was not so sure about that, recalling how angry he had been when she spoke of leaving. But that was tomorrow's worry—today's was her promise to rest.

The duchess pointed at the cot. "Weren't you going to rest?"

"Er…yes, Your Grace."

"I'll help you to the cot, if you need it."

"I can manage," Temperance murmured.

"I realize that," the duchess remarked. "Please do humor me."

Temperance noticed the other woman's eyes looked tired. "Thank you, but who is going to help you?"

"That would be me."

The duchess looked over her shoulder. "Jared, what are you doing here?"

"Coming to remind you it is past time for your midafternoon rest, my darling duchess."

Temperance moved to the cot and sat.

The duchess sighed. "Very well—it seems we both need to

rest, Temperance. If you need anything, the footman will be stationed in the hall."

"Thank you, Your Grace. Enjoy your rest."

The duke slipped his arm around his wife's waist. "I shall see to it that she does."

On that cryptic remark, he swept the duchess from the room. The echoing laughter reminded Temperance of all that she had lost. When the tears threatened yet again, she wondered if mayhap she should not have bottled them up for so long, allowing herself brief moments in the dark of night to weep. Had she given in to them, it may have prevented the flood of them now. Too late for what-ifs…

Lying down, she felt a wave of exhaustion sweep up from her toes. Her heart fluttered at the thought of Flaherty carrying her all the way to the rose garden, and she could not get the image of out of her mind. Closing her eyes, she imagined she heard her daughter calling to him—*Just Flaherty, wait for me!*

CHAPTER EIGHT

F LAHERTY REFILLED HIS powder flask and frowned at Eamon O'Malley. "Are ye certain that's what she heard?"

"Me wife wouldn't be prevaricating," his cousin insisted. "Not to me."

Flaherty checked his pockets for wadding and the small leather bag he used to carry the rifle's .40-caliber lead balls. "I thought Her Grace gave up on that idea before the twins were born."

Eamon spat on the whetting stone in his hand and rubbed it in. "I'm guessing she hasn't." He slipped the knife from his boot and drew it over the stone in swift, sure motions, turning the blade over as he sharpened it. "Abigail is just the right age to be entranced by the fanciful idea of tiny, winged creatures." He ran his thumb over the edge of the blade, nodding when a thin bead of blood welled up. "Sharp enough."

Flaherty held out his hand to O'Malley, who tossed him the whetting stone. "Water horses and faery forts, no doubt."

Eamon grinned. "Helen's mentioned the picture books in the nursery more than once. At least two books have colorful images of the fae, and most any other mythical creature ye can think of."

The urge to smile surprised Flaherty. He hadn't been given to flights of fancy since he was a lad, and then only when Ma rocked him on the nights he could not find his sleep. She'd alternate between singing lullabies and telling stories of magic and heroes of old. "Well now, I'm thinking a certain little ray of sunshine may have had something to do with it."

O'Malley chuckled. "Miss Maddy."

"Aye," Flaherty agreed. "She's got a way about her, convincing ye to do the opposite of what ye planned."

"I'm more than familiar with the tactic," his cousin admitted. "Though I would not have thought too many females knew of it, as it's a warrior's tactic." O'Malley rubbed his chin. "We'd best be on our guard if Her Grace starts getting ideas again."

Flaherty watched his cousin check his pistol's ammunition, reminding him again of the time Wyndmere Hall was under attack. He tucked the memory away, calling up another one from that same year—when the duchess, the duke's sister, and two of her friends had a twilight tea party on the roof. He shook his head, mumbling, "Gargoyles and faeries."

Garahan snorted as he entered the outbuilding where they stored their munitions. "So ye've heard?"

O'Malley nodded and Flaherty grunted.

Garahan held out his hand to Flaherty. "I'll be needing the Kentucky long rifle, as I'll be riding the perimeter."

When Flaherty handed it over, Garahan handed him the pistol from his waistband. "Ye might need to put it off for an hour."

"We'll need Patrick's input on the situation," Garahan warned. "Ye know he doesn't like when we switch shifts without letting him know ahead of time."

"Circumstances do not always allow for careful planning. He will have to bend his stiff neck and understand," Flaherty grumbled.

The door opened and Patrick O'Malley walked in and read the emotion in the room. "I just spoke to His Grace. We'll be putting off our first shifts to guard Her Grace and her entourage."

Eamon scrubbed a hand over his face. "How many women this time?"

"Seven," the head of the duke's guard replied. "Then there

are the children."

Flaherty shook his head. "Too many women to suit me. Little ones should still be abed."

Garahan was shaking his head when he asked O'Malley "Have ye spoken to Humphries yet?"

"Aye," O'Malley replied. "He's assemblin' the footmen we've trained to take over our shifts."

"Did Her Grace think we wouldn't find out about her plans," Flaherty asked, "or do ye think she is going to try to sneak past us?"

"I'm thinking the second," Eamon replied.

Garahan mumbled beneath his breath, "Won't be the first time."

O'Malley stared at his cousins. He nodded to Garahan, who had the rifle over his shoulder. "Ye'll take the position on the roof. The paths to the garden are visible. We don't want any surprise interruptions."

"Anything else I need to know?"

O'Malley shook his head. "I already know the answer, but I'm askin' just the same. Any chance yer wife would sleep in?"

Garahan snorted. "Emily would not want to miss the chance to sneak past us."

"'Tis me feeling about Gwendolyn as well. She'll have Deidre with her." He met Eamon's gaze next. "What about Helen?"

"Our wives have much in common," Eamon reminded him. "Spines of steel and stubborn wills to match."

O'Malley tossed up his hands. "How in the bloody hell did the lot of us manage to find such hardheaded wives?"

"'Tis a weakness," Flaherty said with a grin. "Our das married women just like them."

"Faith, ye aren't wrong," O'Malley admitted. "Eamon, ye'll be on horseback, on the other side of the back wall of the garden. There are too many paths that lead into the thick woods from that point. Flaherty, ye're with me."

Flaherty nodded. "Waiting outside the rear doors to the library."

"Aye. With three women expecting, we need to be prepared for one of them to swoon."

"Where will the duke be?" Garahan asked.

"With O'Malley and Flaherty," the duke announced, stepping into the building. "I will not take a chance that Persephone will stumble, fall, and hit her head."

Flaherty observed Garahan glancing at Eamon O'Malley, who slowly nodded. He wondered if all pregnant women were prone to swoon like the duchess had been while carrying the twins.

Garahan cleared his throat and said, "We could move into our positions after we've safely escorted the women to the garden."

"Her Grace will be carrying Richard or Abigail," Eamon added. "Francis will be involved, too. She'll be carrying the other twin."

O'Malley muttered, "Gwendolyn will be carrying Deidre." He turned to stare at Flaherty "That leaves one other little one to be carried."

"Maddy's sure-footed," Flaherty said. "She'll be walking."

The duke leveled his gaze on each man in turn. "As much as I prefer to have you patrolling and in positions around the garden to start, I think Garahan's suggestion has merit."

"We can have eyes on the women as they sneak out of the nursery," Flaherty said. "And alert the others."

"Excellent," the duke murmured. "Humphries will have the footmen assembled and in positions within the hour. I shall inform him that plans have changed slightly and the footmen are to assume your positions until you relieve them." With a nod to the men forming in a semicircle around him, the duke exhaled. "Thank you, men. It isn't an easy job protecting women who do not believe they need to be."

Flaherty grinned. "I think I'll see if Constance needs me help loading the basket she'll be filling with scones and faery cakes."

And just like that, the tension broke.

The duke shook his head. "It would be best if she doesn't realize we know of their plans."

Flaherty did not hold the same opinion—but once the duke's mind was made up, he rarely changed it.

An hour later, everyone was in place, ready, and waiting.

"MUM? ARE YOU awake?"

Temperance slowly opened her eyes. "Maddy? Do you feel all right?"

"It's time!"

Temperance was slow to wake up, but one look at her daughter's glowing smile and eagerness, and she remembered. "The faeries?"

Maddy bounced on her feet, grabbed hold of her mother's hand, and tugged. "We have to hurry!"

Temperance noticed the wrinkled gown her daughter was wearing had fabric bunched up in spots. "Did you dress yourself?"

"Halfway."

Temperance wondered who had helped her daughter. "Was Merry here already?"

Maddy shook her head.

"Constance?"

Again she shook her head.

"Who helped you?"

Maddy gave an exaggerated sigh. "Just Flaherty."

"Why would he help you?"

"'Cause I couldn't reach my buttons."

Worry filled Temperance. Flaherty was an unmarried man, and he'd helped her daughter dress herself? "Why didn't you wake me up?"

"I tried, Mum."

Temperance swung her legs to the side of the bed and slowly stood. "Tell me exactly what happened."

"I can help you dress first," Maddy told her.

"I'd have to take my nightrail off first."

Maddy giggled. "No you don't."

"Silly thing. Of course I do. Chemise, then gown. Remember?"

Maddy shook her head, walked over to the side of the cot, and lifted the hem of her gown, showing her mother her nightclothes underneath. "See? My gown's on top!"

And Temperance did see. She bent down to her daughter's level and touched the tip of her finger to the end of Maddy's nose. She did not have to worry about her daughter being alone with Flaherty. He was an honorable man, and had probably been aghast at being asked to help Maddy dress. "Who's idea was that?"

"Just Flaherty's."

"I see. Did he ask why you needed to get dressed so early?" Temperance was concerned that the guard would follow them, and she was not certain if the duchess had spoken to him or not. Hadn't Persephone mentioned sneaking past her husband's guard?

Maddy nodded.

"What did you tell him?"

"That it was a secret. Was that right, Mum?"

Temperance opened her arms, and Maddy threw her arms around her mother's neck. "Yes. Mayhap I should put my gown over my nightrail, too."

Her daughter was vibrating with excitement. "Hurry, Mum!"

It was a snug fit, but Temperance managed to pull her gown over her nightclothes. "Do I have time to put my hair up?"

"Can you walk at the same time?"

Temperance snorted, then covered her mouth with her hands, while Maddy giggled.

"Try, Mum. We have to go!"

Rather than risk Maddy raising her voice again, Temperance decided to tidy her braid instead. Untying the ribbon, she unwound the bottom half of her braid, smoothed it out, rebraided it, and tossed it over her shoulder. She held out her hand to her daughter, and they tiptoed to the door, carefully looked from one end of the deserted hallway to the other, and rushed toward the kitchen.

Constance was waiting for them. From the fit of her gown, Temperance suspected that she, too, had pulled her clothes on over her night things. Relaxing, Temperance offered to carry the basket.

"Between the offering for the faeries and our early morning tea, it's too heavy for you to carry." When Temperance sighed, Constance suggested, "Why don't you take hold of one of the handles on the large basket, and I'll hold the other? Between us, it will lighten the load."

Temperance used her free hand to help Maddy open the door to the main part of the house. As soon as she could, Maddy squeezed through and skipped ahead of them down the long hallway. "Constance, is it odd that no one seems to be about but us?" Temperance asked.

The cook smiled. "We do not always see the duke's guard, but they are always watching over us."

"Like guardian angels?"

Constance smiled. "Warrior guardian angels."

Temperance frowned. Was she being untrue to her husband's memory by wanting someone to help protect her daughter? Lately, she'd realized that being strong and willing to work through exhaustion was not enough to ensure that Maddy—and herself—would be safe from those who would mistreat them...or worse.

"Whatever soured your mood, don't let that little moppet see you like this." The cook waited a beat before adding, "We can talk about it later over a nice cup of my special tea."

"Special?"

"I keep a medicinal supply of whiskey on hand. A splash or two in a cup of tea is quite soothing."

"When we had it, I would add a splash of cream."

"And when you didn't?"

"It was a luxury sometimes to have the tea at all."

"Mum, Miss Constance!" Maddy was standing in the doorway to the library, motioning for them to hurry.

"Do you think any of the duke's guard heard Maddy?" Temperance asked.

"Not to worry. The men are always considerate of babes and children."

Temperance added that bit of information to the things she admired about Flaherty. "I did get to see that firsthand when he helped Maddy and me."

They had reached the door and discovered they were the last to arrive. The duchess was carrying Abigail, but Merry was holding out her arms to take the little girl. Francis, the duchess's lady's maid, had Richard on her hip. Patrick's wife carried their precious babe, Deidre, while Helen and Emily—Eamon and Aiden's wives—carried quilts.

"Merry, I can carry Abigail," the duchess said.

"Of course you can, Your Grace, but I would feel better—and I am quite sure His Grace would too—if I carried her outside. You are supposed to be resting and not lifting anything heavier than your smile."

"That is such a lovely thing to say." Temperance wished someone had said that to her while she was expecting Maddy. But her husband had worked long hours underground and was rarely home in the middle of the day when she was keeping house.

The duchess sighed. "My darling duke has hidden depths that he draws upon, saying such sweet things to me."

"You are very lucky, Your Grace," Temperance said.

The duchess's delighted laughter echoed in the darkened library. "Jared has told me that, too…more than once." Gathering the women close around her, she said, "Now then, we must be quiet as mice. Faeries can be quite shy, and we do not want to startle them."

"They like honey cake," Maddy whispered.

"And dandelion wine," Constance added.

"Sounds like a feast," Merry said with a smile.

"Follow me," the duchess said.

The group fell in line, single file, behind the duchess, with Temperance and Constance holding up the rear. Everyone was careful not to bump into any of the chairs or tables and have one of the duke's guard demanding to know why they were up and where they were headed.

At the rear door leading onto the terrace, the duchess put a finger to her lips, opened the door, stepped outside, and gasped.

Temperance heard Francis ask what was wrong before she heard the rumble of a deep voice. She wondered which one of the duke's guard was on the patio, and if he would demand that they forgo their dawn plans.

Constance sighed. "It appears that we shall have escorts. I do hope they will keep their voices down."

"Escorts?" Temperance asked.

"I should have thought of that when the duchess mentioned her plans. The duke is especially protective of her now that she is expecting again."

"He sounds like a devoted husband," Temperance murmured.

"His Grace is the best of men."

"I hear more voices," Temperance remarked. "Who else do you think is out there?" Before Constance could reply, Temperance heard the Irish lilt and suspected it would be one of the married men in the duke's guard—mayhap all three of the married men. Two of the wives were pregnant, and Patrick's wife was carrying their six-month-old daughter.

"It appears all four of the duke's men are waiting for us," Constance said.

"Well now, Miss Maddy," Flaherty said, walking over, "I see

ye woke yer ma. Did ye help her dress?"

Temperance could feel her face flushing at the highly personal question, and hoped it was still too dark for Flaherty to notice. "Maddy is a very good helper."

"So I've heard. Do ye want me to carry ye, Maddy? Ye don't want yer hem to get damp."

For a heartbeat, Temperance wished she were a little girl, and Flaherty was offering to carry *her*. Instead she urged her daughter to let him carry her. The guard was so broad and tall that for a moment she worried Maddy would wiggle too much and topple out of his arms. But as soon as he settled her in the crook of his arm, Maddy hugged Flaherty's neck. She would be safe.

When he offered his free arm to her, Temperance hesitated. Long-dead emotions twisted around inside of her as the musical lilt of his words wrapped around her. "May I escort ye, lass?"

Temperance did not want to be the only one receiving such special treatment, and was about to refuse when she noticed those walking in front of them. The duke carried Abigail on one arm and had the duchess tucked against his other side. O'Malley carried little Deidre and had his wife's arm looped through his. Eamon escorted Helen and Merry; Garahan had Emily and Constance. Looking around her, Temperance asked, "What about the basket?"

"I ran ahead with the basket and quilts," Flaherty replied. "His Grace did not want any of ye to be lifting or carrying. 'Tis still dark enough to trip or lose yer footing."

"Thank you, Flaherty."

"Mum!" Maddy sounded exasperated. "It's *Just* Flaherty."

The rumbling chuckle warmed Temperance's heart, but not as much as the way her daughter clung to the big man's neck. In that moment she was hit by all that Maddy had missed out in life arriving after her father's untimely death. The only memories she had were the ones Temperance had shared with her to keep his memory alive in their minds and in their hearts.

As the group quietly followed the path, Flaherty must have

sensed something was amiss. He bent close to Temperance's ear. "Are ye worried Maddy won't see any of the *fae*?"

Temperance did not want to tell him what troubled her, so she shook her head.

"Ah, 'tis yerself who's worried." The warmth of his breath on the shell of her ear and the deep, rumbling sound of his voice were sharp reminders of all she had lost and what she would never have again. "We are a big group," he continued, unaware of her plight. "If they're feeling kindly toward the wee ones, they may show themselves."

"Do you believe that?"

"Aye. Did yer ma not teach ye to respect the Gentry—the Little People?"

"She read me stories of mythic heroes—Odysseus and Jason."

"Well then, ye must have heard of Cú Chulainn."

"No."

"Fionn mac Cumhaill"

Temperance giggled. "No."

"Lass, we'll need to expand yer education to include Irish legends and heroes."

"Me too?" Maddy asked.

"Aye, wee *cailín*."

Maddy put her hands on either side of Flaherty's face. "It's Maddy."

"Aye, but ye're also a wee *cailín*, a little girl."

She let go of his face and leaned against his cheek. "And you're Just Flaherty."

"That I am, ye wee charmer."

"Mum, I'm charming!"

Temperance felt the warmth of Flaherty's words for her daughter. "You certainly are, Maddy."

Someone in front of them hissed for them to be quiet as they approached the center of the rose garden. Temperance put her finger to her lips, and Maddy nodded until her curls fell into her eyes, causing Flaherty to chuckle as he brushed the hair away.

Before they had to be shushed again, Temperance squeezed lightly on his arm. He turned toward her. In the soft early morning light, she saw a faint flicker of an emotion she had not seen in a long time. Was it due to the moment, or had it meant something more? Before she could decide, he schooled his features until he once more wore a neutral expression—one she could not decipher. *Probably for the best.*

Merry and Francis spread out the quilts for the women to sit on, while Constance unpacked the basket. Flaherty helped Temperance and Maddy to sit and reminded them not to leave until he came back to escort them to the house. The married men bade their wives goodbye, and only the duke and Patrick remained behind, ostensibly to keep a close eye on the duchess, who was doing her best to ignore them.

She motioned for Maddy to help her, and Temperance's heart melted at watching how carefully her daughter carried an acorn top in each hand, filled with dandelion wine, over to one of the rosebushes.

With Francis's help, Richard and Abigail each carried a parsley leaf with a tiny piece of honey cake.

It took a bit of time for the little ones to deliver the faeries' treats, but the duchess insisted that they do so. The fae were usually more willing to trust a child than an adult. Then they all sat down again to wait. To watch.

Maddy's soft gasp had Temperance leaning close to ask, "Do you see something?"

Maddy pointed to the roses farthest from them. Richard and Abigail were transfixed staring at the same bushes. Temperance blinked, rubbed her eyes, and blinked again. "I've never seen dragonflies out before dawn."

"Be careful not to startle the faeries," the duchess warned.

Temperance's heart wanted to believe that they were indeed faeries and not dragonflies, but she could not be certain. If only they were not so far away. The duchess, her maid, and the others were watching just as intently. Was she seeing things, or did that dragonfly just fly over that rose petal, land on it, cup its hands, and pat dew on its face?

A short, sharp whistle broke through the silence. The dragon-flies—mayhap they truly were faeries—flew off.

The duke and O'Malley shot to their feet. "Close ranks," O'Malley ordered everyone.

The duchess scooped up Abigail. Francis picked up Richard. Gwendolyn had Deidre in her arms by the time Temperance had Maddy in hers. Constance and Merry urged the others into a tight circle. Before Temperance could ask what was wrong, Flaherty appeared out of the mist that settled on the garden as the first rays of the sun lit the sky.

Eamon O'Malley and Garahan joined the circle of men sur-rounding the women and children. While the other little ones did not seem to notice the men had drawn their weapons, Maddy did. "Mum," she whispered, "they have pistols."

"To protect us. We're safe here."

A few moments later, one of the tenant farmers approached from the path leading to the stables. "We caught him, Your Grace."

"I'll be along directly to question him," the duke replied. "O'Malley, escort everyone inside and stand guard." He turned to Flaherty. "Go with him."

"Aye, Yer Grace."

"Him who?" the duchess asked.

The duke shook his head. "Later."

All thoughts of magic evaporated as their group was ushered inside. Temperance was concerned, but the other ladies seemed to act as if nothing out of the ordinary had happened. Was no one else worried?

She followed Constance and the others into the kitchen. "Has this happened before?"

Constance sighed. "Aye, but now is not the time to talk—there are mouths to feed and children to be coddled."

The cook's matter-of-fact tone reminded Temperance that

now was not the time for discussion—it was time to prepare and serve a meal. The men would need to eat soon, too. "May I help with the morning meal?"

The cook hesitated, then must have noticed the worry Temperance could not hide. "I could use two helpers. Maddy, would you like to help your mum put the plates and utensils on the big tray? One of the footmen will carry it into the dining room."

While they performed the task, Temperance could not help but wonder who the man they'd captured was. Furthermore, what in Heaven's name he'd expected to do at this hour of the day. The confidence the duke and his guard exuded went a long way toward alleviating her immediate concern for Maddy's safety and that of the other children. Remembering how difficult the first few months of her pregnancy were, she realized it was time to think of others—not herself.

"A good breakfast will set you to rights," Constance said. "That and a cup of my special tea."

Temperance smiled. "That sounds wonderful. Can Maddy and I eat with you?"

The duchess swept into the kitchen and frowned. "Why haven't you joined us in the dining room, Temperance?"

"I... Well... That is to say—"

"We cannot let the food get cold." As she led the way to the dining room, the duchess pitched her voice to just above a whisper. "We keep the women and children with us at times like these. It helps to stay together. Less fretting."

"Thank you, Your Grace."

She slipped her arm through Temperance's, watching Maddy skip ahead of them. "Your daughter is such a joy. Would you like to join us in the nursery after breakfast? Maddy likes to read to the twins and Deidre."

Temperance did not hesitate to reply, "I would love to."

CHAPTER NINE

THE DUKE OF Wyndmere entered the outbuilding his men used for their bare-knuckle bouts to keep their skills sharp. "Where is the prisoner?"

O'Malley tipped his head toward the back corner of the large room, where a young man stood with his hands tied behind his back and his chin resting against his chest. "He's not talkin'."

The duke strode over to the prisoner. "State your name and reason for skulking around my family's home at this hour of the morning!"

The man did not raise his head, nor utter a sound.

"Very well. I shall leave it to my men to extract the information from you." The duke started to walk away, paused, and said, "They have a variety of methods, and I should warn you that they are bare-knuckle champions back home in Ireland."

The sharp intake of breath pleased him, but he did not plan to stay to question the prisoner. It was far more effective for his private guard to do so. Let the rumors continue to abound—the more people who knew that he had a well-trained force guarding himself and his family, the better. "Let me know when you have the information, O'Malley."

"Aye, Yer Grace."

When the door closed, Flaherty, Garahan, and Eamon O'Malley stalked over to stand in a semicircle in front of the man.

Garahan spoke first. "Now then, we'll only be asking once more."

"State yer name," Flaherty said.

"And why ye're here," Eamon added.

O'Malley crossed his arms in front of his chest, and as if on cue, Garahan, Eamon O'Malley, and Flaherty did the same. Every one of them were a full head taller than the man they stared at. Judging by how quickly the man's Adam's apple bobbed up and down, their bid to intimidate him was working.

"Name's Greene."

"Who sent ye, Greene?" Patrick asked.

"She did."

"She who?" Garahan grumbled.

The wild look on Greene's face was a surprise. He shook his head and clenched his teeth.

"Well now," Garahan mused, "if he won't tell us who sent him, we'll have no choice but to begin extracting information." When no one objected, he continued, "I'll start with me right cross."

Eamon spoke next. "I'll be showing off me uppercut."

Flaherty grumbled, "Ye know it's me favorite punch. Now I'll have to pick another." When Eamon O'Malley shrugged, Flaherty said, "I'll be using me jab."

"Right or left?" Garahan asked.

Flaherty felt a wave of satisfaction build as it warmed his chest. "Both."

"Well then I'll be wanting to deliver two blows," Garahan said.

"Two for each of us," Eamon stated.

Flaherty was proud of his cousins. Every one of them made a show of ignoring the prisoner, when in fact they were highly attuned to the way the man's breathing became more shallow by the moment. When beads of sweat trickled down the sides of the man's face, Flaherty knew the prisoner would be telling them who'd ordered him to spy at Wyndmere Hall. Anyone who lived in the village and had not heard of the duke's guard's skills was either living under a rock or daft altogether!

"Her brother will kill me."

"Killing's a sin and a crime," Garahan said. "Best tell us who she is."

Greene's expression was telling—he was either protecting whoever had ordered him to spy on the duke's household, or he'd been bribed, mayhap threatened.

"Which is it?" Flaherty asked.

"What?" Greene looked perplexed.

"Are ye being bribed?" Flaherty asked. "Or threatened?"

O'Malley took one step closer, cracked his knuckles, and slipped out of his frockcoat. "I'm done talkin'."

"M-M-Miss H-H-Harkness."

Flaherty could not believe it. "Is the innkeeper's sister bribing or threatening ye?"

The younger man flushed, and Flaherty wondered if he was younger than they'd pegged him to be. There was only one reason a young man would blush at the mention of a woman's name.

"'Tis a bribe, I'm thinking."

Garahan glanced at him and nodded. "Aye."

Eamon stared at Greene, rubbed his chin, and shook his head. A look of disgust flashed on his face. "She did not offer ye coin, did she?"

Greene's mouth opened and closed, but only a squeak emerged. He did not have to answer when his reaction spoke louder than words.

O'Malley grabbed the front of Greene's frockcoat and lifted him off the ground, shaking hard enough to rattle the man's brainbox. "Ye'll tell me now, or I'll deliver the first blow we promised."

"No coin." Greene swallowed audibly. "She promised me favors."

O'Malley set him on his feet, but did not let go of the man's collar. "Did she now? Ye aren't thinkin' to prevaricate, are ye?"

Greene held up both hands. "Nay. She sent me a message to meet her behind the stables at midnight."

When he paused, Garahan urged, "And?"

"Said she'd make it worth my while, if I rode out here to see if the rumors were true that the black-haired strumpet and the little girl she kidnapped were hiding out at Wyndmere Hall."

O'Malley let go of the man and eased back just in time for Flaherty to push forward. He was incensed on Temperance's behalf. The way Greene's voice modulated to imply that she was a woman of low morals *and* a kidnapper scraped his gut raw. No one would insult the lass or impugn her honor!

Flaherty connected with a solid jab to Greene's throat. The man crumpled at his feet. He drew back his leg to kick Greene, but Eamon shoved him off balance. Flaherty stumbled, but managed to keep from falling on his face. "'Tis me right to avenge the lass's good name."

"Aye. Though now we won't be getting' him to tell us anythin' more about his arrangement with Harkness's sister," O'Malley reminded him. "Get a bucket of water and rouse him."

The order effectively stopped Flaherty, who dropped his fist. Though he nearly hauled off and punched Eamon for trying to trip him.

"Save it," O'Malley warned. "Eamon will feel obligated to retaliate, which would have ye sharing barbs, then blows, if either of ye makes another comment. Remember Her Grace's delicate condition and our promise to His Grace."

Garahan agreed. "We know ye've feelings for the lass. Didn't I help ye question half the people in the inn who were there to witness the innkeeper's sister blatantly ignoring the lass and Maddy when they'd been waiting for her to take their order?" When Flaherty grunted, Garahan continued, "But that doesn't mean ye can put an end to the questioning before we get all of the information we need."

"He slandered Temperance's good name—"

Before Flaherty could work up a head of steam, he realized

he'd let his emotions interfere with his duties. *Bloody hell!* That had never happened to him before. He'd watched his cousins lose their heads a time or two whenever an off-handed comment was made about the women who later became their wives...and rightly so. But this was different. It wasn't just the horrible slur against Temperance's character, it was the suggestion that she'd *kidnapped* Maddy! The last thing he wanted was for the wee lass to overhear such comments and begin to question whether Temperance was her ma.

"And ye know His Grace prefers that we each land *one* punch—not two, nor three, nor more—to encourage Greene to tell us all he knows," O'Malley reminded him.

Flaherty grunted and locked gazes with O'Malley. "I've delivered me punch. I'm going to the inn."

"Ye'll not be going anywhere," O'Malley warned. "'Tis yer turn on the rooftop."

"But I..." Flaherty fell silent. How could he tell his cousin that he'd fallen arse over head in love with the black-haired lass and her pixie of a daughter?

Before he could form the words, O'Malley gave a slight nod. "So that's the way of it?"

"'Tisn't like that," Flaherty began, only to stop when his cousin raised his hand. As the head of their guard, every man deferred to O'Malley, who used the gesture exclusively when he had something to say.

"Ye don't have to explain," his cousin told him. "As Garahan said, we all noticed." All of the pent-up emotion fizzled out of Flaherty, as O'Malley continued, "Ye'd best get over whatever ails ye. We've no time to waste trying to rein in yer volatile temper."

"Aye," Garahan agreed, nudging Greene with the toe of his boot. "What'll we do with him?"

"Same thing we've done with other prisoners," Patrick replied. "We'll ask two footmen to stand guard while the rest of ye return to yer posts. I need to speak to His Grace." He turned his green-eyed gaze on Flaherty. "Ye'll come with me to tell the duke what happened."

Flaherty grunted. "Ye just told me to man me station on the rooftop."

O'Malley narrowed his eyes, and Flaherty clenched his jaw. O'Malley had guessed correctly—Flaherty's heart was taken. "Changed me mind."

Flaherty tried one last time. "I'm asking ye to send me to the inn to speak to Miss Harkness."

O'Malley stared at him until Flaherty could swear he felt the man's fingers sorting through his thoughts. "I'll suggest that ye be the one to go, but 'twill be up to His Grace."

Satisfied that he'd made his request, and his cousin would present it to the duke, Flaherty followed O'Malley to the house. Neither one spoke as they covered the distance. At the rear door to the building, O'Malley put his hand on Flaherty's shoulder. "I've been in yer shoes, torn between duty and finding the other half of me heart. I nearly lost Gwendolyn because I didn't think I could honor me vow to the duke and the one I wanted to say before the vicar when I married her."

Surprised by his cousin's admission, Flaherty told him what he'd already decided: "I'm not certain it's balancing me duty to His Grace and the one to me heart that's needed. But I'm telling ye, I'll not be letting Maddy or her ma leave without telling them what's in me heart." He cleared his throat to add, "If Temperance will have me, I'll marry her and be da to Maddy."

O'Malley dropped his hand. "The tiny lasses have a way of grabbin' hold of yer heart without ye knowin' it. I'm not embarrassed to be admittin' I handed mine over to me daughter when Deidre was minutes old." He shook his head. "Took a bit longer for me heart to realize that Gwendolyn was the only one for me. They're me life, Rory."

"I won't let anyone speak ill of Temperance or Maddy," Flaherty replied. "She's yet to confide what happened to her husband, but I'm thinking 'twas a shock—tragic. It won't matter; she'll come around to realizing she needs me. They both do."

O'Malley's eyes darkened. "What if she doesn't?"

"I'll be marrying the lass in name only, if that'll convince her that I'm meaning what I say. I'm the man she needs to watch over her and protect her and Maddy."

"What if the rumors are based on fact?"

Fury sliced through Flaherty that his cousin would even suggest that Temperance had lied to him. He rounded on him. "Ye'll eat those words now, and never repeat them!"

O'Malley's face was devoid of expression, his voice even as he challenged, "Or what?"

"I'll be resigning from me post. There's no way I can work with anyone who'd question me gut. 'Tis what's guided me through life and kept me safe."

Incredulous, O'Malley asked, "Ye'd break yer vow to His Grace?"

"'Tisn't breaking me vow to resign." Though it gutted Flaherty to do so, he stretched the truth and said, "Working for the duke is like any other position. Ye know when it's time to move on."

O'Malley's lips thinned, but it was the tone of his voice that tipped Flaherty off to the fact that he wasn't merely angry—he was furious. "'Tis a job few can handle, working side by side with family protecting the duke's. Our brothers and cousins have bled for the duke. Our cousin Sean O'Malley nearly lost an arm. Darby Garahan is all but blind in one eye. Emmett, me youngest brother, died—if we can believe what we've been told—and was resuscitated. Yer older brother Seamus nearly bled to death when he was shot in the back...twice!"

Flaherty's anger was raging too close to the threshold where he would no longer be able to control it. "Aren't ye forgetting the times our other brothers, cousins, and ourselves have been shot, knifed, and clubbed over the head?"

"There's no need. We both know the number of times is not the issue. Yer willingness to throw away all that we have built in these last two years working with Coventry and King in our bid to widen our web of protection over the duke and his family and extended family is!"

Flaherty shoved O'Malley out of the way with his shoulder, grabbed the door handle, and yanked. He'd made his decision. He would ask the lass to marry him and promise to protect her and Maddy with his life when she accepted his offer. She did not need to love him—she needed to trust him.

As for the harsh words he and O'Malley had tossed at one another, he'd meant every word. Though family was the glue...he'd given his heart to Maddy and Temperance. If they left, they'd be taking it with them. The shell of the man they'd be leaving behind would be of no good to his family or the duke.

Halfway to the kitchen, O'Malley grabbed hold of Flaherty's arm. "I'll have yer word now that there will be no more talk of resigning until we ferret out the truth."

"Aye, but I'll not be forgetting that ye'd even *suggest* Temperance isn't telling the truth. I cannot work with any man—family or not—who is so quick to judge the woman I love."

O'Malley glared at Flaherty. Flaherty glared back, two hulking brutes challenging one another over hard words, and the one thing neither of them could tolerate or accept...being lied to.

Flaherty knew he owed it to his cousin's position as head of the guard to be the first to capitulate. He gave a brief nod.

O'Malley scrubbed a hand over his face and did the same, and the tension eased. "I'll do the talkin'."

Flaherty snorted. "Don't ye always?"

Though he'd tossed his resignation in O'Malley's face when his temper was up, now that it had cooled, Flaherty realized that he'd meant it. For Temperance and Maddy, he would walk away from the life he and his brothers and cousins had built. The foundation had faltered a few weeks ago when his brother Seamus and their cousin James Garahan had gone so far as to send resignation missives to the duke, due to a situation that involved Viscount Chattsworth and Seamus. Though it had been settled, the idea that the duke's guard was not as tight nor as solid as everyone believed had been brought to light.

Brothers had been known to turn their backs on one another when their core beliefs had been challenged—but they would eventually come around and stand side by side. Cousins did not always have as strong a bond as brothers, and there was often a bit of healthy jealousy between them. Toss together sixteen hardheaded Irishmen—brothers and cousins equal in strength and size—and you had the makings of a melee Flaherty would pay money to be a part of.

Flaherty always preferred using his fists to weapons. It was far more personal. He'd go along with O'Malley for the moment, but if he did not convince the duke to allow Flaherty to go to the inn to question either the innkeeper or his sister, all wagers were null and void.

His future wife and family were being threatened.

CHAPTER TEN

SATISFACTION FILLED FLAHERTY as he rode to the village. O'Malley had convinced the duke that Flaherty be the one to question Harkness's sister, with the caveat that Garahan would accompany him. Garahan would lay down his life for him—and Flaherty would do the same for his cousin. When push came to shove and the choice was between an O'Malley and a Garahan for aid, Flaherty would choose a Garahan any day. His brother Seamus had too.

"Ye gave yer word not to let that hot head of yours rule yer gob," Garahan reminded him.

"Leave me mouth out of it," Flaherty grumbled. "I know what I said."

"Ah, but when the heart's involved, a man tends to lose his better sense."

Flaherty snorted. "Is that happened to ye? Faith, ye haven't been the same since ye married Emily."

Garahan continued to scan his side of the road for possible sharpshooters, thugs, and blackguards. "She's me life, Rory."

"Aye, so ye shouldn't have all that much trouble pulling back on yer decision to use any means to get Harkness's sister to tell us what she knows."

"She'll be telling me."

Flaherty disagreed. "If she tells anyone, she'll be telling me.

Ye fought yer battles and won Emily's heart. Though to hear Emily tell it, she was the one responsible for changing yer mind when ye had that maggot in yer head and were riding away without her."

"I was following orders," Garahan grumbled.

"Ye could not ignore the agony in her voice as she asked ye to wait."

Garahan's lips inched upward before he squelched the urge to smile. "That was then. This is now. I'll have yer word that you will not cause a scene or make the innkeeper's sister cry."

"She wasn't there the last time we thought to question her."

"We were able to speak to guests of the inn," Garahan reminded him.

"Aye, but I need to question her. I gave money to Scruggs to see that Temperance and Maddy were fed. She'll tell me why she refused to serve them and why she spread lies about them. God knows what she planned to do with the information Greene was sent to gather! If the evil harpy doesn't tell me the reason she's started this campaign against Temperance, I'll do—"

"Nothing," Garahan told him. "Ye'll gain nothing if ye come on too strong questioning the woman. Besides, we cannot take the chance she'd taint the food or drink for anyone from the duke's household in retaliation because ye had yer head turned and yer heart yearning for something that isn't meant to be."

Flaherty felt gut-punched. "Are ye saying I'm not worthy of reaching for what ye found? Am I not man enough to hold on to the woman who has me head in a spin, me mind in a jumble?"

"And yer heart?" Garahan demanded when they gently pulled back on the reins to slow their horses as they approached the village.

"I've an ache in me chest where me heart used to be. I've left it behind with Temperance and Maddy."

Garahan held Flaherty's gaze. "I needed to know if ye realized how deep in love ye are. Leave it yerself to fall arse over head with a curly-haired moppet and her widowed ma."

"Bugger yerself."

Garahan grinned. "If only I was that flexible."

Flaherty snorted. "Ye've a foul mind, Aiden."

"Sure and wasn't it yerself that suggested it?" Garahan quipped.

Flaherty snickered. "Shut yer gob."

Garahan nodded. "Are we agreed? I'll take the lead questioning Miss Harkness?"

It was the very last thing Flaherty wanted, but he knew Garahan was right. It would be the best way to get the information out of the innkeeper's sister. Garahan's heart wasn't on the line—Flaherty's was. "Aye. Though I'd rather do the asking."

As they approached the inn, Garahan said, "Here's what I'm thinking. Ye let me do the talking, until ye hear me tell her 'tis fine if she doesn't want to speak with us. That's when ye chime in and say our next stop is to speak with the constable."

Flaherty wasn't certain that Susana Harkness would be afraid of the constable. "Can we trust that she hasn't turned his head with her wiles?"

"We'll find out," Garahan replied. "Though from what we both know, he's a devoted family man."

"Best to be wary," Flaherty warned.

"Two heads," Garahan murmured as he hailed the hostler.

The men dismounted as Scruggs walked over to take their horses. "You're early today."

"Aye," Flaherty replied. "We need to have a word with—"

Scruggs interrupted, "You'd best not press Harkness's sister too hard."

"What makes ye think we've come to speak with her?" Garahan asked.

"I know that Flaherty was the one to ask me to keep an eye on Mrs. Johnson and her daughter for him. I tried to get them to stay. She never said a word about not being served. If I had known, I would have taken care of it for you, Flaherty."

Flaherty inclined his head.

"The next thing I know, Miss Harkness is whispering into any ear that will listen about a widow who is not really a widow, and a little girl who looks nothing like her mother."

Flaherty struggled to keep a lid on his temper. "Are you warning us not to question her?"

"You know I would never stand in the way of yourselves or the other guards. I have a wife and three children and know how it feels to worry for their safety and wellbeing. I'm warning you to be cautious. Harkness is overprotective of his sister, and when cornered, she'll lie."

Flaherty tamped down his frustration. "Thank ye, Scruggs. Know that if ye ever need help, ye've but to ask."

"Thank you."

Garahan asked, "Have ye heard anything else regarding the lass and her daughter?"

"Just what I told you. I will keep my ear to the ground and send word if I hear more."

Flaherty clapped a hand on the man's shoulder. "Thank ye."

Scruggs frowned. "There is one other thing."

"What's that?" Garahan asked.

"One of the stable hands has yet to arrive. He's normally a good lad, arriving early for the day, works hard and doesn't mind a bit of criticism when it's warranted."

"Greene?" Flaherty asked.

Scruggs sighed. "If you know his name, then I don't have to ask where he is."

"He'll be fine," Garahan assured him.

"What happened?" the hostler asked.

"We'll fill ye in later. We need to speak with Miss Harkness first."

"She should be in the main taproom—she's not one you'll find up to her elbows kneading dough."

Garahan snicked, and Flaherty's lips lifted into a crooked smile. "Paints a picture, Scruggs. Thank ye."

"I'll take care of your mounts for you."

They thanked the man, strode across the innyard to the front of the building, and stepped inside.

"There," Flaherty whispered. "By the fireplace, giving that well-dressed nob a healthy view of her charms."

Garahan grumbled, "I'm doing the talking."

Flaherty followed him toward the fireplace.

Garahan approached them. "Miss Harkness, we'd like a word with ye."

Her eyes locked on Flaherty. She slowly straightened in a way that could only be described as sinuous. Flaherty had little use for women who used their bodies instead of words. That kind of a ploy wouldn't work on any of the men in the duke's guard—married or not! A brief look out of the corner of his eye indicated the merchant she'd been reeling in was still paying rapt attention to the woman.

Brushing a hand along the curve of her hip, she lowered her lashes, fluttered them, and finally looked away from Flaherty. "That would depend on what the word is." She stared at him for a few moments. "You're Garahan."

"That's right. Where can we speak privately?"

A smug, satisfied expression settled on her face. "Follow me." When Flaherty and Garahan started to follow her, she smiled. "Both of you want to speak to me?"

"Aye," Flaherty answered. "Unless I'm mistaken, *we* indicates more than one person."

She furrowed her brow and narrowed her eyes at Flaherty, but Garahan distracted her. "I did say *we*, Miss Harkness. Is that a problem?"

Still frowning at Flaherty, she said, "I don't like the tone of your voice."

Flaherty wanted to shake the woman. Before he could speak, Garahan said, "I beg yer pardon, but we are here at the request of His Grace."

Flaherty bit the inside of his cheek to keep from blurting out, *As if ye didn't already know that.*

She licked her lips and twitched her hips, walking ahead of them. Without turning around, she said, "I'm certain I can handle the two of you."

"We have a few questions for ye. It won't take long." Garahan's voice sounded strained, as if he were suppressing the urge to shout.

Flaherty understood the need, for it had him by the bollocks too. The woman's ploy was obvious. Did her brother know how she spoke to the male customers in their inn? He'd be asking Harkness that question himself.

Susana led them to a small room off the kitchen, on the other side of the pantry. Garahan and Flaherty let her enter the room first, but Flaherty moved to block her from reaching around them to close and lock the door. When she started to protest, he cut her off. "'Tis a small space."

"Aye," Garahan agreed, following Flaherty's lead. "Reminds me of that cave-in."

The calculating look in the woman's eyes smoothed out into one laced with concern. "How awful."

"Aye," Flaherty agreed. "How long were we trapped, Garahan?"

Without missing a beat, his cousin answered, "Three days."

That seemed to distract the woman from her illicit thoughts. Flaherty had not minded being seduced in the past. But he'd never been attracted to or tempted by someone who had been pushing her charms into another man's face moments before.

"You must have been terrified."

Garahan shrugged. "I wasn't, but me cousin was."

Flaherty could have happily leveled his cousin with clip to the jaw. But instead he drew in a lungful of air and exhaled slowly. Damned if the woman didn't take that to mean he had been terrified.

Susana patted his arm. "I'm terrified of spiders."

Garahan's lips twitched, though she didn't notice—she was now holding on to Flaherty's arm. "Who isn't?"

"I'm not," Flaherty insisted.

"Someone was sneaking around Wyndmere Hall earlier this morning," Garahan said. "Would ye know anything about that?"

She let go of Flaherty's arm and spat out, "I wasn't there, so how would I know?"

"We apprehended a man by the name of Greene," Garahan informed her.

Flaherty caught the flicker of fear in Susana's eyes. He wanted to press the point, but bloody hell, he'd given his word.

"As he claimed to work here as a stable hand," Garahan said, "we thought ye might have overheard a conversation, mayhap had one with the man."

She lifted her chin, anger blazing in her eyes. "I have little time to fraternize with those who work in the stables." The way she wrinkled her nose, as if she'd caught the scent of something unpleasant, rankled. Flaherty had opened his mouth to speak when he noticed Garahan's raised brow. He pressed his lips together.

"There is another matter that we need to get to the bottom of. Flaherty gave Scruggs coin enough for Mrs. Johnson and her daughter to enjoy a meal and pot of tea the other day. They waited nearly an hour, but were never served."

"We have been inundated with guests lately, especially in the mornings—if we missed serving someone, they should have spoken up."

Flaherty wanted to throttle the woman.

She sniffed. "If that is all you wished to ask, I am needed elsewhere."

When she tried to step around them, Garahan sighed. "Well then, 'tis clear that ye don't appear to be ready to apologize, nor return the coin Flaherty gave to Scruggs in good faith. 'Tis fine if ye don't wish to continue our conversation."

That was Flaherty's cue. "Our next stop is to speak to the constable about what occurred at here at your inn—and at Wyndmere Hall. Greene was quite willing to speak with us."

She froze in place. Flaherty would later swear that he could hear her quietly cursing them. "As I said, we have been unusually busy, and one of the serving girls may not have noticed the woman waiting to be served. As to any of the men working in the stables, Scruggs handles that area for us. Though there have been times when my brother has had to step in to settle disputes or issues."

"Thank ye for yer time," Garahan said, pleasantly enough, though Flaherty caught the anger simmering in his cousin's dark eyes.

"We'll be certain to give the constable yer regards," Flaherty added, before motioning with his hand to have her precede them.

She stomped down the hallway toward the kitchen. When she was far enough away that Flaherty was certain she could not hear them, he snorted. "Did ye see her face? If she had a blade, she'd have used it on ye."

"Me?" Garahan shoved Flaherty out of the way with his shoulder. "She'd be skewering yerself."

"We could have easily disarmed her. We'd be taking her to the constable right now, instead of leaving without the proof we need."

"We aren't through here yet," Garahan said. "She did suggest we speak to her brother. Harkness is a man of business. He won't want anything to discourage customers from coming to his inn."

Flaherty grinned, understand what Garahan wanted to do. "Well now, didn't I hear someone passing through the village the other day commenting on the atmosphere in the taproom?"

Garahan shook his head. "I may have forgotten." They walked back to the main part of the inn where Harkness was speaking to three men. Raising his voice to be heard over the din of a number of conversations, Garahan asked, "Was it the food?"

"Nay," Flaherty answered, keeping a straight face. "'Twas the talk inside the taproom, remember?"

"Ah, now I recall," Garahan said as they drew closer to the innkeeper, who'd stopped talking. The group of men were unabashedly listening to Flaherty and Garahan. Just as they'd hoped. "Rumors—nasty at that. Such that should never be repeated where little ones could hear."

Harkness greeted them, "Garahan, Flaherty. What's this about rumors?" His tone just shy of demanding.

"Disturbing talk that's reached Her Grace," Garahan replied.

Flaherty picked up the conversational thread. "Her Grace is very careful that she does not to expose the twins to conversations that would be unsettling."

"Aye." Garahan nodded. "Especially when the talk involves a young widow and her child a few years older than Her Grace's."

At that moment, Susana's loud, suggestive laughter erupted from the taproom, and the men turned their attention toward whatever was happening. Flaherty did not waste the moment. "I'm afraid I'll have to be telling His Grace that the inn isn't a place where families can bring their little ones any longer."

"Please, wait a moment," Harkness said. "Let me handle this."

The duke's men shared a look and agreed. They watched the innkeeper stalk into the main room of the inn. A few moments later, they could hear a rumble of conversation, but not the words.

"Does this often occur at the inn?" one of the trio who'd been talking to Harkness asked.

Flaherty would not be caught dead in a waistcoat in that shade of yellow. Not wishing to cause the inn to lose business— just to make the innkeeper aware that his sister was causing problems—he replied, "It depends."

The tallest of the trio shook his head. "There are times in a crowded room when one has to pitch their voice above the others to be heard."

The roundest of the group frowned. "One should always be cautious about the topics they discuss in public."

"His Grace insists upon it," Garahan remarked.

The man in the garish waistcoat stared at their uniforms,

lingering for a moment on their identical emblems. "You work for the Duke of Wyndmere."

"Aye. Name's Garahan. Flaherty and I are part of the duke's guard."

Before the group could continue asking questions, the innkeeper rejoined them. Susana stomped toward the kitchen. "My sister has high spirits. Sometimes she forgets we run a family establishment." He cleared his throat. "I have reminded her of that." When no one spoke, Harkness murmured, "It won't happen again."

Garahan inclined his head. "Either meself or Flaherty will be stopping in again. If we see that the atmosphere has changed, then we will hold off bringing a complaint to His Grace."

Harkness held out his hand to Garahan. "Thank you."

Flaherty watched the exchange, adding, "We have eyes and ears in and around the village."

"I understand," Harkness replied. "Thank you."

Before the man could draw them into further conversation, Garahan motioned to Flaherty, who swept the room with his gaze once more. Garahan did the same as they exited the building. Scruggs was waiting for them with their geldings.

A few moments later, they were headed to the constable to apprise him of the situation. It was unfortunate that they did not have enough information...yet.

CHAPTER ELEVEN

D ESPITE THE ABRUPT end to their early morning visit to the rose garden—and what she still could not say for certain was a faerie or a dragonfly—Temperance felt relaxed for the first time in days, sitting beside the duchess in one of the two rocking chairs in the nursery. Rocking the O'Malleys' daughter to sleep, she was swept back in time to when it was Maddy she cradled in her arms. "I miss this."

Gwendolyn smiled as she changed a very sleepy Abigail. "Is it my imagination, or does time seem to go so slowly when you're carrying your babe in your belly, and it flies by once they are born?" She tucked the little one into her cradle and walked over to sit beside Maddy, who was on one of the settees.

The duchess's soft laughter felt like a warm hug. "I couldn't wait for the twins to arrive, and once they did, it seemed as if I would never be able to keep up with feeding them, changing them. I could never have managed it without you, Gwendolyn. I believe the rocking chair benefits both mothers and their babes."

Temperance was in awe of the duchess's ability to remain calm during what could have been an explosive situation earlier that morning. She gave no indication that she was upset as she rocked beside Temperance, who still could not wrap her head around how quickly they had been swept inside while the possibility of a threat loomed.

Taking her cue from the other woman's quiet demeanor, Temperance agreed, "The motion is soothing, and humming or singing lullabies just seems to come naturally."

"Are you certain we are not tiring you out?" The duchess's concern still surprised Temperance. She was not in the same social circle, and could not get past the fact that it did not change the way the duchess spoke to her. There was not a bit of artifice in her tone. Not a mean bone in the woman's body.

"Quite sure," Temperance assured her. "Thank you for worrying, but I truly feel better. I think waiting for faeries this morning, witnessing the children's excitement, was just the boost I needed."

"Patrick mentioned how well you looked after spending time out of doors—and in Flaherty's company."

Temperance felt her face heat at the duchess's statement and wished she wasn't so prone to flushing when embarrassed.

"Just Flaherty is partial to Mum."

Leave it to Maddy to say something to create a stir. "And how would you know that?" Gwendolyn asked.

Temperance watched her daughter tip her head to one side—the same way her father used to when he was thinking over how to answer a question. She wondered what was going through Maddy's mind.

"He told me so."

Shock had Temperance putting her foot down to stop rocking. "What did you say?"

Maddy glanced at Temperance and echoed a reply she herself had used more than once recently in correcting her daughter: "You heard me."

Gwendolyn smiled, and the duchess's happy laughter echoed through the room.

"Ah, music to my ears," a deep voice rumbled from behind them. The duke was standing in the doorway, leaving Temperance to wonder how long he'd been there. Had he heard what her daughter said? Would he be upset with her—or Flaherty?

His expression was contemplative until he walked over to where his wife sat in the other rocking chair. Worry creased his brow. "Are you ready to lie down, darling? You've had a busy day so far."

The duchess shook her head. "I'm certain a little while longer rocking and Richard will stay asleep for at least an hour. Abigail is already asleep in her cradle."

The duke brushed the tip of his finger across their son's forehead. "A few minutes, but no longer. You and our babe—it is only one this time, is it not?"

Temperance thought that an odd question, but she'd only carried one babe in her belly. She supposed a mother would feel movement, mayhap see a heel or elbow stretching the skin of her belly at some point, and know if she carried more than one babe.

The duchess sighed. "I believe so, but it is early yet. Once the babe starts moving, we'll know for certain."

The duke paled, but his loving expression did not change. Temperance felt their happiness fill the room, before grief swept up from her toes. She and her husband had rarely shared moments like this, given his long hours working in the mine.

"Mum's sad again," Maddy whispered, before Temperance heard the deeper rumble of the duke murmuring to the duchess as she placed their son in his cradle and he coaxed her from the room.

Gwendolyn rose to her feet. "Thank you for rocking Deidre, Temperance, while I took care of Abigail. Let me put her down."

Momentarily distracted, Temperance was able to tuck thoughts of her heavenly husband into the special part of her heart that would always belong to him. Instead of gradually becoming accustomed to not having him in their lives, she'd found she missed him more each day. Every time Maddy said or did something out of the ordinary, Temperance wondered if he could actually see her growing and changing. Could he see her mop of blonde curls so like his own from Heaven?

"Temperance?"

She shook herself free from the past. "Forgive me. I was woolgathering."

Gwendolyn settled the blanket around her daughter and walked over to where Temperance was sitting. When Patrick's wife offered her hand, Temperance grasped it and rose to her feet.

"I understand what you are going through." Gwendolyn released Temperance's hand. "I faced the same struggles. I was desolate at first, but needed to earn my keep, so I devoted my life to caring for other people's babes for years."

The woman's sorrow was palpable, a living, breathing emotion.

"I lost my husband and our unborn babe hours apart."

Temperance drew in a sharp breath and held it for a moment. What she could possibly say to this lovely woman who had suffered far more than she had? Finally, she offered what was in her heart. "I am so sorry for your terrible loss, Gwendolyn. If not for Maddy, I would have lost my mind."

Gwendolyn nodded. "There were days when I was on the precipice of doing just that. If you need to talk, at any time, please do not worry that it would be a bother. It won't be. Do you know what shocked me to the bone and healed the hurt I carried all of those years?"

"What?"

"Not what, but who. The hardheaded Irishman whom my heart could not seem to ignore, though the good Lord knows I tried."

"Patrick O'Malley?"

Gwendolyn's smile brightened. "He was by turns an irritation and complication. I tendered my resignation, believing the duke and duchess would not want me to continue caring for their newborn twins if they found out how we felt about one another."

"But you're still here."

"Thanks in part to my brother-in-law Finn and Their Graces."

"That sounds like a story best told over a pot of tea."

"We shall have to make the time. Looking back, I still wonder what I had been thinking to leave the man who'd captured my wounded heart."

Temperance was happy for Gwendolyn and Patrick, but knew her circumstances were different. She was six months along when the accident in the mine had taken the life of her husband and his brother. She still dreamed of him—dreams so real, she swore she felt his solid form holding her close in the night.

Not wanting to put a damper on their conversation, Temperance admitted, "I haven't given a thought to anyone taking Paul's place. We were happy together, though I knew his job in the mines was a dangerous one."

"Mum says Papa and Uncle Matt were the bravest men ever!" Maddy interjected.

Temperance felt tears stinging the backs of her eyes, and could not afford to let them fall, even though it was just herself, Gwendolyn, and Maddy taking care of the babes. She needed to have a clear head, not remain lost in memories. Talking about the mine accident would take her back in time. She quickly changed the subject. "Maddy, didn't Constance mention something about you helping her ice teacakes?"

Maddy's excitement was tangible as she threw herself into Temperance's arms. Holding her tight, Temperance knew that this was what was important now. It would be more than enough because so much happiness radiated out of her daughter.

Enough for three, her heart whispered.

Just the two of us, her mind reminded her.

With Flaherty, it could be three, her heart insisted.

Gwendolyn tugged on the bellpull in the corner, interrupting Temperance's jumbled thoughts. A few moments later, one of the footmen came to the door and Gwendolyn asked him to find out if Constance was ready for Maddy's help.

The young man smiled down at Maddy before nodding to Gwendolyn. "At once, Mrs. O'Malley."

A few minutes later, Francis arrived. "I'm here to relieve

Maddy—and you too, Temperance. Constance is anxious for her special helper to taste-test the teacakes."

"That's me!" Maddy squealed, then covered her mouth with both hands. Glancing to the cradles and back, she whispered, "Sorry, Mum."

"Try to remember not to raise your voice when the babes are sleeping, Maddy."

Deidre whimpered, but fell right back to sleep. "No harm done," Gwendolyn said.

"Yes, Mum. I didn't mean to, but Constance needs me." Maddy puffed up her chest and patted a hand to it. "I'm the bestest tester. She said so."

"I am quite certain that you are, Maddy dear." Temperance held out her hand to her daughter, who took it. "Why don't we go see if there is a job *I* can help Constance with?"

Maddy frowned at her mother. "You're supposed to rest."

"And where did you hear that?" Temperance had her suspicions, but wanted to see if Maddy would tell her without too much prompting.

"You know who." Her daughter's little voice echoed in the servants' staircase as they descended to the lower floor. "He's worried 'bout you, Mum." When Temperance didn't respond, Maddy tugged on her hand. "Did you hear me?"

"Yes, darling. I heard you. It is not polite to ask a question like that."

"Why not?"

"It's intrusive."

"What's that?" Maddy asked.

"Putting your sweet little nose into someone else's business."

"Like when you were asking Just Flaherty why he was following us?"

Temperance had not been certain that her daughter had heard her demand that of Flaherty. She'd best decide how to answer. Maddy would keep asking over and over until she did. So Temperance decided to evade the question. "Did you know that you share a special quality with your father?"

"I do?"

"You definitely do."

"What?"

"You are like a dog with a meaty bone, gnawing away at it until he's satisfied he's finished getting every scrap of meat and fat off it."

"Papa used to chew on bones?"

Temperance laughed. "No. I was giving you an example."

"I didn't like that one."

"I'm sorry. I'll think of another one." She opened the door and stepped into the hallway leading to the kitchen.

"I bet I know who could think of one," Maddy quipped.

Temperance had to agree. "I am quite certain he could."

A short while later, she watched Maddy staring at the array of sweets they'd had a hand in preparing. While Constance sliced sandwiches into tiny triangles and rectangles, Temperance carefully arranged delicate china cake plates on the large tray.

"May I have a teacake, scone, and a berry tart?" Maddy asked.

The cook smiled. "I think your mum will want you to have a sandwich or two first."

Maddy frowned. "But they aren't sweet."

Temperance had to laugh at her little one. Maddy always said what she was thinking. She wished she felt comfortable enough to do the same, but she was not a child any longer. Life was far more complicated once one reached adulthood. Consequences kept most people from speaking their minds.

For some reason, her mind called up the image of a certain broad-shouldered, auburn-haired giant's soft blue eyes. Flaherty had certainly not held back what he had been thinking.

Instead of holding on to the thought that he was controlling, her heart warmed and her mind held on to the possibility that he truly cared for Maddy and her and was trying to protect them.

"Mum? Can I?"

"I'm sorry, my mind strayed."

Maddy's exaggerated sigh had Temperance wondering what that was all about. She did not have to wonder for long, as Maddy blurted out, "Woolgathering."

Constance met Temperance's gaze. "Who was woolgathering?"

Maddy shrugged. "Mum."

"Your mother has been helping almost as much as you have been," Constance reminded her. "Even when she should be resting."

Maddy's green eyes widened as she rushed over to her mother. "Do you need a nap?"

Temperance laughed softly. "I won't sleep a wink tonight if I do."

Her daughter slipped a hand in hers and that mischievous smile slowly revealed itself. "Me neither."

In that moment, when her blonde-haired cherub smiled up at her, Temperance had a feeling her daughter wanted more than iced teacakes. What in Heaven's name would she do if Maddy continued to fawn over Flaherty? Would he understand that it was because she'd never had a father's love and attention? Temperance would have to speak to Flaherty about this and warn him. What worried her was that Maddy had never lavished attention on *any* man. She had singled out Flaherty from the start.

"Teatime." Constance's kind look eased the tension between Temperance's shoulder blades. "I need the two of you to help me serve the tea." She motioned to one of the footmen stationed in the hallway. "Send someone to the nursery and ask Francis to see if the duchess is still resting. If not, she'll be ready to sit down to tea."

The footman reappeared with the news that Her Grace was hungry.

"Well then, please take this tray up to the nursery sitting room." Constance turned and waved her hand at Temperance and Maddy. "I know Her Grace would love to have you take tea with her."

Maddy skipped toward the servants' staircase. Constance lifted her skirts and waited for Maddy to join her. "Can you reach the railing?"

Maddy shook her head. "I hold Mum's hand."

Constance glanced over her shoulder. "Is it all right with you if Maddy holds my hand and you follow behind us?"

Temperance's heart warmed. The duke's cook was a thoughtful woman who enjoyed children almost as much as feeding the duke and his household. "Of course. Maddy dear, pick up your hem like I taught you. I'm right behind you."

The three took their time, as Maddy's legs were not quite big enough to negotiate the height of the risers easily. Halfway up, Temperance knew her daughter was getting frustrated. "What a good job you've done, Maddy. Let me carry you the rest of the way."

"But I want to do it myself," her daughter protested.

"And you have, sweet girl," Constance soothed her. "I wish someone would carry *me* up the stairs."

Distracted, Maddy allowed Temperance to lift her onto her hip. "Know what, Mum?"

Temperance smiled when Constance moved to stand behind them. "Thank you, Constance."

Maddy patted her face to get her attention. "Know what?" she repeated.

"What?"

"Just Flaherty could carry Constance up the stairs."

Temperance had no doubt that he could.

"But he can't."

Intrigued by the way her daughter leaned close to whisper that last comment, she wondered if she had missed something important. "Why is that?"

"'Cause he and Garahan went to the inn."

"Ah, he is on patrol to the village."

Maddy shook her head, leaving Temperance to wonder what she was up to. Normally her daughter would tell her every last detail of news. She braced herself as she asked, "Why else would he go to the inn with Garahan?"

Maddy laid her head on Temperance's breast and sighed. "The mean whispers started there."

Temperance strove to hide the emotions churning inside of her as Constance reached around them to open the door at the top of the stairs. Stepping through into the upstairs hallway, Temperance set her daughter on her feet and asked Constance, "Is there anything I should know?"

The firm set of the cook's jaw surprised Temperance, until Constance put her arm around her and held out a hand to Maddy. "Come along. I'm certain the duchess is waiting to pour our tea."

Temperance had a feeling the mean whispers were about her—and her beautiful daughter. Wherever they went, no matter how kind and caring she and Maddy were, there was always someone ready to hint that she was not all she seemed. The nicest gossip had been that she had not been married. The worst of the tales that had caused them to continue on their journey to another town was the one claiming she wasn't Maddy's mum…and that she'd *kidnapped* her! She could never understand why people who had never met her could hold such a low opinion of her.

Her heart raced again. The evil things strangers assumed—and said—about her sliced through to her soul. She worried that Their Graces would be adversely affected by the slanderous talk. She and Maddy should leave. How could she stay when someone may think to censure the duke for opening his home to her and Maddy? With a heavy heart, she knew what must be done.

Lord, please forgive those who start the rumors. And please, please lead us to a safe haven. I'm so tired…

CHAPTER TWELVE

FLAHERTY AND GARAHAN reined in at Wyndmere Hall to shouts and chaos. "What in the bloody hell is going on?" Flaherty demanded.

One of the tenant farmers stopped mid-stride. "'Tis the little lass—she's gone missing."

Flaherty frowned. "Abigail?"

"Deidre?" Garahan asked at the same time.

Patrick O'Malley paused in the middle of organizing the search parties. "'Tis Miss Maddy."

For the first time in his life, Flaherty understood the saying about one's blood running cold. His mind whirled with questions he needed to ask, but he could not make his mouth work. The cold was debilitating.

"What in the feck is wrong with ye, Flaherty?" O'Malley asked. "Move yer arse and take charge of the tenant farmers. They'll be searching to the south."

Eyes blazing, a tearing pain in his heart, Flaherty sprinted to the back door. Calling her name as he yanked it open, he nearly plowed into Temperance. "What happened? How long has she been gone?"

"We were having tea upstairs when I noticed she was quiet. I carried her to the room we have been using and tucked her in and lay beside her." Tears streamed from her eyes, but she didn't seem to notice. "It's all my fault. I should never have closed my eyes."

Flaherty grabbed hold of her upper arms. "How long ago?"

"But don't you see—"

"Aye, lass. I do. Ye're worried sick, but ye need to snap out of it and tell me, was it one hour? Two? Three?"

Her voice was just above a whisper. "Two." She curled her hands into the lapels of his frockcoat. "Please help me find my little girl! You don't understand—"

Flaherty needed her cooperation, not conversation! He slid a hand to her waist, the other behind her head, and molded his mouth to hers to shut her up. It was a kiss of frustration. Fear. Promise. "I'll find her. Ye need to stay here in case she returns from having a lark, looking for the fae."

"Flaherty?"

He did not have time for this, but he spun around. Walking backward to the door, he growled. "What?"

"If she's lost, she'll be waiting for you to find her. She trusts you."

His resolve clicked into place. "Ye should too." He stalked outside and shook his head at O'Malley. "No time. The wee *cailín*'s counting on me to find her."

"Ye're heading the wrong way!" Patrick shouted.

"The meadow filled with flowers is to the north. Send someone else to the south with the tenant farmers." Flaherty turned to the men waiting, pleased it was the Jones brothers on horseback and their eldest sons on foot. They could handle rifles and pistols and had fought bravely when Wyndmere Hall was under attack. Farmers were used to finding stray sheep and a cow or two. "Ye know the meadow I'm meaning?"

Samuel Jones nodded. "Aye."

"Our daughters pick wildflowers for the duchess in that field," his younger brother Silas added.

Flaherty gave a nod. "I'm thinking two on horseback leading the way, two on foot behind them, while I bring up the rear.

There's a chance the wee lass has tripped and bumped her head, or climbed a tree and got stuck."

"Why do ye think she's headed to the meadow?" Samuel's son asked.

"Earlier this morning we were in the gardens waiting and watching for the fae," Flaherty replied.

Silas nodded. "I remember those days well. Our girls are a bit older now, but every once in a while they'd try to sneak out before dawn for the same reason."

Flaherty was glad for the help, pleased he had a few experts in faerie hunting and flower picking in his search party.

He watched the others move out and lagged behind, waiting, watching, listening. The noise of men gathered and splitting up into groups quieted, until all he could hear was the breeze. Was it his imagination, or did he hear a whisper on the wind? Closing his eyes, he lifted his chin and let it caress his face.

The meadow pond.

Urged on by unseen forces, ones he was Irish enough to trust, Flaherty caught up to the brothers on horseback. "I'm going to the meadow pond. Keep searching!"

They didn't question Flaherty's order. They'd lived near faerie hill forts long enough to have heard voices on the wind and singing in the night. "He'll find her, but we'd best keep looking," Samuel murmured.

"Aye," his brother agreed. "Susana may have sent someone else from the village to spy on His Grace and poor Mrs. Johnson."

"Keep searching, boys!" Samuel said.

With a nod, their sons split up, each taking a side of the road to scour. The pace was slow, but leaving no stone unturned was how they had found their sister the time she ran off chasing butterflies.

MADDY COULDN'T MOVE another step. Exhausted, she sat down

near the pond, wishing she had caught the beautiful faerie with the rainbow wings. She hadn't been watching the path ahead of her, and had tripped and scraped her knee. It stung and was bleeding. Maddy didn't like blood.

Pulling her knees to her chest, she leaned her chin on her hands. She wished Just Flaherty were here. He'd carry her home to Mum, and Constance would give her scones and tea.

Tears welled up and she brushed them away. Mum only cried at night when she thought no one would hear her...but Maddy heard. So she tried to be brave like her mum and not cry. It wasn't dark yet, but she wasn't certain she could find her way home. She'd been looking up, following the faerie that flew above her head, not paying attention to her surroundings.

Now, even the faerie was gone. She was alone, and the sun was hiding behind dark clouds. She was scared. Would she ever see Mum again?

There was a sound behind her. Was it a person or an animal? Maddy wanted to see, but tucked in among the reeds by the pond, she was too short. She'd have to stand up, but she was afraid to. Despite her vow not to cry, a few tears escaped, but she wiped them away. When she lowered her hands, she noticed they were damp and streaked with dirt.

Worried that her knee was still bleeding, Maddy lifted her hem and stared at the trickle of blood that ran from where the skin was scraped off. It looked scary. Her knee hurt and she wanted her mum! She should try to stop the bleeding, but her hands were dirty. Mum would want her to clean her hands before she touched the scrape.

She tilted her head back and watched as two magpies flew over her head. Whenever Mum saw two together, she reminded Maddy that it was good luck! A glance around her, and she wondered—how could her luck be good if no one ever found her? Was anyone looking for her at all? Devastated at the thought that no one but her mother would be looking for her, Maddy sat down hard. "I want my mum!"

Worn out from walking and worrying, she lay down, tucked her hands beneath her cheek, and closed her eyes. She thought she heard a voice, but it sounded so far away that she wondered if it were thunder. Sniffing back the tears that threatened, she drifted into dreams where a big man with red hair and blue eyes rode up on a horse and scooped her off the ground. She nestled into his arms, shivering. But he tucked her inside his big coat. Warm again, she sighed and dreamed the red-haired man would marry her mum.

"YE POOR WEE lass. Don't cry. I've got ye." Flaherty swallowed against the lump of emotion in his throat and sent up a prayer of thanks to God, and another to the fae who had sent him the message on the breeze. He'd found Maddy at the meadow pond, nestled among the reeds.

He ground his back teeth when he noticed the blood on her gown. Carefully lifting it to her knees, he noticed one had a trickle of blood flowing from where it had been scraped raw. "Poor lamb. I'll wrap it up." Removing his cravat, he gently folded it and wrapped it around her knee. Drawing her gown back down, he glanced over his shoulder to where his horse stood patiently waiting for him. "We've found her, laddie. She won't add much to the weight I'll be asking ye to carry." His horse snorted. "She does weigh a bit more than thistledown, but not by much."

Maddy hiccupped and shivered in her sleep. The air blowing in with the storm was chilly. Flaherty knew he had to get her warm quickly. He scooped her into his arms and settled her against his heart, tucking his coat around her. She was a tiny thing, for all of her big personality. Mounting his horse, he shifted the little girl until she was snug against him. "Yer ma's worried about ye, lass. Let's go home."

Home. The word vibrated right through to Flaherty's soul. It had felt like home once Temperance and her daughter were staying at Wyndmere Hall. They'd become a part of his life, and had been welcomed among the rest of the guard and the household staff—and, more importantly, accepted by the duke and duchess as if they were extended family. Would the duke help him if he asked him to obtain a special license? He had for the others. Flaherty hoped His Grace would do the same for him, because he did not intend to go another sennight without asking Temperance Johnson to be his wife and Maddy to be his daughter.

The wee lass sneezed, and he hoped she would not catch cold. There were plans to be made. A woman to woo. And best of all, the possibility of a life he'd never thought he deserved to have just within reach.

All he had to do was ask.

CHAPTER THIRTEEN

FLAHERTY RODE AT an even pace, following the path he'd ridden to the meadow pond. Finding the Jones brothers, he realized they had not been that far behind him.

"You found her?" Samuel asked.

"Aye. Poor wee thing was sleeping in the reeds by the pond."

Silas frowned. "She could have fallen in."

Hadn't Flaherty thought the same thing himself a short while ago? "God watches over lost lambs."

The two men agreed, and Samuel informed Flaherty, "Our sons are just a mile or so behind us."

"Let's head back to Wyndmere Hall," Silas said. "Her mum will be so happy you've found her, Flaherty."

"That she will, Silas. Let's find yer sons."

A mile closer to home, they came upon the boys. Flaherty sensed the tension in the air before they reined in their horses. The boys were a short distance away, huddled together and staring at the ground. "What do you think they found?"

"What makes you think they found anything?" Silas asked.

Sanuel pitched his voice low. "Look at how rigid they're standing."

"Aye, they've found something," Flaherty mumbled. "I don't want to wake Maddy—one of ye dismount and find out."

"Aye." Samuel walked over to the boys. Soon he was leaning

over, studying something on the ground. He shook his head and straightened. "I'll tell Flaherty what you've found, then we'll bury the poor thing. You and Stephen head on back to Wyndmere Hall."

"What about Maddy?" his son Edwin asked.

Samuel smiled. "Flaherty found her sleeping by the pond."

"I'm glad he did."

He patted his son's back. "Me too." Samuel took one last look at the bedraggled pup, shook his head, turned, and heard a yip. "Well I'll be." He knelt and carefully lifted the injured animal into his arms. "We'll take you back to our farm and fix you up."

Edwin was staring at the puppy in his father's arms. "We thought he was dead. He wasn't moving, and the blood…"

Samuel untied the cloth wrapped around his neck. "Wrap this around his belly to stop the bleeding."

Stephen rushed over to where they stood. "The puppy's alive?"

"Aye, let Flaherty know. We'll ask your mother to stitch him back up. I'm not making any promises."

"I understand, Uncle Samuel. We probably won't know if he's damaged on the inside for a day or so." Stephen glanced over his shoulder at his cousin. "The poor pup didn't look like he was breathing, and we weren't sure what to do if he was still alive and possibly dying. Whatever attacked him hurt the poor thing. I know he had to have suffered. Just look at him."

"He seems to be strong enough to make it home if someone carries him tucked inside their frockcoat."

"I'll do it," Edwin called out as he walked toward his father. "I saw him first, so I should be the one to carry him home."

"Sounds fair to me," his cousin replied. "Keep him warm!"

Edwin nodded. "I will."

Three-quarters of an hour later, the group rode out of the woods and onto the duke's estate. Flaherty knew it was necessary to signal to the others that he and his search party had returned. But he didn't want his loud whistle to wake the wee lass.

O'Malley saw him and hailed him. "Garahan had no luck finding the little lass. Neither did Eamon. We'll need to…" He fell silent as Flaherty's coat moved. "Is that who I think it is?"

Flaherty nodded. "The poor wee thing was curled up by the meadow pond. She was cold to the touch, but warmed up quick enough inside of me coat."

O'Malley nodded to Garahan. "Find Temperance!"

Garahan ignored the order to ask, "Ye found her, Rory?"

"With the help of the fae and the Joneses," Flaherty replied.

"What's this?" Patrick asked.

"Ye can think I'm daft, I don't mind. 'Tis the truth."

Garahan ribbed him, "Feck, Flaherty, we already think ye're daft."

"Go and tell—" The words dried up on Flaherty's tongue as Temperance ran toward him, her black-as-night hair slipping from its pins, an expression of hope-tinged fear on her lovely face. He dismounted and slowly walked toward her, meeting her halfway.

"Maddy?" The quiet rasp of her voice had the swell of emotion Flaherty had felt earlier by the meadow pond returning.

He swallowed against the lump in his throat to speak. "She scraped her knee, and it was bleeding. I wrapped it with me cravat. Poor *cailín* was chilled to the bone. We'd best get her in the house and into a hot bath."

"Please wait, just a moment," Temperance said. "I need to see her face."

Flaherty knew better than to argue with a worried ma. "I don't want the night air to give her a chill."

Temperance met his gaze, but did not argue with him. She scooted up close to him. He could see the pulse beating wildly at the base of her throat. Intrigued, he wondered if she was reacting to her daughter being found, or to being so close to him.

"Can you shift the edge of your frockcoat, just a tiny bit?"

Flaherty did as she asked. "See? Safe and sound, although a bit dirtier than when she left, I'm thinking."

Temperance tucked the edge of his coat around her daughter, then placed her hand on Flaherty's arm, lifted onto her toes, and brushed a kiss to his whiskered cheek. "Thank you. From the bottom of my heart. I was devastated when I woke to find her gone. I need to find out why she left, and what she was thinking. Would you help me speak to her? She listens to you."

"I'd be happy to, but I think it may have had to do with the faerie."

"Faerie?"

"We'll talk later. The poor lamb needs a long soak in a hot, soapy tub."

"With rose petals," Temperance said. "Her Grace let Maddy have some in her bath. It's a luxury we have never had before. She loves the scent."

"Rose petals it is," Flaherty rumbled. They walked to the back of the building, and he held the door for her. "After ye."

As soon as they entered, they were mobbed. "Oh, thank Heavens!" Constance pressed her cheek to Flaherty's as she hugged him, careful not to squish the child in his arms. "I'll serve the meat pies and stew I've been cooking shortly." She stared at his hands and frowned. "You have blood and dirt on you. Where is Maddy hurt?"

"It's not serious," Flaherty assured her. "She scraped her knee. I wrapped it up."

Constance pressed her lips together. "I'll direct the footmen to fetch the copper tub and set it up down here. It's closer to the kitchen, and we can get the little darling in the tub faster." As if she realized she had taken over, Constance ducked her head and faced Temperance. "If that is all right with you."

Temperance smiled. "Of course it is. Thank you."

Flaherty noticed some of the heaviness that had settled on Temperance's face had lifted. "Don't forget the rose petals."

Constance laughed. "We won't. Everyone knows how much the little moppet loves them."

A short time later, all of the men who had gathered to search for the little girl returned to their homes with the fervent thanks of Temperance, Flaherty, and Their Graces. Each man carried a basket filled with meat pies, scones, and teacakes as a thank you.

After Flaherty had given his report, the duke pointed out that he had dirt and blood on his shirt. He knew the duke did not want to upset his wife. It was one thing to hear that the wee lass had scraped her knee and another altogether if Her Grace noticed the evidence on Flaherty's shirt. He returned to the outbuilding where he bunked and washed his face where the little one had patted it with her dirty hands. Flaherty never minded a bit of dirt—he'd grown up on a farm. He smiled, thinking how angelic she looked fast asleep bundled in his arms. At one point she started moving until she freed one arm, touched his face, and sighed. Not quite awake, but enough that she was assured she had not been dreaming. She was safe in his arms.

A few seconds later, fear of what could have happened had he not heard the whisper on the wind grabbed him by the bollocks. "Lord, 'tis Flaherty—Rory, in case Ye're thinking it might be Seamus. Although he was the brother most recently in trouble." He paused, for a moment losing his concentration. "Thank ye, Lord, for asking the fae to whisper on the wind telling me where to look, and for sending yer angels to watch over Maddy until I could get to her. I promise to protect and watch over her and her ma for their rest of me life."

His mind wandered to Sussex. He had to ask Garahan if his wife had received a letter from her sister-in-law Melinda lately. Married to James, the eldest of the Garahans, Melinda usually had the most recent family news and liked to share it.

One day, Flaherty thought, they'd all have the chance to be together again, if only for a little while. But the duke's family would have to be gathered together in one spot—most likely Wyndmere Hall, the largest of His Grace's properties. Needing to scrub the fear and what-ifs from his brain, Flaherty started thinking about a reason to gather together. He'd have to ask Patrick what he thought and if he had any notion as to what would be a good reason.

Entering through the side door, he walked toward Humphries. "Thank you for helping to organize the men while Garahan and I were in the village. Ye're the best of us, Humphries."

The older man's lips twitched. "Always happy to be of service. I believe there are two lovely ladies waiting for you in the kitchen."

Flaherty grinned. "Are they now?"

"They're quite the pair. Makes a man contemplate his future."

Flaherty shook his head. "Wasn't I just thinking that?"

The butler chuckled. "I wouldn't know, but if I were you, I wouldn't waste time talking to me."

Flaherty nodded and reached for the door to the servants' side of the house. A cacophony of happy voices reached him as soon as he entered. The dulcet tones of two voices rose above the others, drawing him like an invisible thread. He had come to depend on the two to brighten his days with their smiles, along with Maddy's hugs and the gifts she'd taken to leaving in his quarters. He'd found a drawing on his pillow. It took a bit to figure out what Maddy had drawn before he realized he was looking at it upside down. Sure and wasn't it himself on horseback? Then there was the drawing of himself carrying the lass in his arms to the rose garden with a tiny speck he recognized as a faerie. He loved the little girl's exuberance and imagination... 'Twas time he gave voice to what was in his heart. Time to tell Maddy and Temperance that he loved them!

Rounding the corner, he saw Temperance and noticed she had tucked in the silky strands of her ebony hair that had escaped their pins earlier when she'd run to him. The hope and fear evident in the depths of her expressive green eyes hit him like a blow. He wanted to press his lips to hers then and there, but did not want to listen to his cousins' comments. He planned to kiss her later, if he could convince the lass to take a walk with him after she tucked Maddy in for the night. He had a feeling he was on borrowed time, if the furtive looks Temperance kept sending him meant what he thought they might. His gut told him the lass was still thinking of leaving.

Maddy rushed toward him, flinging her arms around his knees. "Careful of yer cheek, Maddy-lass," he warned. "Ye don't want to bruise it on me kneecaps."

She mumbled something, but her voice was muffled against his knees and he couldn't quite hear it—though Temperance's quiet gasp had him asking the little girl, "What did ye say? My knees heard ye, but me ears are too far away."

Maddy's smile could warm the coldest day of winter. Hanging on to his pant legs, she bent back to look him in the eye. Afraid she would fall over, he bent down and picked her up. Delighted with the joyous sound of her giggle, he was rewarded when she put her tiny hands on either side of his face. "I love you, Just Flaherty."

He melted. Right then. Right there. The little lass with sunshine in her heart loved him. Flaherty wasn't waiting a moment longer, or they'd slip out of his life just as quickly as they'd slipped in. He kissed the little girl's forehead. "Faith, but I love ye too, wee *cailín*."

She giggled. "It's Maddy!"

Everyone was smiling except for Temperance—her eyes were round with surprise and a bit of trepidation—but that would not stop him. Flaherty had made up his mind, and he was not waiting another moment.

With Maddy snug against his chest, her arms wrapped around his neck, he walked over to stand in front of Temperance. He reached for her hand, brought it to his lips, and brushed a featherlight kiss to the back of it. Capturing her gaze, he went down on one knee and offered his heart.

"Temperance, I cannot lose ye or yer daughter. Ye've wormed yer way into me head and me heart. I promise to protect ye always. Ye'll never go hungry, and ye'll always have a roof over yer head. Marry me, lass."

Instead of the immediate yes he'd expected, she wrinkled her brow and opened her mouth, but not a sound emerged. Had she been so overwhelmed by his offer that she'd lost her voice?

"Say yes, Mum," Maddy urged.

When Temperance stared at him with a blank look on her face, a bad feeling slipped up from the soles of his feet. Had he rushed her? Had she not noticed the way he'd made it a point to spend whatever free time he had with them every day? Had he misread what he thought were signs that she felt the same about him? Had he taken a chance and now the woman he loved was going to refuse?

Maddy pressed her tiny lips to his cheek and patted his face, getting his attention. "I'll say yes. Marry *me*, Just Flaherty!"

His heart bled, but no one noticed. He would give his right arm to be a father to the little girl who had wrapped him around her little finger, but her ma had to want him too. Devastated by the lack of response from the woman he'd thought returned his affections, Flaherty slowly rose to his feet. He handed Maddy to her mother, bowed, turned around, and strode from the room.

His heart ached to the point where he wondered if it would simply stop beating. His aching head was crowded with questions he did not have the answers to. Was he not worth loving? Had he done something to warrant her dismissal? *Bloody fecking hell*, he deserved the courtesy of a no…if that was what she couldn't bring herself to say.

He did not make eye contact with Humphries as he let himself out of the side door. He walked around the building and climbed the ladder to resume the rooftop shift he'd pawned off on Garahan.

His cousin frowned at him. "I thought ye had plans to spend part of yer shift with the lass and her ma?"

"Changed me mind."

Garahan held his gaze for a few moments before he muttered, "Bloody buggering hell!"

Flaherty could not agree more. "'Tis where Temperance just consigned me for the rest of me days."

"Ye asked her to marry ye, didn't ye?"

"Aye."

"Just now?" Garahan seemed to want details.

"Aye."

"And she said refused?"

"Aye."

Garahan grabbed him by the cravat and shook him. "Did she say the word no to ye?"

Flaherty frowned. "She didn't say anything. But I watched the light in her eyes dim as she stared at me."

Garahan let go of Flaherty's cravat and shoved him. "Ye're a bloody eedjit. She didn't say anything." When he repeated it matter-of-fact like that, it added another layer of hurt.

"The wee *cailín* kissed me cheek and told me she'd marry me, because *she* loves me."

Garahan slowly smiled. "Well now, that's another thing altogether. And proof that all hope is not lost."

"Temperance doesn't want to marry me."

"But she might."

"Then why didn't she say yes? Ye aren't making sense."

"Yer brain's muddled, and yer heart's breaking. I can all but hear it."

"Ye can have the little bit of time O'Malley granted me. Go say hello to yer pretty wife for me."

"I didn't think I was worthy of Emily," Garahan told him.

Flaherty raked a hand through his hair. "Why is it that after we bleed for the women who have us tied in knots, and receive untold number of knocks on the head for them, we still wonder if we're worthy?"

"I have no idea, but I do know this—if ye give up, ye'll regret it for the rest of yer days. Do ye want another man to marry the lass and be father to that curly-haired pixie?"

Flaherty's hands curled into tight fists. "I do not!"

"Well then. There ye are." Garahan nodded, walked to the ladder, and started to descend.

Flaherty rushed over to the ladder, grabbed hold of it, and leaned over the edge. "What in the bloody hell does that mean?"

Garahan looked up at him and smiled. "Ye have yer work cut out for ye showing Temperance how much ye love her daughter. Maddy's love for ye is obvious to everyone. Did it not occur to ye that the lass has only been a widow for a few years?"

"It hadn't, no."

"Has she spoken of her husband? Do ye know how he died? Was it an accident, and did she see it happen? Was Maddy born already, or did he die before she was born?"

"No and no. I don't know the answer to the rest of yer bloody questions."

"Well, when ye know the answers to those questions, ye might have a better understanding of what the lass has been through. 'Tis plain to all of us that she has had a hard road, but she's been fighting tooth and nail to provide for Maddy—even at the cost of blows to her pride by those who would shred her reputation." Without another word, Garahan descended and walked away.

"Garahan?"

He didn't bother to turn around when he answered, "Aye?"

"I love ye like a brother."

Garahan snorted. "Feck yerself, Flaherty." He made it to the corner of the building before he paused and called out, "Faith, I'm fond of ye, too."

CHAPTER FOURTEEN

T EMPERANCE FELT LIGHTHEADED. Had Flaherty asked her to marry him, or had she dreamed it? By the time she regained her composure and glanced around her, she and Constance were the only two people in the kitchen. "Where's Maddy?"

"She went with Francis to the nursery to read stories."

"I should go too. Maddy shouldn't be alone."

The older woman put her arm around Temperance and led her over to one of the spindle-backed chairs. "Your daughter is loved by everyone here at Wyndmere Hall, including the duke and duchess." Temperance hesitated until Constance added in a firm voice, "Sit down before you fall down. What you need is a bracing cup of tea."

The kindly cook set a cup and saucer in front of Temperance, urging her to drink up. After a sip or two, Temperance could not contain her curiosity. "Did I imagine it? Did Flaherty truly ask…" She could not get the words out. If he had asked her, and she stood there like a statue in a museum, not answering him, what must he think of her?

"To marry you? Yes. Did you hear what your darling daughter said to him after he asked you?"

Temperance shook her head.

Constance frowned. "Then you did not hear what she said when you stood frozen in place?"

"No. I'm sorry, I did not. What did she say?"

"Your dear little girl asked you to say yes. Then she told Flaherty *she'd* marry him, because she loves him."

Tears filled Temperance's eyes, but she did not care. She was gutted and could not believe what had just happened. The man treated Maddy as if she mattered, and enjoyed her company. Flaherty constantly showered Maddy with praise for the little things she did in the kitchen and the nursery.

The auburn-haired, blue-eyed giant of a man had singled her out and *proposed* to her! Why couldn't she have said something—anything? Her mind was riddled with gossip and innuendo that had been nipping at her heels. Every unkind word and slanderous comment had stuck to her, shaking her conviction that she still had worth as a widow.

Sitting in the Duke of Wyndmere's kitchen with his cook, she remembered the last time she had felt as if she mattered. It was hours after the tragedy and the attempts to rescue Paul and his brother. The men her husband and brother-in-law rescued had stood in a semicircle on either side of her with their heads bowed, shoulders slumped, as the vicar said a prayer for the souls of the two brave men who were surely needed in Heaven as warrior guardian angels.

While Constance chatted, Temperance's mind drifted from thought to thought, memory to memory, circling until her head ached abominably. When had she started to believe the slings and arrows, the barbs and taunts of those who did not know her? When had their ugly words seeped into her soul? She had no idea. But she had begun to question her every thought, word, and deed, suspected that the awful things others said about her were true. She was not worthy of any man, let alone the paragon of a man who put his life on the line daily to protect the duke and his family. Temperance had heard the tales of the bravery he and his family exhibited. In spite of the danger, they had taken a vow to give their lives if necessary. It was not a job suited to just any man—Flaherty carried his honor like a shield, upheld his vow, wielding it like a weapon. She could not even manage to maintain a position for longer than a month at a time.

Flaherty deserved someone far better than the much-maligned widow who, some proclaimed, had never been married. Still others whispered that she had either had her child out of wedlock, or she had kidnapped the child.

She had been proud to be a coal miner's wife, had worked hard to keep his home, and was overjoyed when she discovered she was expecting his babe—only to be struck with utter despair when word of the mine disaster reached her.

Tears fell, and she hastily wiped them away. There was no use in crying. "He and his brother saved twenty men," she whispered, accepting a proffered handkerchief without looking up. "Not all of those men were married or had babes." She did finally look up then, and saw the stricken look on Constance's face. "My husband and his brother gave their lives for those men. They must have known the collapse was imminent. None of the other men were as tall or broad as Paul or Matt."

The work-roughened hand that clasped hers held tight. "It sounds as if you are describing Flaherty."

Temperance wondered if that was why she'd felt safe with Flaherty. Was it because he reminded her of her late husband? How could she accept the proposal of another man when she wasn't certain her heart was whole?

"I have nothing to offer Flaherty but a tattered reputation and another man's child."

Constance released Temperance's hand, then reached for the teapot, refilled their cups, and passed the cream. "Drink while it's hot. It will settle your nerves, and Lord knows you have had a trying day—we all have." When Temperance sipped from her teacup, the older woman added, "Give yourself time to accept that your daughter was found, and is safe and sound reading stories to Richard, Abigail, and Deidre."

Temperance set her cup on its saucer. "Thank you for your kindness, Constance. I haven't spoken of my husband in three long years."

"That is a long time to hold grief inside. What you need is to let the rest of it out, and accept that none of us know how many days, weeks, or years we have on Earth before we are called home. You may want to ask yourself if your husband would want a man of Flaherty's character, bravery, and ability to protect Maddy and yourself to offer marriage and step in to help you raise your daughter."

Shocked to the core, Temperance stared at Constance.

"Have you given a thought to the possibility that the Lord planned this for you and Maddy?" the cook continued. "That He has seen you struggle, knows of your hardships, and put you and Maddy in Flaherty's path?" She sighed. "I can see that you have not. Mayhap you should take the time and reflect on what I've said."

"Thank you, Constance. It has been a very long time since I have been treated with kindness and respect." Temperance helped clear their tea things away and started gathering the utensils and linens for the evening meal.

The cook shooed her toward the door. "Go upstairs and lie down for a little while." When Temperance protested, Constance raised a hand. "After what happened, there is not a chance anyone on His Grace's staff would allow that little moppet to leave this house. She will be watched like a hawk, now that everyone knows she has a mind of her own and managed to slip out of the house."

Exhaustion weighed Temperance down. With the cook's assurances, she agreed to her suggestion. "Please do not let me rest for more than half an hour."

Constance nodded and again motioned for her to leave.

This time, Temperance did.

CHAPTER FIFTEEN

"WOULD YOU LIKE me to read a story to you, Maddy, now that everyone else is napping?"

The little girl shook her head. "My tummy aches."

"Oh, you poor thing." Francis opened her arms, and Maddy went willingly into them. Holding her close, Francis rubbed Maddy's back until the tension in her little body eased. "Sometimes it isn't actually our belly that troubles us. It's our hearts."

The little girl lifted her head. "Our hearts?"

"It's true. Sometimes my tummy hurts too. Know why?"

The little girl shook her head. "Why?"

"When I was growing up, my stomach used to hurt whenever I tried to remember my father. I never got to meet him. I only had the stories my mum told me about him. I wish I had a picture of him, but I don't. I realized it wasn't my tummy that hurt, it was my heart, and that's when Mum told me her stomach hurt too."

"But it was really her heart?" Maddy asked.

"That's right. It was because she missed my father too. He was a blacksmith. Three months before I was born, one of the horses he was shooing heard a loud sound and was scared...and kicked my father in the head. Mum said she cried and cried from the moment she received the news until the day I was born."

"Then what happened?"

"She said I had my papa's eyes and his smile, and she knew he would always be with her. All she had to do was look at me and remember how much she loved him, and how much he loved her. How much he would have loved me, too."

Maddy curled into a tight ball, and Francis pulled her closer to her heart. "It's all right to cry. Don't hold the hurt so tight in your heart."

"Mum only cries at night. It's not night yet."

Worried for the little one, Francis suggested, "If you close your eyes, it'll be dark like nighttime. I'll hold you close and you can cry. You'll be safe with me."

Tears spilled from Maddy's emerald-bright eyes as she whispered, "That's what Just Flaherty told me, too."

The floodgates opened, and the little girl cried her heart out. Francis held her close, crooning to her, urging her to let go of her sorrow. When Maddy finally stopped crying, Francis handed her a handkerchief to wipe her eyes and blow her nose. "Now then, it's almost time for the duke's men to change shifts."

Maddy's lip trembled, and Francis felt the sorrow pouring off the child in waves. The poor little one was obviously heartbroken having witnessed her hero proposing to her mum…and her mum not accepting.

Tears welled up in the little girl's eyes. "I want Just Flaherty."

Francis made the decision to interfere. It would be worth a stern talking to if it lightened the heavy load Maddy was carrying. "Gwendolyn should be arriving shortly to relieve me. We can find Flaherty then. Would you like that?"

Maddy threw her arms around Francis's neck. "I love you, Francis."

"Oh, my sweet girl. I love you too."

CONSTANCE LOOKED UP from the tray of teacakes she was icing

and studied the woman hesitating in the doorway. "Come in, Temperance. You look as if you rested. How do you feel?"

"Fine. Where's Maddy?"

Constance wiped her hands on the linen cloth, tucked it in her apron pocket, then smoothed her hands over the apron. "She and Francis went outside a few moments ago."

"It's too dark to be looking for faeries, isn't it?"

The older woman laughed. "Maddy wanted to look for someone a bit bigger than a faerie."

Temperance felt her heart twist in her breast. "Flaherty?"

"Please do not be upset with Francis. She said Maddy was crying buckets earlier, and the only thing she wanted was to see her favorite guard."

Temperance wasn't upset by the fact that her daughter was enamored with Flaherty. Heaven help her, he had turned her world upside down and inside out when he kissed her before promising to find Maddy and bring her back. And he had kept his promise.

Her heart tumbled in her breast when she saw Flaherty holding her fatherless little girl. It was there in his eyes—he cared a great deal more for Maddy than Temperance had realized. But what had she done to repay him? Not a thing.

The unasked question needled at her—would he willingly step into the role of father? Would he truly want to help her raise Maddy? Most days were a challenge because her daughter could be headstrong and independent, even for a four-year-old. How long before the novelty wore off and Flaherty had had enough and washed his hands of them?

"Whatever you are thinking, get it out of your head!"

Flabbergasted, Temperance waited a moment before responding, "You may not approve of me, Constance, but I am entitled to think whatever I like."

Constance folded her arms beneath her breasts and frowned. "You certainly are. However, when it's regarding Flaherty and his obvious affection for your daughter, I cannot let you think he would stop caring for her."

It should not have been a surprise that the cook had read her mind, but it was—Temperance had often been told that her expressions mirrored her unspoken thoughts. She struggled to hide her emotions. "I do not know Flaherty well."

"I do," Constance countered. "And I know that that man is head over heels in love with Maddy. I am willing to wager that Maddy had him wrapped around her little finger the first time she smiled at him."

Temperance had suspected the same, but was not ready to admit it. There was more here that concerned her, namely whether Flaherty was proposing a marriage in name only, so he could protect her daughter and her. He had not said as much, and she had been so startled by his proposal that she had not asked. Ever since Temperance was young, she would freeze, unable to speak, when shocked by someone's words or actions. She had been trying to come to terms with that failing, and it had been working, somewhat...until she'd met Flaherty. He got past all of her defenses.

"Not one of the men in the duke's guard would ever abuse a woman or child," Constance informed her. "They rescue them." The cook slowly smiled. "The ones who have suffered the most seem to be the ones that grab hold of the men's hearts. Their need to protect and defend seems to be synonymous with love and nurture in the minds of those valiant men."

Temperance had sensed that Flaherty loved Maddy. Her daughter was easy to love...but Temperance was not. She had been carrying her insecurities with her since she packed the battered leather bag with what little she had left after having to leave the rented home she and her husband had been living in. A part of her had hoped it wasn't just wishful thinking on her part that Flaherty could possibly fall in love her. Was she ready to open her heart? A heart that no longer felt whole. How much of it was left to share?

"Never underestimate the amount of love one can hold in

one's heart, Temperance," Constance said, interrupting her thoughts.

Temperance sighed. "I wish I were more adept at hiding my emotions."

"From the way you look at Flaherty every time he walks into the room, it is obvious you have deep feelings for the man."

"But I shouldn't," Temperance whispered.

"Nonsense. You are a bright and beautiful woman who is trying hard to make the best of things for your daughter's sake. But it sounds as if you have been faced with insurmountable struggles for the last few years. Would your husband want you to toil until you drop from exhaustion, unable to take care of Maddy?"

Temperance sighed. "Every time I try to imagine where the three of us would be if the accident did not happen, I can't see beyond the worry I faced every time he descended into that mine."

"Life is not for the faint of heart, Temperance," Constance replied. "I suspect you have been striving too hard for too long. You have insisted that you do not need anyone's help, when I believe that you do. There are too many unscrupulous people in this world that would try to take advantage of you and Maddy. A strong man by your side would see that you are protected and cared for. Open your heart and your mind to the possibility of allowing someone else into your life, and Maddy's. You may be surprised that you do have room in your heart for an honest, compassionate bare-knuckle champion like Flaherty."

Temperance couldn't believe Constance had added that. "Bare-knuckle?"

"As a matter of fact, all of the men in the duke's guard at one time or another held the title of champion back in Ireland."

"If they are of a similar age, how is that possible?"

"Different counties, different villages, and just enough of an age difference that the younger brothers took the titles from their older brothers."

"So you're telling me that the duke's private guard are a well-oiled fighting machine."

"That we are, Temperance," Garahan said, walking into the kitchen. "Flaherty wanted me to tell ye he's got Maddy with him."

"Thank you, Garahan." From the look on the man's face, Temperance sensed there was more she needed to know. "And just where are they?"

"On the rooftop watching and waiting for the gargoyle statues to come to life."

"The roof?" Temperance dashed out of the kitchen and raced down the hallway to the rear door. *Good Lord!* Her little girl could not possibly be that high off the ground as dusk darkened to twilight. She opened the back door and bolted around the building to where she'd seen the ladder to the roof.

"Flaherty! Bring Maddy down here this instant!" A deep rumble sounded in reply, but she could not quite make out what he'd said. "Did you hear me?"

"Aye."

"I mean it! Bring Maddy down *right now!*"

"Not yet, Mum. Please?"

"Maddy darling, it's getting darker by the minute and it's not safe up there."

"Just Flaherty is holding me."

Incensed that the man and her daughter were not listening to her demands, or thinking of Maddy's safety, she yelled. "Now!"

"Now what, Mum?"

"Madeline Mary Johnson!"

"Uh oh... Mum used all my names, Just Flaherty."

"Don't worry, Maddy-lass. I'll protect ye."

She heard her daughter gasp, and worry for her daughter's safety and what she could not see had her yelling, "There had better not be any truth to gargoyles of stone turning into gargoyles in the flesh at twilight, Flaherty!"

Her mind envisioned all sorts of disasters happening just out of her sight until she heard Maddy say, "I saw that statue move! Come up, Mum. You can watch them come alive with us!"

Frustration abruptly exploded into fear-laced anger. Incensed, Temperance hiked up the hem of her gown, draped it over one arm, and grabbed hold of the ladder. She would show those two! One rung at a time, she pulled herself to the top of the ladder. She was afraid of heights, but did not give in to the temptation to look down. Reaching the top, she tried to step off the ladder, but her hem got caught, and she made the mistake of looking over her shoulder. The ground seemed so far away!

Just like she had in the kitchen, Temperance froze. Unable to move or make a sound, she gripped the top rung until her knuckles turned white.

"Easy, lass. I've got ye."

Her eyes met Flaherty's. The concern in his gaze was her undoing. She wobbled.

Before she could scream, she found herself wrapped tight in his arms. "If ye're afraid of heights, why in the bloody hell did ye climb up?"

"I did not give you permission to bring my daughter up here!"

"Forgive me. Maddy has been asking me to bring her up. I thought it would make her happy and give ye more time to rest."

"Rest? How can I close my eyes when I'm afraid she'll disappear again?" She hated losing her temper or her composure.

"I wanted to see faeries, Mum. A maid said they live by the meadow pond."

"Why didn't you wake me? I would have taken you."

"You were worried about that man this morning. You would have said no."

How could she respond to that without admitting that her four-year-old knew more about her than she knew about her own daughter? She was more than worried about the man who'd been spying on them—she was terrified. When her emotions were high, she tended to lash out in anger.

As she did so now. "You are never to leave without telling anyone ever again—no matter where we live! Understand?"

Maddy's shoulders sagged. "I *uverstand*."

A deep rumble that sounded like a growl had her glancing at the man standing beside her. "Ye'll not take yer ire out on the wee lamb when 'tis meself ye're truly angry with."

"Are you telling me how to raise my daughter?"

"As she's been following me everywhere these last few days, telling me how many times she's slept in a barn, or under the trees, eaten what she knew was yer last crust of bread? Ye'd best believe that I am! Ye haven't enough sense left to realize that ye need looking after, or that I'm the man ye need!"

Temperance could not believe the gall of the man. "You are not her father." As soon as the words left her lips, she regretted them. But Flaherty absorbed her barb without returning fire. "Well?" she demanded.

"Ye'd be right about that, Temperance." He held her gaze and rasped, "'Tisn't for lack of trying. I offered marriage to ye, but I'm thinking I should have offered to take ye to see the physician so he could examine yer hard head."

"How *dare* you speak to me like that?"

"As a man of sense, how could I not?"

"Maddy, come here." Temperance held out her hand. "We're leaving."

Flaherty slowly smiled. "And just how do ye plan to climb down if ye're afraid of heights?"

"I never said I was."

"Ye did not have to, lass. 'Twas plain as day to anyone watching ye."

She swallowed against the tight lump in her throat, and asked the question she had an overwhelming urge to know the answer to: "Have you been watching me, Flaherty?"

"Aye."

"Why?"

"I'm not blind, lass."

"What is that supposed to mean?"

"Maddy-lass, has yer ma hit her head lately?"

Temperance snorted, then immediately tried to cover up the fact that he'd made her laugh when she was trying to stay mad at him.

Instead of laughing with her, he frowned. "'Tisn't funny, lass. I'm worried about yer brainbox, and ye're standing beside me insisting that ye're going to leave, hauling yer daughter down the ladder, when *I'm* concerned that ye'll drop her when ye pass out from yer fear of heights."

"I am perfectly capable."

He closed the small gap between them and brushed a lock of hair off her forehead. "I never said ye weren't, lass. If ye are bound and determined to leave, let me take Maddy down first. Ye'll have to sit and wait for me to come back and help ye descend the ladder."

"But Maddy will be all alone down there."

"According to ye, she'll be safer on the ground than up here in the dark with the shadows and gargoyles."

He was right. She did not want her daughter on the roof at all.

Temperance inclined her head. "You do make an excellent point."

"Has anyone ever told you that ye're a—"

"Anyone need help climbing down?" Garahan was grinning at the two of them from his perch at the top of the ladder. "We heard the commotion and came to offer assistance."

"Who is *we*?" Temperance asked.

"Patrick O'Malley and meself. He was the one who suggested we both come looking for ye when I told him Maddy was up here with Flaherty and ye'd gone to fetch her. I'll hold on to Maddy and climb down, while O'Malley waits at the bottom of the ladder in case I lose me hold on her."

Flaherty retorted, "*I'll* be bringing the lass down. Then I'll be climbing back up for her ma. Is that clear?"

Garahan laughed in his face. "As mud."

Maddy wrinkled her nose. "Mud isn't clear."

Flaherty sighed. "Ye have the right of it Maddy-lass. Now then, since Garahan is already here, and O'Malley is waiting on the ground to help, why don't I carry ye over to the ladder? Ye're to hold tight to Garahan while he takes ye down."

Maddy was quick to agree. "He can help me because he's not arguing with Mum."

Garahan sounded as if he were choking and about to burst into gales of laughter. Flaherty glared at his cousin, sending a silent message to shut his mouth, or it would be shut for him.

Flaherty led Maddy over to the ladder, where Garahan waited. "Put yer arms around Garahan's neck and do not let go. Understand?"

"I *uverstand*."

"YER MA IS worried about ye being up here with meself and the gargoyles. 'Tis the quickest way down if Garahan takes ye. When ye get to the bottom, let Patrick take yer hand and stay with him. He'll protect ye the same as Garahan and meself would."

Maddy stared at her feet long enough that Flaherty worried that the little girl would refuse to go. Finally she asked, "Why would they help me?"

"Why wouldn't we?" Garahan asked. "Flaherty loves ye like ye were his own. As his cousins, we vow to protect whoever Flaherty takes a shine to." He looked over his shoulder and called down, "Isn't that right, O'Malley?"

"Aye," his deep voice boomed. "Now hurry it up—we've shifts to man, and a duchess's worries to soothe."

Temperance grabbed hold of Flaherty's free hand. "What's wrong with the duchess?"

"Do ye mean ye don't know?"

"I've been up here. How would I know?"

Garahan cleared his throat, and Flaherty scrubbed a hand over his face. "She'll be worried about yerself and Maddy because by now she's heard that ye were screeching at me."

"I never raised my voice to you!"

Flaherty smirked. "How is it then, that Garahan and Patrick heard ye clear as day?"

"Sound carries from the rooftop," Patrick rumbled from the bottom of the ladder.

"There ye have it, lass," Flaherty said. "Sound carries." Turning to Maddy, he asked, "Are ye ready?"

"It's wee *cailín*!"

Flaherty grinned. "That ye are, *mo chroí.*"

"What's that mean?"

"Me heart."

She wrapped her arms around Flaherty's knees. "Will you be my papa?"

He couldn't speak for a moment and had to collect himself. God help him, he wanted to be her da almost as much as he wanted to be husband to her ma. But it was not up to him. Temperance had to accept him for who he was...the duke's sharpshooter! He rarely missed whatever he aimed at. The duke counted on his skill to protect his family. Temperance had not confided much, if anything, about her first husband, but Flaherty had heard the man was rumored to have perished in a cave-in at a coal mine. Would she accept him if he left the dangerous job he'd sworn an oath to?

That was a question for another time. Not now. Now he had to hug Maddy and help her grab hold of Aiden. "Garahan's waiting."

"Will you say yes, if Mum does?"

"In a heartbeat." He passed her to Garahan, and she immediately wrapped her arms around his cousin's neck to the point where Garahan sounded like he was gagging.

"Not so tight, Maddy," her mother implored her.

"Aye, Mum." She loosened just a bit, but it was enough for Garahan.

"There's a lass. Hold tight, don't look down, and above all—don't let go!"

"I won't!"

Flaherty watched the little charmer bury her face against his cousin's neck and make herself into as tiny a ball as possible. Without turning around, he said, "Ye've raised her to be a brave lass, Temperance. Her da is smiling down on ye right now, as pleased as I am."

She placed a hand to his chest. "Do you think so?"

"Aye, *mo ghrá.*"

"What does that mean?"

"Me love."

Temperance leaned into him, close enough that his lips were a whisper away.

"We're safe on the ground!" Garahan said.

O'Malley called out, "Kiss her already, so ye can return to your posts!"

Flaherty did not bother to ask how his cousin knew he was about to kiss the lass, nor did he bother to answer him. Temperance did not bat an eyelash at O'Malley's suggestion. She was waiting to see what he would do.

"Kiss me back, lass." Molding his mouth to hers, he sampled Heaven for the second time and sighed. Easing back from her, he tipped up her chin and stared into her brilliant green eyes. "Whether or not ye believe me, Temperance, ye are me love, and yer daughter is me heart. I'll never intentionally hurt ye, and I bloody well would never lay a hand on Maddy if that's what has ye worrying and not accepting me offer of marriage."

Temperance licked her lips and closed her eyes. "I haven't been kissed in three years." She slowly opened them. "Today, you kissed me twice."

He slid his arm around her waist, anchoring her to him. "The first time involved a promise. Just now 'twas me vow. Will ye think about it? Will ye open yer heart and give me the chance to prove me love for yerself and yer darling girl?"

"Get yer arse down here, Flaherty!" O'Malley barked.

Maddy's giggle floated up to them. "You said a bad word!"

Temperance laughed, a joyous sound that wrapped around Flaherty's aching heart like a hug from the lovely woman herself. Her expression turned to one of concern. "Where will we live? Where will I work? How can I keep Maddy from learning all of the guards' colorful expressions?"

"Bugger it, Flaherty!" Garahan called.

Flaherty winced. "Watch yer language! There're little ears down there." Turning his attention back to the woman in his arms, he answered, "We'll live here on the duke's estate. His Grace has gifted each of the married men in his guard a cottage. As to work, do ye have to? I can support ye."

"I do not know if I can be idle for more than an hour."

He sensed that she did not mean it as a slight against his ability to provide for her, but a need to keep busy. "Well now, I'm thinking Her Grace would be happy to have to ye continue to lend a hand in the nursery. Both Helen and Emily have been feeling poorly and will be moving slower than normal for the next few months until their babes are born. Richard and Abigail are fast, now that they've got their feet beneath them."

"Maddy learned to run as soon as she could walk."

"So Ma has always claimed about me brothers and meself."

"We'd have to ask Maddy, and you'd have to ask His Grace."

Flaherty surprised her by patting his waistcoat pocket. "I've already spoken to the duke."

She was staring at his hand when she asked, "Are you looking for your handkerchief?"

He chuckled. "Nay, lass. I've the special license His Grace procured for me safe in me pocket. We can be married whenever ye like—as long as 'tis soon. I can't give ye the protection of me name until we're wed." He traced the tip of his finger along the curve of her cheek. "I vow to protect ye and Maddy with me life,

Temperance. Say yes."

"Yes."

He crushed her to him and sealed his pledge, and her acceptance, with all of the pent-up need inside of him. When he could bear to end the kiss, he promised, "I'll plan to see the two of ye are safe, happy, and loved for as many days as the Good Lord has in store for me. I've family enough to step in and protect ye, should anything happen to me."

Temperance slid her arms around his neck and urged him closer. He obliged, and this time she initiated the kiss. Her passion echoed his own as she tasted him fully, tracing her tongue over the rim of his mouth and nipping his bottom lip.

"God help me, lass."

The whack on the back of his head had him spinning around, with Temperance behind him. "What in the bloody hell is wrong with ye, Garahan?"

"For feck's sake, Flaherty, if I can't be kissing me wife, ye can't be kissing Temperance."

"She just agreed to be me wife!" Flaherty growled.

"Well now, that's another thing altogether," Garahan said with a smile. "Ye can kiss her once more, then get yer buggering arse to yer post! Eamon is on his way to take his shift on the roof."

"I don't need yer permission to kiss me wife."

"She's not yer wife yet, boy-o."

"He's right, Flaherty—"

"Rory," he corrected her.

Temperance smiled up at him. "He's right, Rory. We're not married yet."

"Why don't we spread the good news and see when the vicar can marry us?"

"Ye'll need to speak to His Grace," Garahan warned.

Flaherty grinned. "He handed me a special license a few hours ago."

"Well then. Ye'll need to speak to *Her* Grace."

"We will. Well?" Flaherty said. "What are ye waiting for? Ye need to get to yer post."

Garahan was laughing as he descended the ladder.

Flaherty took advantage of the moment and kissed the breath out of his wife-to-be. When she sagged against him, he rasped, "Close yer eyes and hold onto me, lass. Don't look down. Don't let go."

"I won't let go in this lifetime for however many days God has in store for the three of us."

Flaherty secured her in his arms. Using his body to shield her, he descended the ladder and kissed her again.

"Took ye long enough to get down," Garahan grumbled.

"Where's Maddy?" Flaherty asked.

"She told O'Malley she needed to ask Constance to bake an iced teacake for her ma and Just Flaherty."

"You still need to ask her, Rory," Temperance said.

"That I will, lass. That I will."

CHAPTER SIXTEEN

SUSANA HARKNESS WAS fuming. "How could he prefer that haggard, skin-and-bones harpy to *me*?"

The cook did not bother to reply, which irritated Susana even more. She stomped over, raised her voice, and said, "I asked you a question."

The older woman shook her head. "Any louder and everyone in the taproom will hear you. Do you really want to drum your brother out of business?"

Susana leaned close. "I do not care in the least if he loses this inn. I do not want to work here. I was meant for a far better life than this, and I plan to see that I get it!"

The cook ignored the outburst and continued to stir the pot of stew. "Shouldn't you be making the rounds and taking orders from our guests?"

"I am not a serving girl!" With that, Susana spun on her heel and stalked out of the kitchen.

A few moments later, her brother strode through the doorway. "Where's Susana?"

The cook sighed. "She just left in a huff after reminding me for the umpteenth time that she was not a serving girl."

The innkeeper frowned. "It's been hard on her since our parents died. I know she can be difficult, but I need her where I can watch over her. I cannot leave the inn and take her to London."

"You're a good man, Tom Harkness," the cook told him. "You pay a fair day's wages and treat your employees well. I'm going to risk making you mad, but you should know Susana just told me that she was meant for a better life and was going to see that she got it."

Tom raked a hand through his hair, making it stand on end. "Which way did she go?"

"The side door that leads around back."

He nodded. "I'll divide Susana's tasks among the others." He paused in the doorway, slapped his hand against the wall, and looked over his shoulder. Anger was evident in his posture and his expression, but he controlled it. "Thank you for telling me."

"She has had her heart set on snagging one of the duke's men for a while now."

Tom's fierce frown was worrisome, but his tone was even when he asked, "Which one?"

"Flaherty."

He nodded and left.

⤐⟫⟫⟫⟪⟪⟪⤏

SUSANA SNUCK INTO the back of the stables. The rough-looking man her brother had recently hired was mucking out stalls. She sashayed over to where he worked spreading fresh straw in the stall he'd just cleaned. Pitching her voice low, she purred, "I have been looking for you."

His gaze met hers and she saw a flare of heat in his dark eyes. "You found me."

Not the reply she usually received. Men usually bent over backward to do whatever she asked. Of course, she repaid them with certain favors she was well used to doling out, and most of the time she enjoyed the quick tumble most expected in return. She knew she was beautiful and had a shapely body that men craved.

She inhaled and watched the flash of heat she was watching for. He was interested, but did not want to cede control. She had played that game before and won.

"I need a favor, and you look to be strong enough and intelligent enough to do it for me."

He slid his gaze from the top of her head, settling it on her full breasts and hips, until she had no doubt what he wanted. "What do I get in return?"

"My brother doesn't pay me enough to purchase hair ribbons. I do not have any coin to pay you with, but I'm certain we can come to an agreement." She moved close enough to feel the heat pouring off his body and nearly laughed, knowing she had him in the palm of her hand.

Susana dipped one shoulder and felt her gown slip low on one side. She had her necklines lowered to show off her large breasts to any and all interested in sampling them. From the desire in the eyes of the man ogling her *décolletage*, she knew he wanted a taste of her.

Maybe she'd give him one. She turned her back to him and glanced over her shoulder. "If you want a sample of what I'm worth, follow me."

He set the pitchfork against the wall, removed his gloves, and put his hands on her waist. "I may have time for more than a sample."

Neither one of them saw or heard the young stable hand who walked around the corner toward the empty stalls, in time to hear her sultry laughter as she pulled the man toward the tack room at the back of the stables.

CHAPTER SEVENTEEN

F LAHERTY ESCORTED TEMPERANCE to the rear door of the building and held it open for her. "I'm certain O'Malley has already spoken to Their Graces by now—'tis his job as the head of the duke's guard to keep them informed. But I don't want Maddy to hear it from anyone else first. Can ye bring her over to the stables? I'm certain Garahan will allow me a few more minutes before I head out to guard the perimeter."

Temperance brushed a kiss to his cheek and hurried down the hallway, calling for Maddy as she neared the kitchen.

"In here, Mum!" Her daughter's smile was radiant, and her eyes sparkled.

"Have you already heard the news?"

Maddy pursed her lips and shook her head.

Temperance had a feeling that word had spread to the kitchens already, but she did not want to spoil her daughter's mood. Summoning all of the hope and happiness she'd felt when she accepted Flaherty's offer, she knelt in front of her daughter, took hold of her hands, and asked, "Do you remember what you asked me earlier?"

Maddy frowned. "I asked you lots of things."

"Flaherty would like to ask you something. He's waiting by the stables." Temperance straightened, caught the knowing look on Constance's face, and smiled. "I need to borrow your helper for a short time. We'll be back shortly."

The cook waved them away. "Take all the time you need."

Maddy caught on to the excitement and started to run, tugging her mother behind her. "Hurry, Mum. Just Flaherty needs me."

To keep her daughter from tripping in her haste to get to her hero, Temperance scooped her up and carried her to the stables. "I think someone's been feeding you boulders for breakfast. You're heavier than you were."

Maddy patted the side of her mother's face. "Constance is always trying to feed me, even when I'm not hungry."

"There they are, laddie," Flaherty said to his gelding as he walked his horse over to meet Temperance and Maddy. "Thank ye for coming to speak to me. I only have a few minutes, or Garahan'll be skinning a strip off me hide for being late to me patrol."

Temperance shot him a worried look. "Will he really?"

"Nay, lass, it just feels like it when he uses his I-can-beat-ye-with-me-hands-tied-behind-me-back-blindfolded look."

Maddy giggled. "Can he really?"

"Nay, I let him think he can."

The little girl leaned toward Flaherty, who took her from her mother's arms and held her on his hip. "Then what happens?"

He grinned. "I beat him!"

Maddy wrapped her arms around his neck and pressed her cheek to his. "Mum said you wanted me."

"THAT I DO. Can I be yer da? I asked yer ma to marry me, and she said yes."

Maddy squealed, kissed his cheek, and then eased back. As she looked into his eyes, her expression swiftly changed from ecstatic to thoughtful. "You'll need to ask him."

Confused, Flaherty glanced at Temperance, who shrugged and shook her head. Turning back to Maddy, he asked, "Him who?"

"My papa. Mum says he's my guardian angel… He's in Heaven."

"Ah, *mo chroí*, she told me that too." He met the intensity of Temperance's look with one of certainty. "Will you help me ask him?"

Maddy nodded. "We have to kneel down and fold our hands."

Flaherty set her down, told his horse to mind his manners, and let go of the reins. Well-mannered horse that he was, the gelding stood still. Maddy reached for his hand. Flaherty knelt and urged her to kneel beside him.

"Now fold your hands together like this," she told him.

He mirrored the little girl's movement, interlacing his fingers. "Since I've not been properly introduced to yer da, would you do the honors?"

She furrowed her brow, was silent for a few moments, then slowly smiled. "I will. Now close your eyes."

He closed his eyes.

"And bow your head. No peeking until I say so!"

He bowed his head. "Aye, Maddy-lass."

"Papa?" Her soft voice was reverent, as if she were used to praying. "I'm here with Just Flaherty. He rescued Mum once, and me twice, and wants to protect us and love us." She paused and patted him on the shoulder. "Just Flaherty?"

"Aye?" he asked without opening his eyes, lest she remind him she'd said no peeking.

"Do you want to love us and protect us?"

"With all me heart and every bit of me strength." She kissed his shoulder, and he vowed to move Heaven and Earth if Maddy or her ma asked him to.

"Papa, I had to check. Just Flaherty wants to love us and protect us, and I want him to…but only if you say so."

How in the bloody hell did she expect her departed father to give his blessing? He had no idea how to navigate the hurt that would surely follow when the little girl's request went unanswered. *Dear Father in Heaven, help me!*

A blast of warmth hit him in the heart and spread to his limbs, shocking him to the core, as a feeling of peace seeped into his very soul. He nearly opened his eyes, but he'd given his word, and he would keep it.

"Thank you, Papa! Open your eyes, Just Flaherty!"

He did as the little girl bade him.

"Did you hear what he said?"

"Nay," he answered, "but I felt as if the warmth of the sun was pressing on me heart and soul a moment ago...and then peace filled me."

"My husband just gave his daughter and you his blessing," Temperance rasped. "I felt the same warmth you experienced, Rory."

He held his women in his arms and breathed slowly as he thanked God for the miracle that they'd all witnessed. "I promise to protect the both of ye with me life, and if the Lord takes me first, ye'll have yer da and me—two guardian angels—watching over ye."

"Flaherty! Move yer arse!" shouted.

"Language, ye bloody *eedjit!*" Flaherty's gelding nudged him between his shoulder blades. "Well now, if me horse is poking me in the back, I'd best be going. Promise me the two of ye won't be getting into any trouble while I'm guarding the perimeter."

"We promise—don't we, Mum?"

"We promise, Rory."

"Can I still call you Just Flaherty when you marry my mum?"

"Aye, *mo chroí.*" He kissed Maddy's forehead, and Temperance's cheek, slowly stood, and helped them to their feet. "Off with the two of ye now. I've work."

Temperance held out her hand to Maddy while Flaherty vaulted into the saddle. "Be safe, Rory."

"I will, lass."

"Bye, Just Flaherty!"

"Bye, wee *cailín*." He urged his horse forward and rode toward the front of the building. At the bend in the drive, he turned and waved to them. "God, thank ye for me latest blessing, and thank Maddy's da for me and tell him 'twill be me mission in life, and an honor, to love and protect his wife and daughter."

Picking up the pace, Flaherty scanned both sides of the road, seeking anything out of the ordinary that would indicate trouble lurking nearby. As he rode past the section of meadow on both sides of the road, he added to his prayer, hoping Maddy's father was still listening. "Just so ye know, should anything happen to me, I've three brothers, four Garahan cousins, and eight O'Malley cousins who will stand in me stead and protect Temperance and Maddy with their lives."

The warmth returned, more intense than the first time. Flaherty had his answer. As he continued on his patrol, all was right with his world.

The dense forest was up ahead on the left. He slipped his rifle off his shoulder, ready to fire off a warning shot or return fire. Flaherty never worried that any sharpshooter would be able to shoot him before he got a bead on the gunman first. His O'Malley cousins in America had sent Kentucky long rifles to Patrick O'Malley as a gift when they first learned they had pledged their lives to protecting the duke and his family. No other rifle that he'd ever possessed was as accurate at four hundred yards. His thoughts drifted to the woman he would marry instead of the densely wooded area.

He heard the shot before he spotted the sharpshooter. Pain seared his cheek, momentarily distracting him. Just as suddenly the pain receded, and he felt a sudden urge to duck. He did, and a second shot whistled past, missing him. He concentrated on the direction the shots were coming from and fired. The grunt of pain told him he'd hit his target. Loading his rifle quickly, he took aim and fired again. The resounding crack and thud that followed had him racing toward the broken limb and the man who had fallen with it.

Flaherty dismounted and muttered a curse. The nick to his face wasn't serious, but would be if it got infected. He grabbed hold of the saddle as thoughts of Temperance and Maddy filled his mind. Would they worry about him every time he went on patrol? Would his being injured, even slightly, cause them to change their mind?

The slash of pain surprised him and had him wondering why the graze to his cheek bothered him now, when it hadn't until he'd shot his attacker off his perch. The answer surfaced—the intensity of the moment had passed. He recognized the feeling. It had happened before when he'd been clubbed or stabbed fighting to protect his duke and his family. 'Twas part of his make-up to stand his ground, even when injured, until the threat had been contained. Then pain would make itself known.

Flaherty walked over to the prone man. He swiped at the blood that trickled from his wound. Frustrated and angry, he growled, "Who in the bloody hell sent ye?"

The man had a hand clamped around his upper arm, but it didn't do much to stop the bleeding. Flaherty nudged him with toe of his boot, but did not receive the reaction he expected.

The man who'd had the bollocks to shoot at him glared. "Wasn't worth it."

"Getting shot, or getting caught?"

"I'll tell you, if you help me bind my arm. I can't manage it one-handed."

"Where's yer knife?"

The man surprised Flaherty by chuckling. "There's one in my left boot."

Flaherty kept his eyes on his attacker while he disarmed him. Intrigued, he wondered why the man did not seem worried that he'd been injured. Moreover, why had he capitulated so quickly? Nothing about the attack or aftermath made sense. It wouldn't until he had the name of whoever was behind it—and how much the sharpshooter had been paid. "I'll take yer pistol too."

"Coat pocket. If I had known who you worked for, I would not have shot you. We could have been friends otherwise."

"I usually offer me hand in friendship—not a lead ball," Flaherty grumbled.

"I'm sorry I let a woman talk me into this."

"As I got yer shooting arm, I'm not surprised. I'll bind yer wound if ye promise not to club me in the cheek that ye grazed."

"You have my word."

"That would take a leap of faith on me part to trust ye, but I've been known to do so when me gut urges me to. What's yer name?"

"O'Brien."

Flaherty noticed the hard gleam in the man's eyes had been replaced by one of interest. He pulled the spare cravat from his frockcoat pocket, folded it into a square, and placed it on O'Brien's wound. "Hold that." Flaherty untied the cravat from around his neck and wrapped it around the man's upper arm. "That should slow the bleeding, but ye'll need threads to stop it. Me lead ball went clean through."

"Felt like it. Hurts like bloody hell."

"I'm more than familiar," Flaherty muttered. "The chunk of me cheek that's now missing best not disfigure me after she said yes."

O'Brien stared at him. "You offered marriage recently?"

"Aye. Twice in the same day." Satisfaction filled Flaherty. "She accepted the second time." He did not bother to go into detail, to mention Maddy's request or the angelic approval that followed.

"As we both managed to shoot one another," O'Brien murmured, "we'll call it even and be on our way."

Flaherty snorted. "Why would I do that, when ye haven't told me who sent ye?"

O'Brien scrubbed a hand over his face and shook his head. "If I had known you were one of the Duke of Wyndmere's guards, I would never have agreed."

"But if I had been anyone else, ye would have?"

O'Brien stared at him for a few moments before answering. "Aye. It isn't because I fear any one of you—it's because I respect the oath I've heard you and the others have sworn to protect the duke and his family."

"Then ye'll understand that as it is His Grace I work for, I have rules I must follow."

The other man nodded. "I expected as much as soon as you walked over and I saw you were wearing black and recognized the symbol of Ireland embroidered over your heart."

"If ye don't cause any more trouble, and are willing to tell me the name of the woman who sent ye—though I have a fair idea who it was—the constable and I may be able to sway His Grace into putting ye to work for the duke instead of being taken to the gaol."

"The innkeeper's sister, Susana Harkness."

Anger had Flaherty clenching his fists. "The woman has caused a great deal of heartache to me betrothed and her daughter with her slanderous lies. What in the bloody hell did I ever do to her to have her send ye to kill me?"

"I was to wound you—not kill you," O'Brien replied.

Flaherty shook his head. "Ah well, that's all right then, isn't it?"

"You're not dead," O'Brien said.

"Neither are ye. If it had been daylight, and ye hadn't been hidden in the thick of the trees, my aim would have been true, and I'd be carting yer lifeless body to the undertaker."

O'Brien didn't bother to argue. "I may have to learn to shoot left-handed."

Flaherty eyed the man. If what O'Brien was claiming were true—and Flaherty believed it was—then he deserved a second chance. "How are ye at bare-knuckle fighting?"

"I hold me own."

"The lot of us, me brothers, cousins, and I, were bare-knuckle champions back home."

O'Brien flashed a grin. "I wouldn't mind going a few rounds with you."

The longer Flaherty talked to the man, the more he believed what O'Brien was saying. Thinking of Greene, he asked, "Did she offer ye certain favors if ye shot me?"

O'Brien's eyes widened. He shook his head, turned, and spat on the ground. "She's done this before." It wasn't a question.

"Aye. Though I'm certain ye'd be a fine catch for any lucky young lass—as long as ye change yer ways and aren't duped into shooting a man for performing his duties. A man ruled by his bollocks doesn't always think things through. But I'm willing to give ye a second chance. Are ye interested in one?"

O'Brien struggled to lift his arm, but managed to put his hand over his heart. Sweat beaded at his temples and trickled down the sides of his face. It was obvious he was in pain. "I am." He let his hand drop to his side and blew out a breath, panting.

"Any man who would go to the trouble of swearing a vow with the same arm he'd just been shot in is a man worthy of being given a second chance. It'll take some fast talking and maybe surviving a round of bare-knuckle with all four of us."

"I thought there were more than that."

Flaherty grinned and cursed. Every time he shifted his facial muscles, his face hurt like bloody hell. "There're sixteen of us in all, but we're spread out, as the duke has more than one estate that needs guarding."

O'Brien's shoulders slumped and he hung his head. "The way word travels in this village, and if Susana hears what happened before you speak to her, no woman would have me after what I've done."

Flaherty's ancestors had been pitted against similar situations for years. He wasn't a stranger to such tactics. "We've countered lies and slander successfully before. But if ye prefer, and if His Grace agrees, I'm certain we can find a spot for ye in London."

"I'll confess my sins to the vicar, and apologize to the duke, if you will convince him to give me a second chance."

"I'm thinking Miss Harkness needs to be confessing her sins," Flaherty grumbled. "She embroiled another man who worked for her brother in her schemes that I wouldn't have minded adding to our number, but it's out of me hands now."

O'Brien's frown was fierce. "I have only been working for Harkness for a sennight. His sister tried to tempt me into more than a few lascivious kisses." He shook his head, looked up, and met Flaherty's gaze. "But bloody hell! We were in the stables. Anyone could have interrupted us."

Flaherty nodded, more than pleased that his gut feeling was bearing fruit. "Ye have principles. But I'm needing to know what had ye accepting her offer in the first place."

"I won't lie to you, it was the way she walked and sidled up next to me that set me on fire. I haven't had the pleasure of bedding a woman in a while."

"Working for His Grace, it has been some time for me as well. If ye work for him, ye won't have time to even think about a quick tumble. Ye'll be dodging lead balls, cudgels, knifes—"

"All manner of weapons," O'Brien interrupted.

"Aye. Grab on to me arm, and I'll help ye up."

O'Brien stood and seemed grateful for the aid. Flaherty waited a moment for the man to stop swaying on his feet. As he'd been shot before, Flaherty knew O'Brien was fighting the pain, hoping it would subside to a bearable level. "If yer aim had been slightly to the right, me cousins would be praying over me corpse this night. It would have put off me wedding."

O'Brien's shout of laughter had Flaherty smiling. "Wouldn't that be a tale to tell, that a lass in the Lake District married a corpse!" O'Brien's laughter died as his expression changed. "She didn't mention that you were getting married. When is the wedding?"

"As soon as the vicar has five minutes."

O'Brien sighed. "Maybe someday I'll find a woman that puts that kind of look in my eye."

"Look?"

"Aye. You're head over heels."

Flaherty drew in a deep breath and slowly exhaled. "That I am, O'Brien, though me cousins prefer telling me that I'm arse over head."

"A more apt description."

"I'll not tie yer hands behind yer back if ye give me yer word ye won't try to escape."

"You have it."

"Where's yer horse?"

O'Brien pointed. "I left him just behind the oaks grouped tightly together."

"Whistle for him. If he doesn't come, then I'll fetch him."

O'Brien whistled, a rustling sounded, and a few moments later a horse pushed his way through the branches, and trotted toward them. "Good lad," Flaherty crooned, reaching for the gelding's halter. "I know yer arm must be paining ye. I'll give ye a leg up." O'Brien groaned as Flaherty helped him gain the horse's back, careful not to let the man topple over the other side of his horse. "Ye've a fine horse."

O'Brien smiled as his horse lifted his head as if agreeing. "He knows it."

"I'm thinking we made a friend, laddie," Flaherty told his horse as he vaulted into his saddle. "But it'll take more than me horse taking a shining to ye to convince His Grace to help ye. I'll need all me powers of persuasion, and yerself to be honest with the duke when he questions ye. Can ye do that?"

"I will do that." O'Brien's gaze latched on to Flaherty's. "I may need to ask a favor."

"Ye can ask, but I won't guarantee that I'll be able to do it."

"Are you handy with a needle and thread?"

Flaherty's laughter was his answer. "We'll see that yer wounds are sewn back together, with boiled threads and a sharp needle that has been seared to lessen the chances of infection."

"I don't deserve your kindness after letting me cock make

decisions for me."

"Well now, ye wouldn't be the first man to be led astray by a wanton woman," Flaherty replied. "Ye won't be the last." His horse snorted, and Flaherty apologized, "I'm sorry to have mentioned it."

O'Brien stared. "How long have you been having conversations with your horse?"

"Any Irishman has the gift—he just has to open his mind and become attuned to what his horse is thinking."

"No wonder you offered me a second chance," O'Brien grumbled. "You're insane."

Flaherty's answering laughter followed them back to Wyndmere Hall.

CHAPTER EIGHTEEN

GARAHAN'S MOUTH GAPED open. "Have ye lost yer mind? The man shot ye in the face!"

Flaherty shrugged. "Grazed me cheek. 'Twill be a scar worth talking about."

"Unless yer ugly mug scares Temperance or Maddy into changing their minds about marrying ye."

Flaherty wished his cousin hadn't mentioned the one point that had burrowed into the back of his mind and taken root on the ride back to Wyndmere Hall. "They're both made of sterner stuff than that. They won't."

"Are ye asking or telling me?"

Flaherty used his shoulder to knock his cousin off balance as he stepped around him. "I've got to take O'Brien to the outbuilding. I told him that's where the four of us would interrogate him." He slowly smiled. "I may have hinted that fists would be involved." Garahan cackled with laughter, and Flaherty shook his head, "Ye sound more insane than meself, Aiden."

That shut his cousin up. He strode toward Flaherty and handed him a clean handkerchief. "Press this on yer face. I'm thinking ye need a stitch or two to stop the bleeding."

Worried that his cousin wouldn't be open to listening, Flaherty asked, "And ye'll hear O'Brien out? Ye won't interrupt?"

"'Tis me right to interrupt." At Flaherty's grunt of disapproval, Garahan added, "But eventually he'll get to tell the whole tale, and yes, I'll listen."

"'Tis all I'm asking. The real culprit is the innkeeper's sister. If O'Brien hadn't recognized me as one of the duke's private guard, he may have seriously injured me."

Garahan studied Flaherty's cheek. "As ye mentioned, 'tis but a scar."

Relief filled Flaherty. Only two more cousins to ask. The sainted O'Malleys would be the hardest to convince. He was deeply concerned about the innkeeper's sister causing more trouble. She'd already spread her poison among the good people in the village, turning them against Temperance, and snared two men with promises to repay them with her allurements. Some men were weaker in that regard than others. Susana had managed to root out ones that were. "We need to have His Grace speak to the constable again. I'm thinking this will prove that the woman is a threat and unhinged."

"'Tis three things she's done now," Garahan replied. "The duke will have to agree that once may have been an error in judgment and unintentional, two instances suspect, but three times? Intentional."

Relieved his cousin had come around to his way of thinking, Flaherty added, "We'll need the footmen to stand in our stead while we question O'Brien."

"I'll speak to O'Malley first, then Humphries. Ye take care of O'Brien."

"I will. Garahan?"

"Now what?"

"As it's nearly shift change, will ye ask O'Malley if he wants me to forego the last bit of the perimeter patrol and man me post outside the nursery?"

"Don't be forgetting he's been in yer shoes, Flaherty. He'll see right through yer request and know it for what it is—a chance to see Temperance and Maddy."

"Doesn't matter as long as he grants it. I'll take O'Brien to the outbuilding next to me quarters. Would ye ask Constance to have boiled threads at the ready? O'Brien'll need to be stitched up."

"Anything else?"

"If I think of anything, ye'll be the first to know."

"Lucky me," Garahan muttered. He walked toward the front of the building and headed toward the ladder leading to the roof. He called over his shoulder, "What if O'Malley wants ye to finish out yer perimeter patrol?"

"He won't." Flaherty was confident that his cousin would agree. The next difficult conversation would be the one with Temperance about his minor injury. He hoped she would not change her mind. He sensed she was a strong and courageous woman, but she needed to believe herself able to accept the daily possibility that he would walk into a dangerous situation at any given time. She had to trust in his strength and ability to handle himself against overwhelming odds. Their future depended on it.

"Lord, 'tis Flaherty again—er, Rory. I could use a bit of Yer divine intervention convincing Temperance she's brave enough to handle whatever happens to me while performing me duties."

As his concern faded, he nodded to O'Brien, who dismounted. The two men walked their horses to the stables and turned them over to the stable master. "Don't be forgetting extra oats for both horses."

"I haven't forgotten yet, Flaherty."

"Faith, ye're a good man and finest of stable masters." Flaherty turned and nodded to O'Brien. "This way."

O'Brien was silent as Flaherty led him along the path from the stables to the outbuildings—one was the guards' quarters where they all used to sleep before his cousins got tangled up with the women they'd rescued and started marrying the lasses to protect them.

Just like you are now.

Lord willing.

⋙⋘

HUMPHRIES OPENED THE door and greeted the frazzled-looking man standing on the duke's doorstep. He looked vaguely familiar. "May I tell His Grace who is calling?"

"Harkness—I own the inn in the village."

"Ah, Mr. Harkness, please come in." When the innkeeper entered, Humphries closed the door behind him. "If you'll kindly wait here, I will see if His Grace has time to meet with you."

"Thank you." Harkness glanced around, wondering how receptive the duke would be to helping him find his sister. It was almost ludicrous to ask, considering his sister's recent actions. But the duke had been generous in offering his staff and his personal guard when one of the villagers needed help. And he needed help. "Why did you have to stir up trouble for one of the duke's men, Susana?"

He turned at the sound of footsteps approaching.

Humphries inclined his head. "If you'll follow me, His Grace will see you now."

Unused to being in such grand surroundings, Harkness glanced at his surroundings once more. The staircase was enormous, and there were footmen stationed at various points above him, and in the entryway and hall. He wondered how the duke became accustomed to having so many servants. He was often surrounded by people, but they were not usually members of the *ton*. The Duke of Wyndmere wasn't just a member of Society—he was among the top tier.

Humphries knocked and was bidden to enter. "Mr. Harkness from the inn, Your Grace."

"Thank you, Humphries."

Dismissed, the butler retreated, leaving Harkness alone with the duke. The topic of his sister weighed heavily on him. He'd been responsible for her after their parents died, and given her behavior of late, he felt as if he'd failed both their parents and his sister. She was not demure or gracious, nor could even be called a hoyden. Susana Harkness was a hellion!

"Harkness, welcome to Wyndmere Hall. Won't you have a seat and tell me what brings you here today?"

"Thank you, Your Grace." He sat in one of the leather wing-back chairs in front of the fireplace. Shifting to the edge of the seat, he didn't know where to start. Should he ask for help finding his missing sister? If the rumors circulating were false, then Susana had knowingly caused irreparable damage to an innocent woman's reputation, and that of a child. He needed to find her and demand to know why she would do something that vile. But how to frame the apology so that the duke would understand and be swayed to help him? His Grace needed to understand that Harkness was to blame…not his younger sister.

"It would appear that whatever brought you here is weighing heavy on your mind. Have you come for advice? I regularly offer sound advice, but my darling duchess rarely heeds it. Though she does have the courtesy to listen before ignoring it."

Harkness snorted, then cleared his throat. "Forgive me, Your Grace. I meant no disrespect. My sister has the same unfortunate habit."

"Ah. Have you come to speak of Miss Harkness?"

The tone of the duke's voice hinted that he knew what Susana had done. "You Grace, I must apologize for my sister. You see—"

"Is that why you came?"

Harkness stared at the floor. "In part, Your Grace."

"Why don't we get to the other part of why you came first? Then we can discuss the rest."

He lifted his head and met the duke's steady gaze. "My sister is missing—she's a few hours overdue for her shift in the taproom. She has a habit of strolling in late, but never this late. I've asked the vicar and the blacksmith to help form a search party, and they agreed to help—if one of your men would organize it, as they graciously have in the past."

The duke rose from his seat. "Patrick O'Malley, the head of my private guard, is the man we need for this. How late is she?"

"Three hours."

"Then we'd best make haste, Harkness. We'll use the side door at the end of the hallway. The path to the stables is right outside the door."

Before the duke reached the door, Harkness stepped in front of him. "Forgive me, Your Grace, but there's something you need to know before you enlist O'Malley's help."

The duke raised one brow in silent question.

"My sister has developed an attraction to one of your men...Flaherty. I thought it was an infatuation and would pass, but it hasn't."

"I see."

He wrung his hands. "To be honest, Your Grace, I have learned this is not the first time my sister has used her wiles to get her way. Our cook informed me that Susana convinced one of our younger stable hands to spy on Flaherty."

"I know."

"You do?"

"My guard has eyes and ears in places you would not even think of. Anything else?"

Harkness swallowed what pride he had left. "Aye, Your Grace. A recently hired stable hand walked out a few hours ago, after only mucking out half of the stalls. My hostler hired the man and was confident that O'Brien would be an asset to those already working in our stables. He's never misjudged a man before."

"And you believe this O'Brien has lured your sister away from the inn?"

Harkness felt his throat tighten, and knew it would be a struggle to tell the duke the rest, but he had to impart what he'd just learned. "I suspect, but do not have evidence. One of the younger hands reporting to Scruggs said he saw my sister leading O'Brien to the tack room at the back of the stables."

"I see."

Before the duke formed the wrong conclusion, Harkness went on to explain, "Curious—the young man hung around to see how long they would be gone before reporting it to Scruggs. 'Twasn't long enough to..." He could not bring himself to say anymore.

The duke inclined his head. "You need not say any more—however, I can relieve your mind on one point. I happen to know where O'Brien is. Your sister is not with him."

"Where?"

"My men are currently interrogating him."

He felt the blood rush from the top of his head to his feet. "Please do not tell me the man came here to cause trouble."

"Actually, that may have been his intention until he realized whom he had in his sights. O'Brien was perched in a tree on the road leading around the southern perimeter of my estate."

"Perched?" Harkness felt his gut roil. *Tree?* "Bloody hell, who did he shoot?"

"Flaherty."

Harkness slumped against the wall. "I had no idea. I was inside tending to our guests. I cannot be in two places at one time—"

"No one would expect you to be. Now that you know where your sister *isn't*, let's speak to O'Malley and organize a search party to find her."

"She's the only family I have left. I am so sorry that she's caused you trouble, and I have no right to ask. You see, I have been trying to balance the running of our family's inn and her behavior. I've sheltered her when I should have been stern with her. Susana has no idea what could befall a young woman on her own."

The duke placed a hand on Harkness's shoulder. "I have been in your position with my younger brother, and managed to encourage him onto the right path. You'll do the same, Harkness. Let's find O'Malley."

CHAPTER NINETEEN

T HE DUCHESS BEAMED. "You are going to be a beautiful bride, Temperance."

Maddy bounced on her toes. "Me too?"

"You'll be the most beautiful daughter of the bride, Maddy," the duchess replied.

Maddy giggled. "I know."

"I have a feeling I know who may have already told you that," Francis said.

Maddy twirled across the upstairs sitting room and landed at her mother's feet. "Just Flaherty told me. And you know what?"

The three women were smiling when Francis asked, "What?"

"I heard him tell Mum that she would be as lovely as a May morning, and taste just as sweet."

Temperance covered her mouth with her hands, but it was too late—the duchess, the maid, and her daughter heard her inelegant snort. Highly embarrassed, she told Maddy, "You should not be listening to other people's conversations." When her daughter opened her mouth to speak, Temperance frowned. "Nor should you repeat private conversations."

"But he said he's going to be my da—that's the same as a papa, right?"

"Yes, darling, but you cannot—"

Maddy interrupted, "But you aren't a scone or teacake. So

why would say you'd taste sweet?"

Temperance felt her face flame, but she ignored it. "I shall tell you when you are a bit older. Then we shall have a serious talk."

"Mum and papa stuff?"

"Exactly."

Maddy sighed. "All right." She was quiet for a few minutes, and Temperance wondered if that would be the end of her daughter's embarrassing questions.

"How much older do I have to be before we talk?"

Apparently it wasn't.

"At least five years."

"But I'll be nine by then."

"Just the right age to have that talk with your mum, Maddy," the duchess remarked. "Why don't you go with Francis? She will help you change out of your new dress. You'll want it to be nice and clean for tomorrow afternoon."

"'Cause Mum and I will marry Just Flaherty tomorrow?"

Temperance opened her arms, and Maddy flew across the room into them. "Because Rory and I will be married tomorrow, and we'll be a family."

"I'll have a papa?"

"Yes, Maddy. Now go along with Francis. I'll be there shortly."

As soon as the door closed behind Maddy and Francis, the duchess burst into laughter. "Is this what I have to look forward to in a few years with Abigail and Richard?"

Temperance brushed a lock of hair out of her eyes and shrugged. "This was a first for me. I hadn't even thought of having a talk with Maddy about marriage and babes yet."

"You'll need to have the conversation about her monthlies by then, too," the duchess advised. "I still remember how awkward it was when my mother shared that information with me. I plan to make it less so when I talk to my daughter."

"I cannot even begin to imagine having to describe the marriage bed and birthing babes," Temperance admitted.

The duchess sighed. "I hope I'll be able to impart more information than my mother shared with me. As it was, I had to muddle through, but thankfully my husband was understanding."

Temperance confided, "My mum told me to close my eyes and it would be over in a few minutes."

They were still laughing by the time Temperance had changed into her gown. They arrived in the nursery sitting room in time to find their tea was ready and waiting for them.

Temperance was sipping her second cup of tea, and Maddy eating her third—and last—iced teacake when the duke appeared in the doorway. "I thought I'd find you ladies here. Temperance, Flaherty needs to have a word with you before he leaves."

"Leaves? Where is he going?"

"We've organized search parties. He wanted to speak to you before he heads out."

Worry filled Temperance. "Is it another lost child?"

"In a way, but no, not really."

At the duke's oddly evasive answer, Temperance told Maddy to stay with Francis and the duchess and followed the duke to the servants' staircase. "He's waiting for you at the foot of the stairs." The duke paused before adding, "He's leading one of the teams from the village."

"I see. Thank you for telling me, Your Grace." She placed her hand on the railing, lifted her hem so she wouldn't trip, and descended. The door opened before she reached the bottom step.

"Ah, lass. I was wondering what kept ye. Did the duke tell ye I'm needed?"

Temperance noticed the wound slashing across his cheek. "You've been hurt."

"'Tis but a scratch."

She counted five stitches. "It must have bled quite a bit."

"Wounds to the head and face always do. I need ye to listen."

Temperance stared at his injury, fighting to hold on to her composure. "I'm listening, Rory."

"What else did the duke say?"

"He mentioned that you're leading one of the search parties."

He inclined his head. "I am. She's been gone nearly four hours now. Her brother is worried sick."

"Her poor brother. How old is she?"

Flaherty sighed. "He didn't tell ye who's missing, did he?"

"His Grace only said it wasn't a child."

"She most certainly is not."

A shiver raced up her spine. "Do I know the woman?"

"Aye, and ye know of her—'tis Miss Harkness."

Aghast, she tried to keep from raising her voice, but it was a struggle. "The woman who said vile things about me and hinted that Maddy was born out of wedlock?"

"Aye. But that isn't important now. The length of time she's been missing without a hint of what happened is vital. She could have been abducted—"

Temperance felt the hold on her temper slip. "Like she said *I* abducted my own daughter?"

Flaherty tucked a wayward curl behind her ear and traced the tip of his finger along the curve of her cheek. "Aye, lass. Try to let go of yer anger and say a prayer for her. I'm thinking she's a lost soul."

Chastised, temper simmering, the best Temperance could do was choke out, "I'll try."

"The sooner I leave, the sooner we'll find her. Her brother is worried sick."

"You said that already. I understand his worry, but not the reasoning behind her destructive words or deeds."

The intensity in Flaherty's steady stare had Temperance letting go of her anger. She accepted that this was most likely how the rest of her life would be—Flaherty in danger, getting shot at, then leaving to find lost children or, Heaven help her, women. She closed the distance between them and slipped her arms around his neck. "You'd best kiss me like you mean it, so I have something to hold on to while you're gone."

His blue eyes darkened with desire. It was a heady feeling that her words would have such an immediate effect on him. He bent his head until their lips were a breath apart. "Make it count, *mo ghrá*. We could be gone for a few hours."

Temperance poured everything she had been feeling for him into her kiss. When he parted her lips to taste her fully, she melted into his embrace.

"Ye'll be the death of me, lass. One taste of ye will never be enough."

She slipped out of his arms and cupped the side of his face. "I'll be waiting for you. Be careful, Rory."

"Count on it, lass. I have two beautiful women to come back to."

Unable to stop herself, she followed him to the door, watching as he signaled to a group of riders and rode off. She sighed, then rasped, "I'd best get used to his coming and going and make myself useful while he's gone."

But Temperance was also thinking of the kiss she planned to share with Rory when he returned.

She ascended the stairs and returned to the nursery sitting room.

"That took longer than expected," the duchess remarked.

Maddy was quiet, and had a look of concentration on her face before she blurted out, "Did Just Flaherty taste you more than once?"

The musical sound of the duchess's laughter eased some of Temperance's embarrassment, but not quite all of it. Needing to have the last word, she replied. "Yes, Maddy dear, he did."

Satisfied, Maddy asked, "Can I have two more teacakes?"

FLAHERTY WONDERED IF Garahan was having any luck finding Miss Harkness. He and the men he'd been assigned to lead had been searching between the village and Wyndmere Hall for hours with not a sign of the irritating woman. He dug deep to find some sympathy for her, but she had been the cause of so much heartache for Temperance and her daughter. Flaherty settled for accepting her as someone he was tasked to rescue, and by all that was holy, he'd been doing his damndest to find her! It was time to join Garahan's search party to see if his cousin was having any better luck.

Pulling on the reins, Flaherty looked over his shoulder and whistled to get the attention of the men. They immediately responded. Those that had dismounted and were searching alongside the road, in the wooded areas, turned toward him. The two others on horseback—one man riding out front, the other bringing up the rear—did as well. Every man stopped in his tracks.

"Did you find her?" one asked.

Flaherty shook his head. "We'll ride into the village, and join Garahan and the men who are searching on the other side of it. He may need our help, if he's found her."

One by one, the men nodded—or shrugged—leaving Flaherty to realize that they were only there for the sake of Harkness, who was well liked among the villagers and tenant farmers. His sister had been a troublemaker from the moment they'd taken over the running of their parents' inn. While the locals were always up for a bit of gossip, he couldn't think of more than a handful of women who claimed to be friends with Miss Harkness.

Riding through the village, Flaherty let his mind wander— just for a minute—to what Temperance and Maddy were doing right now. 'Twas past teatime. Were they helping with the evening meal? Were they worried about him?

"Flaherty!" the man riding ahead called out.

His mind snapped to attention and he heard raised voices in the distance. "Aye. Sounds like Garahan's run into trouble— er...found the woman. Follow me!"

He took the lead and increased the pace as they cleared the village proper. The high-pitched screech, followed by a wail of distress, had him shuddering. Praise God, neither Temperance nor Maddy acted in such a way. He'd seen them at their lowest, and they never exhibited such behavior.

Flaherty could see Garahan up ahead. His cousin and the men of his search party had formed a ring around Miss Harkness, who, thankfully, had stopped screeching when she noticed Flaherty and his men riding toward her.

"I can't walk!" she shouted.

"Did she break a leg?" Flaherty asked as he reined in alongside Garahan.

His cousin growled. "Nay."

"Sprain an ankle?"

Garahan scrubbed a hand over his face. "Nay, but she refuses to get up, even after I had two other men check for breaks or sprains, both of whom pronounced her well enough to walk."

Flaherty's gaze connected with the woman's. He frowned, and she crossed her arms and lifted her chin. Unable to tolerate the sight of the woman now that she was relatively safe, he turned to his cousin. "Well then, why in God's name is she still sitting on that boulder?"

"I've ruined my only pair of kidskin slippers!" she shouted. "Are all of the men in the duke's guard as lack-brained as Garahan?"

Flaherty didn't mind being insulted, but no one insulted his family. "Ye'll apologize to me cousin," he ground out. "Then ye'll get off that rock, walk over here, and apologize to the men for taking them away from their families, and missing their evening meal to search for ye."

Miss Harkness didn't bother to do anything Flaherty asked. She shot to her feet—thankfully, the top of the boulder was relatively flat—and put her hands on her hips. "I refuse! If you have more than one search party, my brother must have gone to the duke for help. You and Garahan work for the duke, and the tenant farmers over by the edge of the group rent land from the duke." She narrowed her eyes, skimming her gaze over the other half of the men gathered. "The rest of you live in the village and count on the duke's support of the village. How do you think His Grace will react when I tell him how horribly all of you have treated me? That not one of you were kind enough to carry me, when I was unable to walk—no one asked if I was hurt or—"

Flaherty had heard enough. There was not going to be any reasoning with the woman. He motioned for the blacksmith to fetch her. The man grimaced, but dismounted and swept Miss Harkness off the large rock and onto his horse. When he hesitated to mount behind her, Flaherty realized the woman had made more enemies than friends in the village.

"'Tis a sorry thing to have ruined yer best slippers," Flaherty said. "Have ye no sturdy half boots ye could wear?"

The woman glared at him. "I refuse to wear them. They're ugly."

"'Tis a pity ye didn't wear them," Flaherty continued, keeping his voice low and even. "Else ye would not have ruined yer kidskin slippers. Now would ye?" He rode toward the blacksmith. With a heavy sigh, the man mounted behind Miss Harkness and put his arm around her.

"Do not touch me! You reek of sweat and horse."

"Best let go of her, otherwise we'll be here all night," Flaherty said.

"But she'll—"

"There are times when one must reap what they sow." Flaherty fought the urge to smile, knowing what was about to happen. "Are ye and yer men ready to move out, Garahan?"

"Aye," his cousin replied. As one, both groups turned their horses toward the village.

The shriek of distress, and muffled laugher, had Flaherty silently thanking the Lord that the blacksmith moved like lightning and saved the lass from falling off the horse and onto her hard head—or well-padded backside.

"I told you not to touch me!" she screeched.

"Enough!" Flaherty shouted. He looked over his shoulder at

the men holding in their laughter. Pointing at two of the shortest, lightest men, he told them, "I need ye to ride double—and give yer horse to Miss Harkness to ride, as ye know she's unable to walk the distance."

The fair-haired man dismounted, walked his horse over to Flaherty, and handed him the reins. "She's a bit fractious, but a fine mare if treated well."

"Thank ye, Miller. I'll let ye grandma know of yer generosity and will have one of the men bring your mare home to ye a bit later tonight." The young man returned to the horse he would be riding double with his friend.

"Thank all of ye, men," Garahan told the group. "I'm sure Harkness and His Grace will be thanking ye themselves tomorrow or the next day. But know this—both men value yer service and diligence in looking for Harkness's lost sister."

"We're grateful as well," Flaherty announced for the both of them. "Ye're free to go."

The men broke off into pairs or smaller groups and bade Garahan and Flaherty goodbye to return to their homes and farms. Only Miss Harkness, Garahan, Flaherty, and the blacksmith remained. Flaherty took pity on the man. "Thank ye for rescuing the lass off that boulder. Garahan and I will take the reins and keep Miss Harkness and her horse between us on the way back to the inn."

The relief on the man's face was quickly masked with a look of indifference. "Happy to help…anytime."

"Thank ye," Garahan called to the blacksmith as he rode toward his forge and his house just beyond it.

"Fine man," Flaherty murmured.

"He stank!" Miss Harkness said.

"Shut yer gob!" Garahan barked.

The stricken look on the woman's face did not erase her intentionally cruel words. They hung in the air between them. Flaherty suspected the woman had never given a thought to anyone but herself in her life. 'Twas past time that she did.

"Because ye have no idea what it means to work hard enough to work up a sweat, let alone to toil over a forge that is hotter than the fires of hell, I won't tell ye what I think of yer words and actions that caused those good men to leave their homes to search for ye."

"For feck's sake, Flaherty, just tell the harpy she's a pain in the arse, no one likes her, and be done with it!" Garahan said.

The wail of tears that followed did not abate, even when they turned Miss Harkness over to her profoundly grateful brother. Flaherty started to explain to the man that she was not injured, but her tears were for her ruined slippers. When the woman's wails grew louder, Garahan told her to shut her gob a second time, earning a fierce glare from both Harkness and his sister.

"Tell him it isn't true, Tommy!" Susana begged. "Tell him he's wrong!"

"What isn't true and who's wrong?" Harkness asked.

"I'm not a harpy," she shrieked, "nor a pain in the arse, and everyone likes me!"

The sorrowful look on Harkness's face had Flaherty almost feeling sorry for the man. He and Garahan gave Harkness suggestions as to how his sister could make reparations to those she had slandered and mistreated. The innkeeper was in full agreement. Their mission complete, Flaherty and Garahan took their leave.

When they rode past the last building in the village, Garahan cackled with laugher. "Did ye see that poor *eedjit's* face when his sister demanded he tell her she's not a harpy or pain in the arse?"

Flaherty chuckled. "I was right there beside ye when she did."

"Everyone likes me," Garahan mimicked in a high-pitched voice, before lowering it again to add, "I'm willing to wager not one person likes her!"

Flaherty sighed. "I almost feel sorry for her, as I'm thinking ye have the right of it, Aiden. No one likes that woman."

⇒⇒⇒⋘⋘⋘

A FEW HOURS later, the search parties returned. Maddy had been asleep for some time, but Temperance was still wide awake, worrying, hoping that the men did not have to spend half the night searching for the difficult woman.

Tiptoeing from their bedchamber, she made her way to the servants' staircase, grateful that the door at the bottom had been left open. She'd forgotten to bring a candle in her haste to see Flaherty.

She followed the sound of voices to the kitchen in time to hear Constance ask, "Where did you find the poor woman?"

"Garahan was the one to find her—on the other side of the village, hidden by a hedgerow, sitting on a rock, weeping."

Temperance entered the kitchen, her gaze immediately riveted to the side of Rory's face. Thank goodness the stitches did not look inflamed. She was relieved, and at the same time irritated that she felt obligated to ask, "Was she injured?"

Constance paused, smiled, then continued fixing a pot of tea and arranging a plate of meat pies for the men. Temperance wondered at the cook's reaction until she noticed Flaherty's eyes lit with humor.

"Nay, lass, but the soles of her kidskin slippers were worn through."

"Why would anyone wear kidskin slippers outside, especially if they were walking?"

"Not everyone is practically minded, lass," he reminded her.

"Garahan, would you mind carrying the tray for me?" Constance interjected. "The others should be arriving in the servants' dining room in a moment."

Garahan glanced at Flaherty. "I'll save ye two meat pies, but if ye take too long, I'll be eating them." He winked at Temperance before grabbing the tray.

Flaherty watched them leave. "Me ma is a practical woman,

and it would seem ye are as well. Ma's going to love ye—and Maddy too."

"When will I meet her?"

Flaherty shrugged. "Garahan and I were discussing that a few weeks ago. None of us have been able to visit home in a few years. 'Tis costly. If we aren't working, we aren't getting paid. Nor will we be able to send money home to our parents, which is why we came to England in the first place."

Temperance put her hand on his arm. "You must miss her."

"That I do, and me da as well, but we keep in touch through letters. Me elder brother, Seamus, recently wed. Ma and Da will be happy to hear that, along with the news of our married cousins who are expecting babes."

"Do you really think she will love Maddy?"

"How could she not? We do."

Temperance slid her arm around Flaherty's back and leaned against his side. "I must be dreaming. I never thought Maddy would have family, and now she'll have grandparents!"

"Is yer ma gone?"

"Both my parents are."

"Well now, me ma and da will be pleased to add another daughter—and granddaughter—to our family."

"Maddy will be so excited at the prospect of having grandparents."

"Do ye think she'd draw them a picture of us to send to me parents?"

Temperance smiled. "Yes. She's liable to draw a picture of your horse, and your cousins, too!"

"Well then, that would be grand. I'd best be leaving, lass—tomorrow's a busy day and ye need yer rest."

At his pointed look, she asked, "I will?"

Flaherty kissed the breath out of her. "Aye, lass, you will."

"I'm certain a few hours sleep is all I will need to be ready for our vow taking."

He stared deep into her eyes. "I'm thinking ye missed me

meaning. Ye'll need yer rest for *after* we wed."

Temperance felt the flush sweep up her neck to her forehead. "Er… Y-yes, of course."

"Am I making ye nervous, *mo ghrá*?"

"N-no. Not at all."

He pressed a kiss to the tip of her nose. "'Tisn't a good habit to get into, prevaricating when I embarrass ye, lass."

"I do not get nervous," she huffed. "I am a bit *unsettled*."

His snort of laughter relieved her worry. He wasn't angry with her.

"I'm meaning what I said, though, Temperance. There'll be no lies between us—not even tiny ones to make yerself of meself feel better. Understand?"

"Yes, of course. I agree with you. I've always been honest with Maddy. I will always be honest with you, even if it makes you mad or sad."

"Well now, that's fine, then." He pulled her into his embrace one more time, kissed her soundly, and set her away from him. "Come, I'll walk ye to the stairs."

She shook her head. "That won't be necessary. Please go eat. I can find my way."

"Sure and I know that, but I'll be able to get one last kiss in—unless ye've had yer fill."

Temperance tugged on his hand and hurried down the hallway. Standing in front of the door, she smiled up at him and whispered, "Make it a good one."

She was still sighing when he nudged her up the stairs and closed the door behind her. Rory Flaherty fulfilled his promise and kissed her until she couldn't see straight. As she slowly ascended the stairs, she realized there was a part of their marriage that she was a bit hesitant about, though she enjoyed his kisses.

Temperance wondered what Flaherty would have to say when she asked him if he meant for their marriage to be in name only. They had yet to discuss expectations. As she entered the bedchamber she was sharing with Maddy, she knew she'd find out soon enough.

Climbing into bed, she smiled when Maddy rolled over and snuggled against her. There were going to be big changes come tomorrow. Maddy would be sleeping in her own bed. Temperance listened to the sound of her daughter's snores and realized tomorrow was already turning out to be fraught with difficulties.

CHAPTER TWENTY

T HE DUKE WALKED into the servants' dining room and nodded to his men. "Thank you for stepping up once again to lend aid to our villagers. They have come to rely on your aid, as I have." When O'Malley pushed back from the table, the duke placed a hand to his shoulder. "Your report can wait until you have eaten your fill. Take your time. I'll be in the library."

A short while later, the duke looked up at the knock on the open door. "Come in, men. I trust you ate every crumb."

Garahan chuckled. "Ye know us too well, Yer Grace."

"Constance is an excellent cook," O'Malley added.

The chorus of *ayes* pleased the duke. "We're lucky she was not tempted to leave with the other servants." It still rankled that his elder brother had all but bankrupted the dukedom and tainted the family name. But it had taught him one thing—to toil until he'd refilled the family coffers. With the help of his younger brother, they had restored their family's good name.

"If ye're ready," O'Malley said, "I'll let the others give their reports separately, as they each led a separate search party."

The duke inclined his head. "Proceed."

Eamon O'Malley gave his summary first. "I can tell ye the men riding with me got to see firsthand that Yer Grace has well-trained geldings in yer stables."

"Indeed. What happened?"

"A vixen shot out from beneath a hedgerow and tore across the road in front of our horses. Spooked half the horses, but not the ones from yer stables, Yer Grace."

The duke smiled. "I hope they have been bedded down for the night and treated like the champions they are."

"Aye, Yer Grace," O'Malley replied. "I took me men to the west of the village, and though it would have been a sight to see, we did not run into any vixens—human or fox."

The duke smiled, watching the reaction ripple through his men. They were bound by blood and their vow of fealty to him. He'd nearly lost Patrick, as head of his guard, due to his unbridled fear after his twins were nearly kidnapped. He'd let pride, and his unreasonable expectations at needing O'Malley to be in more than one place at a time, color his better judgment. Thankfully, they'd come to an understanding. He'd offered O'Malley a second chance, though the stubborn Irishman felt he did not deserve one.

Eamon O'Malley's serious expression had the duke wondering if the man's wife was still suffering from nausea. That made three women under his protection—and his intrepid private guard—that were expecting: Eamon's wife, Garahan's wife, and his own darling duchess. No wonder there had been a bit more tension among his men when Flaherty added another rescued woman, and her daughter, to those they'd vowed to protect.

"Anything untoward occur during your search, Eamon?"

"Nay, Yer Grace." He paused, then grinned. "Unless ye count one of the tenant farmers' sons chasing after their milk cow."

The duke could not hold back his smile. "Gertrude again?"

"Aye," Eamon replied. "They cannot afford to let her run off. Gertrude's milk churns into the tastiest butter—"

"Don't forget the cream she provides that Constance whips up and serves with her scones," Flaherty added.

"Are you men still hungry?" the duke asked.

"Nay, Yer Grace." O'Malley frowned at his cousins. "But they'll always make room for scones."

He chuckled at hearing the chorus of ayes from his men.

"Any trouble during your search, Flaherty?" the duke asked.

"None. We've good men who stepped up from the village, and our tenant farmers. I'm proud to continue to work with them."

"As to that, men, I'm grateful and proud of the protection you provide on a daily basis. The recent threat to the foundation we've built had me reevaluating your core mission. I know most of you have already heard part of it, but let me reiterate and assure you that your wives and babes are just as important and in need of your protection as my duchess and the twins.

"My brother and I have fought alongside you men, our footmen, and tenant farmers when we were under attack. When our call goes out for reinforcements from Captain Coventry or Gavin King of the Bow Street Runners, no matter which one of my estates requires it, you band together and work alongside whoever arrives. You defend not only my family, but your own. My thanks will never be enough, but you have it. In return for your unstinting loyalty to me and mine, you shall have mine for you and your families."

The intensity and gratitude gleaming in the eyes of his men showed their trust and dedication to him—giving the duke yet another reason to show his faith in their decision by agreeing with Flaherty's earlier request. "As I have been given a second chance to rebuild what my brother Edward and I thought we had lost, I agree with your suggestion regarding O'Brien, Flaherty." The looks of awe and relief were expected, but welcome just the same. "After speaking to him, I believe he will be a welcome addition to your ranks here—on a trial basis. See that he is proficient in all manner of weapons, though it may take a bit longer while his arm is healing." His lips twitched as he slowly smiled. "By the by, excellent aim, Flaherty—but I expect no less from my sharpshooter."

Flaherty grinned. "Any man intelligent enough to admit to his mistakes, and vow not to make them again, is a man worth knowing."

"Now then, Garahan. I understand Harkness left your search party before you found his sister. Is there anything in particular you learned after finding Miss Harkness weeping over her ruined slippers?"

"She's headstrong, self-centered, and, if I am not mistaken, will have just received her first dressing-down from the brother who has always doted on her. Flaherty and I did not stick around to hear it," Garahan answered.

"And?"

"I'm thinking she's realized the damage she had done to not only Greene and O'Brien's reputations, but Temperance and Maddy's, her brother's, and her own."

"I understand how Harkness felt," the duke remarked. "And the reason he blamed himself for his sister's actions. I have been in his shoes, though it was my brother—my sister is another tale for another time. Her issue was her overexuberance once she recovered from being held at knifepoint."

O'Malley cleared his throat. "I seem to recall Baron Summerfield having a different opinion on the matter regarding her exuberance."

The duke chuckled. "Indeed. Any further information or observations, O'Malley?"

"Harkness has promised his sister will make amends to Temperance and her daughter by admitting she made up the gossip she spread about them. She promised to share the news with any and all visitors to the inn. She will also stop by every shop in the village to apologize for sowing the seeds of dissension."

"An excellent start," the duke replied. "What of Greene and O'Brien?"

O'Malley replied, "I stopped in to speak with Harkness after Garahan and Flaherty dropped her off. The man was loath to admit it, but finally confided that the attention Susana was getting by using her face and form went to her head. She's promised to speak to the vicar and repent."

"I had not expected that," the duke admitted.

"As I witnessed her epiphany," O'Malley said, "I was not surprised. She truly had not given a thought to her actions before that moment. Apparently, her brother's disapproval—loudly stated—meant more than his approval."

"Thank you, men, for your steadfast loyalty to me and mine. I'm grateful, and I know Harkness is too. As I discovered, it isn't always our love and approval that the ones we are guiding need. Sometimes it is the stark reminder that they are in the wrong and need to realign their thoughts, words, and deeds to become the person they were meant to be." Flaherty, Eamon, and Garahan were staring to the point where the duke had to ask, "Don't you agree?"

"Aye," Flaherty answered. "I may not speak for me cousins, but as I'll be a da tomorrow, I've taken yer words to heart and only just realized 'tis what me ma and da did for me brothers and meself growing up."

Garahan squared his shoulders and laughed. "Faith, I'm glad I have time to get used to doing battle with me own son or daughter." Turning to Flaherty, he grinned. "I'll be praying for ye, Da."

The duke chuckled. "O'Malley, I expect you've put the plans in place for the footmen to stand guard when the vicar arrives to marry Flaherty and Temperance so you can all be in attendance?"

"I have."

He thanked the men and dismissed them. Following them out of the library, he took the stairs two at a time. His duchess was no doubt expecting to hear *his* report, while he was looking forward to talking her into waiting until he undressed her before giving it. He was smiling when he knocked and then entered their bedchamber.

"Have I told you today how very much I love you, Persephone?" She furrowed her brow as if she could not recall. Unable to wait to hold her in his arms, he scooped her off her feet and kissed her soundly. "Minx!"

Persephone was laughing when she finally answered, "Why

yes, my darling duke. I believe you said that just this morning when you pressed your lips to my belly."

He eased back to stare into her dark eyes. "How remiss of me not to say it again. That was *hours* ago."

She turned her back to him. "Unbutton me, and I'll let you make it up to me."

"With pleasure, my love."

CHAPTER TWENTY-ONE

TEMPERANCE FOLLOWED MADDY into the kitchen in time to see Constance pulling loaves of bread out of the oven. "Let me help you with that."

The cook shook her head. "I have it, thank you." Brushing her hands on her apron, she beamed at the two. "Are you ready for your big day?"

Maddy bounced on her toes. "I am." She leaned close and in a stage whisper confided, "Mum's nervous."

Francis entered the kitchen. "Morning, everyone. Are you ready for this afternoon?"

Temperance put a hand to her stomach. Before she could reply, Constance asked, "Maddy, would you and Francis please set the table in the main dining room?"

"We'd be happy to," Francis said. "Wouldn't we, Maddy?"

"We would!" Delighted to be asked, Maddy led the way, while Francis carried the tray from the room.

Constance poured a cup of tea and nodded at Temperance. "Sit down and tell me what has you so concerned this morning. You have not changed your mind, have you?"

Temperance bit her lip and sat. "No."

The cook set the cream next to Temperance. "Fix your tea, have a few sips, and tell me. If you are this rattled, and it's not even seven o'clock in the morning, you'll be a complete wreck by noontime."

Temperance added a splash of cream to her tea and sipped. "I haven't told Flaherty about my late husband yet."

"He knows you were married and that your husband passed away. What more does he need to know?"

"It's been over three years since he's been gone, and I'm not certain that I can...or will be able to... Botheration!"

Constance reached over to pat Temperance on the hand. "I have an idea of what might be plaguing you...the marriage bed."

Temperance sighed. "I said vows and have kept them, even after Paul lost his life in that mine."

"I hope you don't mind my asking, but is it Flaherty's being a giant of a man that worries you?"

Temperance shook her head. "My husband was built like Flaherty, and an inch or so taller."

Constance refilled the cup Temperance did not realize she'd already emptied. "Well then, a little Maddy-bird told me that she's seen him kiss you and that you were smiling." When Temperance felt the heat rise up from her toes, Constance sighed. "From the way you're flushing, I would venture to say that you enjoy his kisses."

Temperance rested her elbows on the table and put her head in her hands. "Too much! What if... You see, I'm worried that... I do not want him to feel as if—"

The cook nodded. "This calls for something extra sweet. Here's the jam and cream I just whipped."

Temperance eyed the bowls and waited for Constance to set the plate of scones in the middle of the table and sit. "I'm afraid I'll compare them."

Constance nodded. "I had a feeling it was something like that."

"I'm afraid to tell Rory, and at the same time, I'm afraid *not* to tell him."

"You do realize that not many widows are lucky enough to find another man who vows to love her and another man's child?

But you have. Flaherty's heart is pure gold. Everyone has noted the way he cannot take his eyes off you every time he sees you. And we all know that your curly-haired moppet stole his heart. I hope you won't feel slighted when I confide that I think he fell for her first."

Temperance felt the knot in her belly ease. "I do know it, and it warms my heart. Paul never had the chance to meet Maddy. He would have doted on her."

"Have you ever noticed that men are as prone to gossiping as women?"

Temperance frowned. "I have never been around a group of men before. By the time my husband returned from the mine, he was usually exhausted. It took a bit of time to scrub the coal from him. Then it would be time to eat, and he'd fall into bed exhausted, only to begin again the next day."

"When the duke and duchess first arrived at Wyndmere Hall, they arrived with the entire guard. Sixteen of the tallest, broadest, handsomest men than I had ever encountered before. Each and every one of those men were charmers. During their shift changes, they would stop in the kitchen and ask if I had a few extra scones for a starving man."

Temperance laughed. "I can imagine them asking, but cannot envision cooking for that many men at one time—aside from the staff and His Grace."

"It was a challenge, but at the time Mollie and Francis were helping me."

"Mollie?"

"She married one of Patrick's younger brothers, Finn. They are stationed at Penwith Tower on the coast of Cornwall."

"I see."

Constance moved the plate of scones closer, and Temperance took the hint and helped herself to one, then added jam and a spoonful of cream on top. As she bit into the delicious confection, the cook regaled her with stories of the men and their antics.

"Sparks flew from the moment Gwendolyn stepped down off

the carriage. She was hired to take care of the newborn twins."

"Sparks, you say?"

The cook put her hand over her heart. "Oh my, yes. And of course his brothers had something to say. It was as if they knew he was smitten with the nanny and were pushing him to declare himself. Once things settled down, and the duke's extended family were added to those the men were to protect, the duke decided to divide up his men and assign them to his properties, and those of his distant cousins, the viscount and the baron."

Nibbling on her second scone, Temperance asked, "Did the men stop talking about one another?"

Constance laughed. "They became *more* obvious. When the men in the duke's guard fall in love, they fall hard and fast. Which is a blessing, because with their duties, they do not have a lot of time to spare."

"I see—and you believe Flaherty really cares for me too?"

"I'll tell you after you answer a question honestly. How do you feel when he kisses you?"

Temperance bobbled her teacup, but caught it before it crashed onto its saucer.

The older woman smiled. "I thought as much. My best advice to you is to tell Flaherty how you are feeling and what has you worried."

"And you do not think he will be angry with me for even suggesting that I might be thinking of my husband while we… Before we… When—"

"Since it has you tied up in knots, yes, you should. From what I know of the Flahertys and their cousins, I suspect he would see it as a challenge to ensure that you think only of him when you are in your marriage bed."

Temperance could not feel the top of her head, and was grateful for the anchor Constance provided when she grabbed hold of her hand.

"The Irish are passionate men." Constance winked at her. "Be very grateful that you'll be married to one."

When Temperance found her voice, she rasped, "I believe I will."

Constance rose from her seat, put her arm around Temperance, and gave her a hug. "Trust me, I know that you will. I'm certain those two are finished setting the table by now. Will you tell them it is all right to come back in the kitchen?"

"Oh, I did not realize they were waiting."

"You needed to share your worry, and I am always happy to listen. Now, off with you. Fetch those two so we can have breakfast ready for the staff and Flaherty."

"What about the other men in the guard?"

"They're married and have their first meal of the day in their cottages with their wives. Last night, the duke asked me to prepare a special basket with your evening meal to be delivered to your new cottage."

"Flaherty mentioned the duke and duchess's overly generous gift."

"His Grace gifted each one of the men and their wives a cottage when they married. The cottages are not far from here, on the road leading to the tenant farms."

"And you're certain there is one for Flaherty, Maddy, and me?"

Constance sighed. "Quite certain. Now then, tonight and for the next three days, the duchess would like Maddy to stay with Francis to give you and Flaherty time alone."

"I'm overwhelmed by their generosity and that of everyone here at Wyndmere Hall. Not one person has made Maddy or me feel as if we are interlopers."

"No one thinks that, Temperance." Constance smiled. "Flaherty is due to return from his dawn patrol to the village any minute. You don't want him to get the wrong impression on your wedding day, if he sees your eyes welling with tears."

Temperance wiped her eyes and looked up in time to see Flaherty striding into the kitchen. "Lass, what's wrong? Is it Maddy? Whatever's happened, tell me, and I'll take care of it."

Constance leveled a look at Temperance, as if to say, *I told you so*. Temperance wanted to say something, but suddenly Flaherty had her by the hand and was pulling her along behind him. "Excuse us, Constance. I'm thinking the lass needs privacy to tell me what's happened with Maddy."

Alone in the hall with Flaherty, Temperance had no idea where to start. Should she begin with her worry about tonight, or ask him if he meant for them to seal their vows and then go on to lead separate lives? They had not talked about expectations for their marriage—or even babes. Did he want them? Did *she*?

It only took a few seconds for her to decide. Yes, she did want Maddy to have brothers and sisters. Heaven help her, she wanted a marriage with all of the trimmings, and she hoped Rory did too!

He tipped up her chin with a knuckle. "Now then, lass. Tell me what's happened. Where is our wee *cailín*?"

The intensity in his crystal-blue eyes scorched her. For the life of her, she didn't want to spend the time to wonder what he was thinking. She could not think past what he'd just said.

"Our?"

FLAHERTY FROWNED. "I already think of her as ours. The vicar will make it official this afternoon. Were ye thinking to keep our daughter all to yerself?"

"No, but—"

"Are ye thinking I wouldn't want to adopt her?"

"Well, I—"

"How could ye think that I would not want to give her the protection of me name, too?" His frown was fierce when he asked, "Are ye thinking to tell me ye want a marriage in name only?"

"Rory—"

"Why can ye not verbalize what ye're wanting from me? I'm

not an intimidating man!"

That comment snapped Temperance out of her inability to speak. She put her hands on her hips and glared up at him. "You most certainly are! And you keep interrupting me! I do not want a marriage in name only. For Heaven's sake, *look* at you!"

Flaherty glanced down at himself, then at her. "Do I have a spot on me waistcoat?" She narrowed her eyes at him, and he told her, "I look the same as I did this morning when I got dressed."

"You are too handsome for your own good."

"'Tis good of ye to notice."

"You are well over six feet tall."

"And have been since I was six and ten, lass."

She spread her arms out to her sides. "And your shoulders are broader than my arm span, fingertip to fingertip!"

"Same as it was the day I found ye and Maddy in the grave-yard."

"And the breadth and depth of your chest... It's massive."

His frown changed to a glower as he moved a half step closer so they were toe to toe. Faith, but the lass did not give an inch. "Are ye explaining...or complaining? If ye're explaining, there's no need. I'm well aware of me manly attributes. Women love them." He bent closer until his mouth was a hairsbreadth from hers. "I've never had a woman complain about me face and form. Ye'd best be telling me now what bug has gotten up yer—"

He clamped his jaw shut before he insulted the woman. How had she managed to get under his skin and spark his temper so easily? He would never intentionally speak crudely to any woman, let alone the one who'd be his wife.

"Well?"

The feisty lass was staring at his mouth. When he licked his bottom lip, her eyes widened. *Ah, so that's the way of it,* he thought. *Poor lass won't stand a chance once I get her in bed. She'll be putty in me hands, and screaming me name in ecstasy before the night is over. Thank God she doesn't intend for our marriage to be in name only!*

He glanced down to see the pulse thrumming at the base of

her throat, and a wave of tenderness swept over him. "Ah, lass. If ye're worried about me crushing ye when I make love to ye tonight, don't. I'll be bracing most of me weight on me forearms." When she closed her eyes, he brushed a kiss over her lips. "Open yer eyes, lass. Don't fear me."

She slowly did as asked. "I don't fear you, exactly."

"What are ye afraid of, then, *exactly*?"

"Too many things all tangled together," she confessed.

He pulled her into his arms and kissed the top of her head. "I will treat like the treasure ye are, Temperance," he rasped against her ear before he nipped her earlobe. "I'll go slowly, so ye can accustom yerself to me size."

"Oh, but I'm not worried about how wide your shoulders are."

He chuckled. "I was referring to another part of meself altogether, lass."

"Oh, Lord!"

Flaherty could not contain the snort of laughter that erupted.

The smack to the back of his head had him swallowing the laughter. He eased back and stared down into her emerald-bright eyes. "God help me, lass, I never thought I'd meet a woman as feisty as me ma." She placed her hands on his chest and pushed, but he did not give an inch. "I've got ye now, lass, and I'll never let ye go. Ye can complain—or explain—like ye were trying to do just now, and it won't matter. Ye're the woman I've been praying for, but I truly never thought I'd meet anyone as perfect as yerself. And do you know what?"

Temperance tried to look away, but he put a finger against her jaw to turn her head back. He whispered, "Don't look away from me, lass." When she met his gaze again, he molded his mouth to hers. Her scent—roses and raindrops—surrounded him as he plumbed the depths of her honey-sweet mouth, tasting, nibbling, kissing her supple lips.

A cool breeze made him look up in time to see Garahan standing just inside the back door behind Temperance. His arms were crossed, and he was frowning. "Ye're late for yer shift, Flaherty. Move yer bleeding arse!"

Temperance gasped, glanced over her shoulder, and asked, "How can you even see the back of him, let alone if he's injured his backside?"

Flaherty had the satisfaction of watching his cousin's eyes widen a moment before Garahan roared with laughter. "Faith, ye've found a woman just like yer ma. Aunt Sorcha will be busting her buttons with pride when Emily adds the news to the letter she's writing."

"Ye'll not be the first to tell me ma I'm getting married. *I* will!"

Garahan grinned. "Well, boy-o, ye've missed the boat entirely if ye haven't written home to tell her about Temperance and Maddy yet."

Flaherty's temper simmered. "I wasn't going to tell Ma anything until I asked Temperance to marry me, and she agreed."

Garahan slipped his arm around Temperance. "Just so ye know, lass, I was cursing at yer husband-to-be, though I don't think the English use *bleeding* interchangeably with *bloody* when they curse. We Irish do."

When Temperance snorted, Flaherty sighed. "Adorable sound, isn't it, Aiden?"

Garahan chuckled. "I just thinking the same."

Temperance snorted louder this time. "Please don't make me laugh. I sound like a cow with a bellyache."

"Nay, lass." Flaherty removed his cousin's arm from around his bride-to-be. Pulling her into his arms, he rasped, "Ye sound like one of the pigs on me family's farm back home."

For the second time in less than ten minutes, the lass smacked him in the back of the head… Harder this time.

"What in the bloody hell was that for?"

Her eyes were narrow slits of green. The angry set of her jaw told the rest of the story. She was *incensed*.

"Well? Ye'd best be telling me, so I don't do whatever it was that had ye hitting me poor head again."

"Don't ye mean yer soft head?" Garahan asked. "Even I know that no woman would want to be compared to a pig—whether it reminded ye of home or not." Turning to Temperance, his cousin apologized, "Ye'll have to excuse me cousin—he has not been in his right mind since he clapped eyes on yer daughter and yerself. He's smitten."

"Garahan! I thought you were going to tell Flaherty to move his arse?" Eamon O'Malley called out as he walked toward them. "Are we having a family meeting? Where's Patrick?"

"'Tisn't a meeting, and we don't need another hardheaded Irishman's opinion on me bride-to-be's snort." Flaherty mumbled.

Eamon glanced at Flaherty, Temperance, and then Garahan. "Well now, a snort can be adorable, especially if it sounds like a wee piglet."

Flaherty nudged Temperance. "Ye see? I'm not the only one who thinks pigs sound adorable when they snort."

Her eyes were full of fire. Lord, he loved riling her. He sensed that beneath the surface was a passionate woman. After witnessing her temper, he could not wait to unleash it tonight.

He noticed his cousins quietly slipping away and was relieved. He needed to tell the lass what was in his heart.

"Eamon said piglet—that's a baby pig," Temperance reminded him. "You said pig—that is a much larger, and not terribly attractive animal."

Flaherty shook his head. He'd never understand females, but knew he would enjoy *trying* to figure out the woman glaring at him. "I love ye, lass."

She sagged against him. "Why would you say that now, when I'm mad at you?"

"'Tis the perfect time, because now ye'll have to make it up to me." He kissed her tenderly, then whispered against her lips, "Say it back to me, lass."

"'Tis the perfect time."

He laughed, scooped her into his arms, and kissed the breath out of her. "God help me, lass, but ye've got spirit!"

She placed her hand to the side of his face. "Rory?"

"Aye, lass?"

"I love you too."

The fire in her eyes called to him, and he started walking toward the kitchen door at the end of the hall. He opened it, and was about to walk in when the back door opened and O'Malley barked, "Put that woman down and get to yer post!"

Flaherty laughed as he kissed her full on the mouth. "Ah, lass. It seems I'm needed elsewhere." He winked at her. "We'll have to wait until tonight to have our discussion. I'll never last until the noon hour if I don't eat now, but I'll have to be quick about it." He turned around with Temperance in his arms. At O'Malley's arch look, he grinned.

"Ye're a bloody *eedjit*, Flaherty."

"Ye'd be knowing, O'Malley. Ye're a right *eedjit* yerself." He could hear his cousin's heavy footsteps behind him, following them. He wasn't worried. O'Malley wouldn't be tossing any punches at him while he had Temperance tucked against his heart. He brushed a kiss to her temple. "What are ye plans for the morning? I'm thinking me shift would improve greatly if I could hold ye in me arms."

Temperance tilted her head to one side. "Where is your next shift?"

He grinned and lifted his shoulders up to his ears, protecting the back of his head as he answered, "The rooftop."

Instead of hitting him, as expected, she kissed his cheek. "Will the rest of our lives be like this—you trading barbs with your cousins while you haul me around in your arms?"

He glanced at O'Malley, who grunted.

"That grunt was a distinct *no* from the head of our guard. Though it would certainly make for a more interesting shift, I'd best not take ye with me." He looked over his shoulder at his cousin.

"Shut yer gob, before I'm tempted to shut it for ye."

"Do ye see what I have to put up with, lass? O'Malley's always picking on me."

O'Malley snickered and ordered him, "Hurry it up, and put Temperance down so she can eat." He nodded to Constance and retraced his steps.

Flaherty waited a moment, then called out, "Did anyone ever tell ye that ye're a pain in the arse, O'Malley?"

His cousin laughed, and Constance shook her head at Flaherty. "Set Temperance down and let her eat."

Flaherty knew the time for teasing the lass was over. "Aye, Constance. Do ye have any meat pies left from last night? I could take one or two with me and head to the rooftop before O'Malley sets the dogs on me."

"You have dogs here?" Maddy asked as she and Francis entered the kitchen. "Where are they?"

Before he could reply, Constance said, "Flaherty is in a playful mood this morning. His Grace doesn't have any dogs—yet, though I did hear him mention something about one of the tenant farmers' dogs having a litter. Then there are the kittens in the barn."

"I told ye about them the other day, Maddy," Flaherty added. "I'm thinking the little black one would be perfect for ye."

Maddy's gaze locked on her mum. "I've always wanted a dog—or a black kitten."

"Eat your breakfast, Maddy dear. We'll talk about it later."

"'Tis a fine suggestion, Temperance," Flaherty said. "I'm thinking we'll have just enough room in our cottage for a pup *and* a kitten. And our wee *cailín* and her pets could grow up together."

"Flaherty?"

"Aye, *mo ghrá?*"

"Eat your breakfast."

CHAPTER TWENTY-TWO

F LAHERTY PACED FROM the sitting room fireplace to the French
doors leading the terrace and back. He paused to glare at the
open door before resuming his pacing.

"Ye're giving me a pain in me head," Garahan grumbled.

"Ye've been a pain in me arse all day!"

"Ye have no reason to be nervous, Rory. She's been married
before and won't be fearing the marriage bed."

Flaherty grunted. "But that's the problem! What if her expectations are high? 'Tisn't like I could ask her about her experience
with lovemaking. Can ye imagine me asking, *How many times did
ye make love before ye fainted from the orgasms yer husband gave ye?*"

Garahan snorted. "Ye might not want to lead with that question, but it would be good to know."

"Ye see? I *need* to know. What if she's cold as ice, and never
felt anything?"

"I'm thinking ye'd get a hint of whether or not she'd be passionate from kissing her." Garahan stared at his cousin's back.
"Stop pacing and pay attention!" When Flaherty spun around and
stalked over, his cousin said, "I know ye've kissed her more than
once—as I've walked in on ye and caught the two of ye in a
passionate embrace. So what is the real reason yer bollocks are in
a knot?"

Flaherty raked both hands through his hair until it stood on end. "What If I cannot satisfy her in bed?"

Garahan scoffed. "Ye wouldn't be any cousin of mine, nor an Irishman worth yer salt, if ye couldn't figure out to how bring a woman to the gates of Heaven, boy-o."

When Flaherty remained silent, Garahan sighed and placed a hand on his cousin's shoulder. "Ye've been with more than one woman—have ye not been able to bring one of them to peak?"

Flaherty shoved Garahan and growled, "I'll be willing to wager, I've satisfied more lasses than ye have!"

"Did ye worry about whether or not ye'd satisfy any of those other lasses beforehand?"

"Nay. I've never left a woman's bed without hearing her cry out me name at least five times."

Garahan snorted. "There's the cousin I love like a brother, confirming what we all heard back home… That ye had a score of women fawning over ye, following ye around begging for crumbs."

Flaherty swore without any heat behind it. "Sorry I shoved ye, Aiden. I let me temper loose for a few minutes. I've contained it. I'm an arse."

"That ye are, but faith, I'm fond of ye. About tonight—don't let doubts plague ye. Woo the lass with kisses, and when she's pliant in yer arms, whisper of the things ye have in mind. Ye'll know if she's experienced any of them by her reaction."

"Is that what ye did?"

Garahan eyes darkened with grief and anger before he masked it. "I know ye heard what happened to me wife. 'Tisn't something I willingly speak about. Emily was attacked at that inn—ye remember the bruises on her face, and Helen's too—but I stopped the blackguard before he forced himself on her. On our wedding night, I treated her as if she were made of fine china." He scrubbed a hand over his face and rasped, "Asking permission before I touched her—even to brush a finger along the line of her jaw—went a long way to earning her trust."

Flaherty nudged Garahan with his shoulder. "Yer temper is

equal to mine, ye showed restraint and patience, and 'tis plain for anyone with eyes in their head that ye healed her invisible scars. Ye're a far better man than meself, Aiden. Here I am worried about whether or not I'll be up to the challenge of competing with the memory of her dead husband in bed, while ye had the worry of doing or saying something that would remind yer bride of what happened to her during the attack."

When Garahan didn't reply right away, Flaherty pulled his flask out of his waistcoat pocket and handed it to him. "Take it. I won't need it tonight. Ye can give it back to me tomorrow—but it'd best not be empty."

Garahan nodded. "Ye won't say anything to Temperance about what happened to Emily, will ye?"

Flaherty put his hand over his heart. "Ye have me word."

"Thank ye."

"Vicar Digby," Humphries announced from the doorway.

The vicar walked toward them with his hand outstretched. "Congratulations, Flaherty. I've heard about your bride-to-be and her daughter."

Flaherty shook the vicar's hand. "Whatever ye heard, 'tisn't true."

The vicar frowned. "I'm sorry to hear that. I was led to believe that she was a God-fearing widow who has been raising her four-year-old daughter on her own since her husband died in a coal-mining accident."

"Ye mustn't mind himself," Garahan said. "Flaherty's worried about tonight."

Flaherty glared at his cousin, then turned to the vicar. "Forgive me. There's been rumors circulating about me intended that simply aren't true—though what ye've just said *is* true. I'm sorry that I jumped to the conclusion that ye heard only the vicious lies."

The vicar sighed. "I did hear those terrible rumors, but then I heard the other story as well. I'm a firm believer in judging a person for myself. And while I have not had the pleasure of meeting your intended, Her Grace sent a note singing Widow Johnson's praises."

"Thank ye, vicar. I shouldn't jump to conclusions, but to be honest, I never thought to marry—let alone be lucky enough to find a woman as lovely inside and out as Temperance. I've confessed that her Maddy's bravery, when I rescued her and her ma, touched me heart. Temperance doesn't mind that I loved her daughter first, because she knows I do not love her less."

Vicar Digby smiled. "You are a good man, Flaherty. I know you will be a good husband and father. Now, do I have time for a cup of tea, or is your bride ready?"

"His Grace plans to escort her downstairs," Garahan announced. "I'll check with Humphries to see if he knows."

"Thank you, Garahan. Now then, Flaherty, would you care to tell me what's worrying you about tonight?"

Flaherty snorted, then begged the vicar's forgiveness. "Thank ye for the offer, but no."

The vicar chuckled. "If you change your mind, just let me know."

"I won't."

TEMPERANCE BRUSHED MADDY'S curls until they shone, and held the looking glass close so her daughter could see her reflection. "You look beautiful, Maddy."

Her daughter touched her curls, then turned and threw her arms around her mother's neck. "You do too, Mum. I'm ready, are you?"

Temperance laughed at her daughter's excitement. "I am, but we need to wait for His Grace—he's going to escort us downstairs."

A few minutes later, the duke knocked on the open door to their bedchamber. "Temperance, are you ready to get married?"

"I am, Your Grace, but I do have a small favor to ask."

"Of course. What can I do for you?"

"Would you escort the both of us? Flaherty might be marrying me, but he's gaining a daughter at the same time."

"He is a very lucky man. I have a feeling he will have his hands full protecting the both of you, but is more than up to the task." The duke held out his arm to Temperance, and his hand to Maddy. They walked to the staircase, where he stopped. "I'd prefer to carry you, Maddy—that way you won't trip. May I?"

"Yes, Mr. Duke."

The duke chuckled. "Thank you, Miss Maddy." He did not let go of Temperance when he scooped her daughter up and placed her on his hip. "How is the view from up here?"

Maddy hugged his neck and kissed his cheek. "Wonderful!"

The duke was still smiling when he entered the sitting room. He kissed his wife and greeted the vicar before addressing Flaherty. "It is an honor to escort these fine ladies, but also my solemn duty to inquire whether you accept the responsibility of honoring and protecting Temperance and her daughter."

"Aye, Yer Grace. I will honor and protect them with me life."

The duke inclined his head, then passed Maddy to Flaherty first. Once she was settled on his hip, with her arms wrapped around his neck, the duke took hold of Temperance's hand and urged her toward Flaherty. "By placing these women in your care, I am letting them know that I trust you with their lives as I have trusted you with my wife and twins—and the growing list of those you have sworn an oath to protect."

"Thank ye, Yer Grace."

When the duke walked over to stand beside his wife, the vicar nodded to the gathered group and smiled. "It is my pleasure to perform the marriage of Rory Flaherty and Temperance Johnson this afternoon—"

Maddy interrupted, "Don't forget me!"

"I would not dream of it. As I was saying," the vicar continued, "as well as asking him to willingly accept Maddy Johnson as his daughter and to treat her as if she were his own."

Temperance had trouble listening to what the vicar was saying. She could not stop looking at the way Maddy was holding on to Rory as if she would never let him go. Had she missed not having a father that much? Of course she had. Maddy must have noticed other children with their papas and wondered if she would ever have one.

Temperance was still smiling when the vicar told Flaherty to kiss his bride, but Rory surprised everyone by kissing Maddy's cheek first.

The little girl giggled when he kissed Temperance with gusto. "Why didn't you kiss *me* like that?"

Flaherty touched the tip of his finger to the end of her little nose. "Because ye're me daughter, and yer mum is me wife."

She wrinkled her nose as she considered his answer. "Oh. All right. But do you promise to tuck me in and kiss me every night and every morning when I give you your good morning hugs?"

Temperance's heart filled with joy as she watched the auburn-haired giant's eyes well with tears. Tears he didn't bother to hide. "I promise, *mo chroí*. God has truly blessed me this day."

Maddy turned to the vicar. "That means my heart. I'm Just Flaherty's heart, and Mum is his love. Tell him, Just Flaherty!"

"Ye are me heart, *mo chroí*. Yer mum is *mo ghrá*, me love."

Maddy poked Flaherty in the back of the head. "Kiss Mum later. I want cake!"

CHAPTER TWENTY-THREE

HOURS LATER, MADDY was holding on to Francis with one hand and waving goodbye to her parents with the other. The carriage waiting for them was a surprise. "I thought we would walk to our new home," Temperance said.

"Ah, but His Grace thought it would be easier—and faster—if we borrowed one of his carriages. Do ye mind?"

She smiled. "No. It was thoughtful of him. I must have thanked him and the duchess three times for their generous gift." Flaherty handed her into the coach and settled on the seat beside her. "Have you seen our cottage?"

"I haven't, though I have seen me cousins' cottages, and they are similar to what the lot of us were used to living in before we came to England. I think ye'll like it, but if there's something ye want to change, I can always ask His Grace—"

Temperance placed her fingers to his lips, then replaced them with her mouth. Flaherty's lips were firm and warm, and he was more than willing to stop talking in favor of returning the kiss she'd initiated.

"I hope ye aren't worried about tonight, lass."

This was the opening she had been waiting for. "Actually, I *am* a bit concerned."

That seemed to rattle him. "About what?"

"I have been married before, and know what to expect when

we seal our vows." He held her gaze but didn't say anything. A bit unnerved, she added, "I know we have to consummate our marriage, or else we won't be legally wed."

"Aye." He paused for a moment, then asked, "Are ye afraid I'll rush ye and not treat ye with care?"

"No! It's just that I have no idea what you will expect me to know or be accustomed to."

Flaherty chuckled. "It would seem we have a similar concern, Temperance. That being the case, I'm thinking we should leave our expectations outside our home. I know I'm going to enjoy finding out how ye will react when I press my lips beneath yer ear."

His lips brushed against the sensitive skin beneath her ear. It tingled, then heated when he nibbled her earlobe.

"I'm thinking we'll add that to the list of where ye'll want me to kiss ye." Flaherty kissed her until she was no longer anxious, but brimming with anticipation.

The coach slowed down all too soon. "Just when I was about to trail kisses along yer collarbone to the base of yer throat." He ran the tip of his finger along the bone, watching her eyes while he dipped his head, and touched the tip of his tongue to the soft skin that pulsed madly. "Yer scent intoxicates me."

While she struggled to regain her composure, he opened the door and stepped down from the carriage. Reaching for her hand, he leaned close and rasped, "Remind me to pick up where we left off once we're inside."

Temperance shivered. He smiled, thanked the coachman, and waved him on his way before turning to open their brightly painted yellow door. He scooped her into his arms and entered their cottage.

She noticed the basket on the table by the fireplace, and recognized it as the one Constance had been filling for them earlier in the day. "Are you hungry?"

He closed the door with his foot and strode over to the bed covered with a quilt in the softest shades of cream and green.

"Starved."

"Oh, well why didn't you set me down over by the table?"

His eyes darkened to the color of a midnight sky. "I'm hungry for ye, lass—not food."

Temperance decided to stop worrying and kissed him with all of the hope and love in her heart.

"Now then, lass," Flaherty said, setting her on her feet beside their bed, "where were we?"

She sighed and turned her back to him. "If you undo my buttons and help me remove my gown, I'll help you with your frockcoat and waistcoat, and then remind you."

He deftly undid the tiny buttons before placing his hands on her shoulders. Pressing his lips to her neck, he slowly turned her around to face him. "Are ye wanting yer gown off before or after ye help me undress?"

Temperance slowly smiled. "Now, please."

"'Tis me goal tonight, lass, to please ye with me lips, me tongue, and me teeth. But don't worry—I won't bite ye *too* hard."

Her hands were trembling as she helped him out of his frockcoat, shaking too hard to undo his waistcoat buttons.

"Let me." Instead of folding his clothing, as he'd done to her gown, he tossed them on the chair. Temperance watched them slide to the floor and bent to pick them up. Flaherty surprised her by lifting her off the floor and laying her on the bed. "I believe I was about to kiss yer collarbone."

Words were no longer necessary as he knelt on the bed and slowly lowered himself until he pressed her firmly into the mattress. He leaned most of his weight on his forearms and said, "I hope I didn't crush ye, lass." Before she could tell him he hadn't, her husband trailed a line of kisses where he'd promised, interspersing them with nips and licks as he worked his way slowly to the dip at the base of her throat. "Ye taste of raindrops and rose petals."

Undone by the tender way he kissed her, Temperance slipped her arms around his neck and pulled his mouth to hers. She tormented him with nibbles, licks, and kisses to his mouth, his jaw, and his neck, until his breathing grew heavy and he groaned.

Temperance forgot everything but the taste and feel of her husband as he slid the chemise off her shoulder, bit it, then soothed it with a kiss. "Where else will ye taste of rose petals, lass?"

Her eyes bored into his. "Everywhere. Her Grace sent a container of rose petals along with the hot water for my bath."

Flaherty's eyes glittered with passion. "Why don't I undress, then I'll help ye out of yer chemise, and we'll test yer theory?"

"Theory?"

"Aye, lass, *everywhere* is a bit vague. There's a particular bit of skin on the underside of yer belly, and the top of yer thigh, that I'm wanting to sample, if ye'll let me."

Temperance was lost in the sensation of Rory's powerful body pressing her deeper into the mattress as he rose from the bed to remove his boots, socks, and the rest of his clothes. Her eyes nearly popped out of her head when he stood before her in all his naked, muscled glory. Wanting to show that she did not fear him, she lowered her gaze and nearly swallowed her tongue. "I don't think you'll fit."

He motioned for her to sit up, then helped her take off the last article of clothing between them. "Not to worry, lass—we have all night. Ye'll be more than ready to receive me, and I'll have ye writhing beneath me, begging for me to fill ye to the hilt."

She would have answered, but was too busy responding to his urgent, all-consuming kiss. It lit a fire deep inside of her—in a places she had forgotten existed. Slowly, meticulously, and with tenderness, he paid homage to her breasts, drawing them into his mouth as he coaxed a response from her.

"Roses," he whispered. "Here, too."

"It's my turn to taste you."

"Not yet, *mo ghrá*." He sucked her breast into his mouth and slid his hand beneath her other, to test its weight. Watching her closely, he rolled the nipple between his fingertips and cupped the fullness, all the while devouring her other breast with his lips, teeth, and tongue. His eyes darkened as if he sensed the shift in her moans a heartbeat before she cried out as the climax slammed into her.

"God in Heaven, lass. Ye're exquisite. I want to see ye come again before I test ye to see if ye're ready."

Temperance couldn't catch her breath, and was mindless to try when Rory switched to her other breast. His hands and mouth worked their magic and she felt herself begin to fly.

FLAHERTY COULD NOT believe how responsive his wife was. He'd barely gotten started finding all of the places he knew would excite her when she came apart in his arms a second time. He was desperate to settle between her legs and feel her warmth as he slid inside of her, but he had not plumbed her depths with his fingers yet. The last thing he wanted to do was to hurt her.

"Lass, I need to see if ye're ready to take me."

She opened her eyes and held his gaze before whispering, "Hurry."

He lowered his forehead to hers and drew in a deep breath. "I've married a lusty wench."

Temperance's hands slid from his shoulders along his sides, and lower still until she grabbed his muscled buttocks and squeezed.

Flaherty's eyes crossed, and he nearly gave in to the need to plunge into her, but stopped himself. "Soon, lass." He slipped one finger, then two, inside her, drawing them out slowly at first, and then a bit faster each time he pumped them into her, mimicking what he desperately wanted to do with his aching shaft.

Like magic, her inner walls clenched around his fingers and softened until he was able to slip in a third finger. Her gasps and the way she lifted her hips told him she was beyond ready to receive him.

He withdrew his fingers and, settled between her thighs, poised at her core, rasped, "Now and forever, *mo ghrá*." Her eyes closed as he slid into her warmth. He stopped and urged, "Open yer eyes, lass. I want to see them cloud with passion when ye come apart again."

Her dark lashes fluttered against her cheeks, and slowly lifted until he was riveted by the desire and need in the depths of her brilliant green eyes.

"There's a lass. Don't close yer eyes. Watch me, see me need for ye. See me love for ye as I fill ye."

He withdrew, then slowly filled her to the hilt. Her gasps and moans pushed him to increase the pace, until he was mindless to everything except the pressure building inside of him. She cried out his name, her inner walls clenched, and he drove home, spilling his seed inside of her.

Capturing her lips, he kissed her until he stopped pulsing inside of her. Her hands fell to the mattress as she shook with aftershocks of the pleasure they'd shared. Worried that he'd been too rough, he kissed her cheek, her temple, her forehead. "Lass, did I hurt ye?"

Her sweet moan told him he'd satisfied her, but he needed her to tell him that he had not been too rough their first time. He straightened his arms to look down at her. "Ye need to answer me, lass."

"If I say no, will you make love to me again?"

He snorted with laughter as his shaft hardened inside of her. "Don't be leading me on, wife. I'm wanting and answer—not yer distractions."

She reached up and slipped her arms around his back, urging him closer. "I feel alive again, Rory. I may be sore tomorrow, but I'm not right now." In a move that took him by surprise, she hooked her legs around his waist and lifted her hips. "Take me to Heaven again, Rory."

He kissed her tenderly, slid his hands beneath her backside, and thrust into her, setting the pace and the rhythm that had her panting and meeting him thrust for thrust.

"Rory!"

He drove into her one last time and shuddered, releasing his seed into her welcoming warmth.

"If I'm dead in the morning, lass, be certain to tell me cousins I'm wanting a fine wake, and there'd best be a bottle of the Irish when they send me off."

Temperance pinched his buttocks. "You will not be dead in the morning—you'll be too busy making love to me as the sun rises."

He brushed a tendril of hair off her forehead. "Will I now, lass?"

"Aye, *mo ghrá*. So get plenty of rest tonight."

"Ye're a bossy bit of goods, lass, but faith, I'm thinking I might live long enough to pleasure ye again in the morning."

She laid her cheek on his heart and sighed. "Tomorrow I get to taste you...everywhere."

Legs tangled, bodies sated, and hearts filled with the miracle of the love they'd made, they drifted off to sleep.

CHAPTER TWENTY-FOUR

Three days later...

"**D**O YOU HAVE to leave now? I haven't had a chance to make breakfast for you."

Flaherty pulled his wife into his arms and rolled over until she was beneath him. "I'm onto yer tricks, woman. Ye're a lusty wench, but ye cannot fool me. I've realized yer idea of breakfast is making a meal out meself!"

"You haven't complained until now."

He grinned, kissed her until she sighed, and chuckled. "I'm not about to start, but O'Malley will be sending Garahan or Eamon to fetch me. I'm due to patrol the perimeter this morning."

"It's too dark to be morning," Temperance grumbled.

"Ah, so ye've finally shown yer true nature. Ye're all sweetness and light until ye don't get yer way. I never would have thought that of ye."

Feisty lass that she was, his wife pinched him hard on the buttocks—again. He rolled over until she was on top of him. When she smiled that sensual smile he'd grown accustomed to in the last few days, he pinched her back. Instead of complaining, she slid down, pressing her curves against him until his eyes crossed.

The loud knock on the door had her stiffening. He cupped her head in his hand and kissed her thoroughly. "Not to worry—

the door's locked."

"Time's up, Flaherty!" a deep voice boomed.

"Ah, O'Malley sent Garahan." He kissed the tip of her nose, looked over his shoulder, and shouted, "Come back tomorrow."

"The bloody hell I will! Get yer fecking arse out here now!"

"Can't. One of the tenant farmers' sons could be walking past on the way to their fields. Me manly form would shock them."

"Put some fecking clothes on! Ye have five minutes before I break the door down."

"Will he really do that?" Temperance asked.

"Depends on what's been happening while we've been co-cooned in our own world, lass."

"I'm helping him dress now, Garahan," Temperance called out. "Please don't break down our pretty yellow door."

A deep groan—followed by the sound of something heavy hitting their door—had Temperance jumping out of bed. She tossed Flaherty's trousers at him. "Hurry!"

He slipped on his pants, fastened them, and cupped her face in his hand. "That sound was his head. Garahan would never intrude on our privacy, lass. Surely by now ye've noticed he's more bluster than bite."

Temperance handed him his cambric shirt. "Put this on," she whispered. Then she yelled, "We're hurrying, Garahan!"

Flaherty laughed when he heard his cousin's head hitting the door again. "Ye're making him daft, lass. Say something else."

"But his head might crack our door if he hits it again!"

"It'll be worth it to see the huge knot on his forehead." When she pressed her lips together, Flaherty sighed, found her chemise, and slipped it over her head. "Now yer gown, lass. I won't be opening the door until ye're dressed. No one but meself will see ye like this."

She lifted to her toes and kissed him before letting him slip her gown over her head. Turning her back to him, she let him do up her buttons. "Now for your waistcoat. Do you want help with your cravat?"

"Nay, I hate wearing the bloody thing."

"It won't take but a moment." She didn't wait for him to agree—the lass tied the fabric faster than he'd ever done. "There." She patted his chest and smiled up at him. "All you need is your coat."

"That's not all I need, lass." He pulled her flush against him and kissed the breath out of her. "*That's* what I need."

"After I straighten up, I'm going to spend the day in the nursery again. Maddy loves reading and playing with Abigail, Richard, and little Deidre. But I think she's ready to sleep here in her new trundle bed instead of sharing a room with Francis."

There was another groan from the other side of the door, and Flaherty kissed her forehead. "With the way ye've been begging me to make love to ye—more than once a night and twice before dawn—ye may be carrying our babe. Maddy will be a wonderful big sister."

Temperance's hands covered her mouth, but not the squeal of happiness.

"Flaherty!" barked. "Step away from yer wife and get out here. Now!"

His wife's musical laughter filled Flaherty's heart. "I'm coming."

"That's what I'm afraid of," Garahan grumbled.

"Is this what I can expect every morning? To have one of your cousins pounding on our door telling you to get dressed?" Temperance asked.

Flaherty slipped his arms around her waist and drew her into his arms. "Only on the mornings me insatiable wife insists that I make love to her until I don't have the strength to stand."

Instead of the response he expected, she furrowed her brow and then slowly smiled. "We'll have to get up earlier to give you time to recover."

Flaherty was still laughing as he opened the door. "Get yer arse moving, Garahan, or we'll be late to our shifts."

Once Garahan started walking, Flaherty turned around,

sprinted back to his door, and pulled his wife into yet another hug. "Don't lift anything heavier than yer smile until I get home. If ye want, I can bring Maddy home midmorning—it'll give ye time to rest."

She smiled at him. "I'm not the one who's tired."

Flaherty was whistling when he caught up to Garahan.

"It looks good on ye, Rory."

"What does?"

"Love."

Flaherty shoved his cousin with his shoulder. "How's Emily feeling this morning?"

"Her stomach's finally settled."

"I can't wait."

Garahan chuckled. He understood what Flaherty couldn't wait for. "Ye'd best hurry up—that way our babes will be only a month or so apart."

Flaherty grinned. "More babes for Maddy to play with."

"God's granted us a good life, Rory."

"Aye," Flaherty agreed. "God is good."

EPILOGUE

Five years later…

FLAHERTY AND TEMPERANCE stared down into the face of their newborn son. "He looks just like you, Rory."

The knock on the door had him rising to his feet. He bent and kissed his wife's forehead and then their son's. "That'll be Emily with Maddy with the twins."

Flaherty opened the door and smiled at their newest stable hand. "Thank ye for escorting Mrs. Garahan and me girls, Tommy. Will ye wait and escort Mrs. Garahan back home?"

"Aye. Though I'm to bring her back to Mrs. O'Malley's house. We dropped her boys off there before coming here."

"Ye're a good man, Tommy. I'll be sure to put in a good word for ye with Garahan."

"I appreciate it. Ready, Mrs. Garahan?"

"I am." Emily hugged Maddy and her little sisters, then kissed Flaherty on the cheek. "Congratulations. Tell Temperance I'll visit tomorrow."

"Walk slowly and mind yer step," Flaherty reminded her.

"Yes, Flaherty. I'm ready, Tommy. Bye, girls!"

"Bye, Aunt Emily!" the lasses called in unison.

Flaherty smiled at his daughters. "Are ye ready to meet yer new brother?" They cheered, and he grinned and put a finger to his lips. "Quiet now—yer ma is exhausted, and so is the babe. I'll lift ye onto the bed, but don't be touching or jostling yer brother now. Ye hear?"

Their chorus of "aye, Da" warmed his heart.

Maddy waited until Rose and Honey were on the bed before scooting in next to Honey, whose fingers were twitching to touch the babe. "Did you and Mum decide on his name?" she asked.

"We've talked about calling him Donal."

"After your da's favorite uncle," Temperance added.

Flaherty smiled watching their daughters stare at their newborn brother with awe. "But," he said, "I've been thinking Donal should be his middle name." He watched his wife's face for her reaction. "Paul will be his first name."

Maddy smiled. "Would you really?"

Flaherty smiled back and, with a nod from his wife, replied, "After all, I asked permission from him to marry yer ma. He gave it, and I don't think a powerful guardian angel such as himself would mind adding a fourth babe to watch over."

Maddy reminded her sisters, "My papa is your guardian angel, too."

Flaherty stared at his wife and the picture she made with the babe in her arms, and their three little girls surrounding her on the bed. "I'm thinking we'll name our next son after me other favorite uncle—Patrick. He's been watching over our brood since I married yer ma."

Temperance sighed. "Rory, you do know that I love you, don't you?"

"Aye, lass."

"If you continue to talk about me having another babe *hours* after I just gave birth, I will have to hurt you."

Maddy frowned. "Mum, don't hurt Da. He loves you. He loves us."

"That I do, *mo chroí*," Flaherty said.

"Uncle Aiden and Aunt Emily have sons," Rose added.

"Three of them!" Honey piped up.

"And we have three darling girls—and a son," Temperance said.

"That's enough talk for now, girls," Flaherty interrupted.

"Maddy, will ye read to yer sisters while I speak with yer ma?"

"Yes, Da."

He helped the twins off the bed and scooted them to the other side of the cottage, then waited until they were settled on the settee and listening intently while their older sister read them a story about a princess and a castle in the air.

He walked back and sat on the edge of the bed. "That glint is still in yer eye, lass. It has me thinking I shouldn't close me eyes tonight. Should I remind ye that ye love me?"

Temperance leaned against him. "I love you to distraction, Rory. Paul Donal takes after you with broad shoulders."

He winced. "I'm sorry the birthing was hard on ye, lass."

"The twins were smaller. This time our babe had more room to grow."

"Rest against me, lass. I've got ye both." He pressed his lips to her temple and inhaled the faint scent of roses and raindrops. "Ye're braver than meself, lass. Closer yer eyes now and sleep." He'd rather be surrounded by a host of blackguards wielding blades, cudgels, and pistols than give birth!

Nestled in his arms, their babe fell asleep first, then his brave and courageous wife.

Flaherty silently said a prayer of thanks for his wife, his children, and his life. He was surrounded by family, and had the honor of working for a man he admired. The duke had had the foresight to understand that his men's wives were of equal value to his own…and above all, in the eyes of the Lord.

Listening to the lilting sound of Maddy's voice as she read to her sisters soothed Flaherty. The delicate snore of his wife and the tiny sounds from their new babe warmed his heart and had him praying for just one more son—after Temperance fully recovered from giving birth.

Nine months later to the day, Temperance gave birth to healthy twin sons. And, much to his delight, she agreed to name them Patrick and Aiden.

About the Author

If we have not met yet, I'm delighted to meet you. Here's a little bit about me…

I have been writing romance novels for almost half my life—well, at least for the last thirty years. I'm a die-hard romantic and have to confess the broad shoulders and wicked glint in the brilliant green eyes of a stranger had my breath snagging in my breast, my heart beating madly, and my future flashing before my eyes. At the age of seventeen, I'd met the man I knew I was going to spend the rest of my life with.

I write Historical & Contemporary Romance featuring characters that I know so well: hardheaded heroes and feisty heroines! They rarely listen to me and in fact, I think they enjoy messing with my plans for them. Over the years I have learned to listen to them. I have always used family names in my books and love adding bits and pieces of my ancestors and ancestry in them, too! Visit my website to learn more about my books.

Sláinte!
CH

C.H.'s Social Media Links:

Website: www.chadmirand.com
Amazon: amazon.com/stores/C.-H.-Admirand/author/B001JPBUMC
BookBub: bookbub.com/authors/c-h-admirand
Facebook Author Page: facebook.com/CHAdmirandAuthor
GoodReads: goodreads.com/author/show/212657.C_H_Admirand
Dragonblade Publishing: dragonbladepublishing.com/team/c-h-admirand
Instagram: instagram.com/c.h.admirand
YouTube: youtube.com/channel/UCRSXBeqEY52VV3mHdtg5fXw

www.ingramcontent.com/pod-product-compliance
Lightning Source LLC
Chambersburg PA
CBHW050614200925
32905CB00016B/1174